**Mary Higgins Clark** is the author of twenty-two
worldwide bestselling novels and a memoir.
She lives with her husband in Saddle River,
New Jersey

Praise for SECOND TIME AROUND
and **Mary Higgins Clark**

'There's something special about Clark's thrillers,
and it's not just the gentleness with which the
bestselling writer approaches her often lurid subject
matter . . . special above all is the compassion she
extends to her characters. Grace, charm and solid
storytelling' *PUBLISHERS WEEKLY*

'Another cracking tale from the ex-president of the
Mystery Writers Club of America' *HELLO*!

'Clark plays out her story like the pro that she is . . .
flawless' *DAILY MIRROR*

'Mary Higgins Clark is a master plotter, seeding [her
stories] with crimes, clues and psychopathic quirks
that pay off' *NEW YORK TIMES*

'One of the best storytellers ever. Yes, you won't put
it down' LARRY KING

'As well-oiled as a fine-tuned engine' *NOTTINGHAM
EVENING POST*

# MARY HIGGINS CLARK

## SECOND TIME AROUND

POCKET
BOOKS

LONDON • SYDNEY • NEW YORK • TOKYO • TORONTO

First published in Great Britain by Simon & Schuster UK Ltd, 2003
This edition published by Pocket Books, 2004
An imprint of Simon & Schuster UK Ltd
A Viacom Company

13 5 7 9 10 8 6 4 2

Simon & Schuster UK Ltd
Africa House
64–78 Kingsway
London WC2B 6AH

Simon & Schuster Australia
Sydney

www.simonsays.co.uk

A CIP catalogue record for this book is available from
the British Library

ISBN 0-7434-6773-6

Typeset by SX Composing DTP, Rayleigh, Essex
Printed and bound in Great Britain by
Cox & Wyman Ltd, Reading, Berkshire

# Acknowledgements

The end of writing a story is the beginning of expressing gratitude to those who made the journey with me.

My gratitude is endless to my longtime editor, Michael Korda. It is hard to believe that twenty-eight years have passed since we first started putting our heads together with *Where Are the Children?* It is a joy to work with him and for the last twelve years his associate, senior editor Chuck Adams. They are marvelous friends and advisors along the way.

Lisl Cade, my publicist, is truly my right hand – encouraging, perceptive, helpful in ways too numerous to mention. Love you, Lisl.

My gratitude continues to my agents Eugene Winick and Sam Pinkus. Truly friends for all seasons.

Associate Director of Copyediting Gypsy da Silva has once again been marvelous and meticulous. Many, many thanks and kudos to you always.

My gratitude to her associates Rose Ann Ferrick,

Barbara Raynor, Steve Friedeman, Joshua Cohen, and Anthony Newfield.

Again and always thanks and blessings to my assistants and friends Agnes Newton and Nadine Petry, and reader-in-progress, my sister-in-law, Irene Clark.

My daughter and fellow author Carol Higgins Clark is always my valued and helpful sounding board. We continue to communicate the highs and lows of creativity – the high begins when the book is finished.

I am so grateful to Clinical Research Associate Carlene McDevitt, who so willingly answered the questions I posed: Suppose? What if? If I got any details wrong when she answered those questions, I plead guilty.

I close with my thanks to my husband, John, and our wonderful combined families, children and grandchildren, who are named in the dedication.

And now, my dear readers, the tale has been told. I truly hope you enjoy.

Once Again

For my nearest and dearest –
*John Conheeney* – Spouse Extraordinaire

The Clark offspring –
*Marilyn, Warren and Sharon, David, Carol,* and *Pat*

The Clark grandchildren –
*Liz, Andrew, Courtney, David, Justin,* and *Jerry*

The Conheeney children –
*John* and *Debby, Barbara, Trish, Nancy* and *David*

The Conheeney grandchildren –
*Robert, Ashley, Lauren, Megan, David, Kelly, Courtney,
Johnny, Thomas,* and *Liam*

You're a grand bunch, and I love you all.

# SECOND TIME
# AROUND

# Chapter 1

The stockholders' meeting, or maybe the stock-holders' *uprising* is a better way to describe the event, took place on April 21 at the Grand Hyatt Hotel in Manhattan. It was an unseasonably cold and wintry day, but suitably bleak considering the circumstances. The headline two weeks earlier that Nicholas Spencer, president and chief operating officer of Gen-stone, had been killed in the crash of his private plane while flying to San Juan had been greeted with genuine and heartfelt grief. His company expected to receive the blessing of the Food and Drug Administration for a vaccine that would both eliminate the possibility of the growth of cancer cells and bring to a halt the progression of the disease in those already afflicted – a preventive and a cure that he alone was responsible for bringing to the world. He named the company 'Gen-stone,' a reference to the Rosetta stone that had unveiled the language of ancient Egypt and allowed the appreciation of its remarkable culture.

The headline proclaiming Spencer's disappearance was followed in short order by the announcement from the chairman of the board of Gen-stone that there had been numerous setbacks in the experiments with the vaccine and that it could not be submitted to the FDA for approval in the foreseeable future. The announcement further said that tens of millions of dollars had been looted from the company, apparently by Nicholas Spencer.

I'm Marcia DeCarlo, better known as Carley, and even as I sat in the roped-off media section at the stockholders' meeting, observing the furious or stunned or tearful faces around me, I still had a sense of disbelief in what I was hearing. Apparently Nicholas Spencer, *Nick*, was a thief and a fraud. The miracle vaccine was nothing more than the offspring of his greedy imagination and consummate salesmanship. He had cheated all these people who had invested so much money in his company, often their life savings or total assets. Of course they hoped to make money, but many believed as well that their investment would help make the vaccine a reality. And not only had investors been hurt, but the theft had made worthless the retirement funds of Gen-stone's employees, over a thousand people. It simply didn't seem possible.

Since Nicholas Spencer's body had not washed ashore along with charred pieces of his doomed plane, half the people in the auditorium didn't believe he was dead. The other half would willingly have driven a stake through his heart if his remains had been discovered.

Charles Wallingford, the chairman of the board of Gen-stone, ashen-faced but with the natural elegance that is achieved by generations of breeding and privilege, struggled to bring the meeting to order. Other members of the board, their expressions somber, sat on the dais with him. To a man they were prominent figures in business and society. In the second row were people I recognized as executives from Gen-stone's accounting firm. Some of them had been interviewed from time to time in *Weekly Browser*, the syndicated Sunday supplement for which I write a financial column.

Sitting to the right of Wallingford, her face alabaster pale, her blond hair twisted into a French knot, and dressed in a black suit that I'm sure cost a fortune, was Lynn Hamilton Spencer. She is Nick's wife – or widow – and, coincidentally my stepsister whom I've met exactly three times and whom I confess I dislike. Let me explain. Two years ago my widowed mother married Lynn's widowed father, having met him in Boca Raton where they lived in neighboring condominiums.

At the dinner the evening before the wedding, I was as annoyed by Lynn Spencer's condescending attitude as I was charmed by Nicholas Spencer. I knew who he was, of course. The stories about him in *Time* and *Newsweek* had been detailed. He was the son of a Connecticut family doctor, a general practitioner whose avocation was research biology. His father had a laboratory in his home, and from the time that Nick was a child, he spent most of his free time there, helping his dad with experiments. 'Other kids had dogs,' he had explained to interviewers. 'I had pet mice. I didn't know it, but I was being tutored in microbiology by a genius.' He had gone the business route, getting an MBA in business management with the plan of owning a medical supply operation someday. He started work at a small supply business and quickly rose to the top and became a partner. Then, as microbiology became the wave of the future, he began to realize that was the field he wanted to pursue. He began to reconstruct his father's notes and discovered that shortly before his sudden death his father had been on the verge of making a major breakthrough in cancer research. Using his medical supply company as a base, he set out to create a major research division.

Venture capital had helped him launch Gen-stone, and word of the cancer-inhibiting vaccine had made the company the hottest stock on Wall Street. Initially offered at $3 a share, the stock had risen as high as $160, and conditional on FDA approval, Garner Pharmaceutical contracted to pay $1 billion for the rights to distribute the new vaccine.

I knew that Nick Spencer's wife had died of cancer five years ago, that he had a ten-year-old son, and that he'd been married to Lynn, his second wife, for four years. But all the time I spent boning up on his background didn't help when I met him at that 'family' dinner. I simply was not prepared for the absolutely magnetic quality of Nick Spencer's personality. He was one of those people who are gifted with both inherent personal charm and a genuinely brilliant mind. A little over six feet tall, with dark blond hair, intensely blue eyes, and a trim athletic body, he was physically very attractive. It was his ability to interact with people, however, that came through as his greatest asset. As my mother attempted to keep the conversational ball going with Lynn, I found myself telling Nick more about myself than I had ever revealed to anyone at a first meeting.

Within five minutes he knew my age, where I lived, my job, and where I grew up.

'Thirty-two,' he said, smiling. 'Eight years younger than I am.'

Then I not only told him that I had been divorced after a brief marriage to a fellow MBA student at NYU, but even talked about the baby who lived only a few days because the hole in his heart was too big to close. This was so not like me. I never talk about the baby. It hurts too much. And yet it was easy to tell Nicholas Spencer about him.

'That's the sort of tragedy our research will prevent someday,' he had said gently. 'That's why I'll move heaven and earth to save people from the kind of heartbreak you've experienced, Carley.'

My thoughts were quickly brought back to the present reality as Charles Wallingford hammered the gavel until there was silence – an angry, sullen silence. 'I am Charles Wallingford, the chairman of the board of Gen-stone,' he said.

He was greeted with a deafening chorus of boos and catcalls.

I knew Wallingford was forty-eight or forty-nine years old, and I had seen him on the news the day after Spencer's plane crashed. He looked much older than that now. The strain of the last few weeks had added years to his appearance. No one could doubt that the man was suffering.

'I worked with Nicholas Spencer for the past eight years,' he said. 'I had just sold our family retail business, of which I was chairman, and I was looking for a chance to invest in a promising company. I met Nick Spencer, and he convinced me that the company he had just started would make startling breakthroughs in the development of new drugs. At his urging I invested almost all the proceeds from the sale of our family business and joined Gen-stone. So I am as devastated as you are by the fact that the vaccine is not ready to be submitted to the FDA for approval, but that does not mean if more funds become available, further research will not solve the problem – '

Dozens of shouted questions interrupted him: 'What about the money he stole?' 'Why not admit that you and that whole bunch up there cheated us?'

Abruptly Lynn stood up and in a surprise gesture pulled the microphone from in front of Wallingford. 'My husband died on his way to a business meeting to get more funding to keep the research alive. I am sure that the missing money can be explained – '

One man came running up the aisle waving pages that looked as though they had been torn from magazines and newspapers. 'The Spencers on their estate in Bedford,' he shouted. 'The Spencers hosting a charity ball. Nicholas Spencer smiling as he writes a check for "New York's Neediest." '

Security guards grabbed the man's arms as he reached the dais. 'Where did you think that money was coming from, lady? I'll tell you where. *It came from our pockets!* I put a second mortgage on my house to invest in your lousy company. You wanna know why? Because my kid has cancer, and I believed your husband's promise about his vaccine.'

The media section was in the first few rows. I was in an end seat and could have reached out and touched the man. He was a burly-looking guy of about thirty, dressed in a sweater and jeans. I watched as his face suddenly crumpled and he began to cry. 'I won't even be able to keep my little girl in our house,' he said. 'I'll have to sell it now.'

I looked up at Lynn and our eyes met. I knew it was impossible for her to see the contempt in my eyes, but all I could think was that the diamond on her finger was probably worth enough to pay off the second mortgage that was going to cost a dying child her home.

The meeting didn't last more than forty minutes, and most of it consisted of a series of agonized recitals from people who had lost everything by investing in Gen-stone. Many of them said they had been persuaded to buy the stock because a child or other family member had a disease that the vaccine might reverse.

As people streamed out, I took names, addresses, and phone numbers. Thanks to my column, a lot of them knew my name and were eager to talk to me about their financial loss as well. They asked whether or not I thought there was any chance of recouping some or all of their investment.

Lynn had left the meeting by a side door. I was glad. I had written her a note after Nick's plane crashed, letting her know I would attend a memorial service. There hadn't been one yet; they were waiting to see if his body would be recovered. Now, like almost everyone else, I wondered if Nick had actually been in the plane when it crashed or if he had rigged his disappearance.

I felt a hand on my arm. It was Sam Michaelson, a veteran reporter for *Wall Street Weekly* magazine. 'Buy you a drink, Carley,' he offered.

'Good God, I can use one.'

We went down to the bar on the lobby floor and were directed to a table. It was four-thirty.

'I have a firm rule not to have vodka straight up before five o'clock,' Sam told me, 'but, as you're aware, somewhere in the world it *is* five o'clock.'

I ordered a glass of Chianti. Usually by late April I'd have switched to chardonnay, my warm weather choice of vino, but feeling as emotionally chilled as I did after that meeting, I wanted something that would warm me up.

Sam gave the order, then abruptly asked, 'So what do you think, Carley? Is that crook sunning himself in Brazil as we speak?'

I gave the only honest answer I could offer: 'I don't know.'

'I met Spencer once,' Sam said. 'I swear if he'd offered to sell me the Brooklyn Bridge, I'd have fallen for it. What a snake oil salesman. Did you ever meet him in the flesh?'

I pondered Sam's question for a moment, trying to decide what to say. The fact that Lynn Hamilton Spencer was my stepsister, making Nick Spencer my stepbrother-in-law, was something I never talked about. However, that fact did keep me from ever commenting publicly or privately on Gen-stone as an investment because I felt that might be considered a conflict of interest. Unfortunately, it did not keep me from buying $25,000 worth of Gen-stone stock because, as Nicholas Spencer had put it that evening at dinner, after this vaccine eliminated the possibility of cancer, there would someday be another to eliminate all genetic abnormalities.

My baby had been baptized the day he was born. I'd called him Patrick, giving him my maternal grandfather's name. I bought that stock as kind of a tribute to my son's memory. That night two years ago Nick had said that the more money they could raise, the faster they would have the tests on the vaccine completed and be able to make it available. 'And, of course, eventually your twenty-five thousand dollars will be worth a great deal more,' he had added.

That money had represented my savings toward a down payment on an apartment.

I looked at Sam and smiled, still debating my answer. Sam's hair is a kind of grizzled gray. His one vanity is to comb long strands of it over his balding dome. I've noticed that these strands often are somewhat askew, as they were now, and as an old pal I've had to resist saying, 'Surrender. You've lost the hair battle.'

Sam is pushing seventy, but his baby blue eyes are bright and alert. There's nothing babyish behind that pucklike face, however. He's smart and shrewd. I realized it wouldn't be fair not to tell him of my somewhat tenuous connection to the Spencers, but I would make it clear that I'd actually met Nick only once and Lynn three times.

I watched his eyebrows raise as I filled him in on the relationship.

'She comes through as a pretty cool customer to me,' he said. 'What about Spencer?'

'I would have bought the Brooklyn Bridge from him, too. I thought he was a terrific guy.'

'What do you think now?'

'You mean, whether he's dead or somehow arranged the crash? I don't know.'

'What about the wife, your stepsister?'

I know I winced. 'Sam, my mother is genuinely happy with Lynn's father, or else she's putting on one hell of a performance. God help us, the two of them are even taking piano lessons together. You should have heard the concert I got treated to when I went down to Boca for a weekend last month. I admit I didn't like Lynn when I met her. I think she kisses the mirror every morning. But then, I only saw her the night before the wedding, at the wedding, and one other time when I arrived in Boca last year just as she was leaving. So do me a favor and don't refer to her as my stepsister.'

'Noted.'

The waitress came with our drinks. Sam sipped appreciatively and then cleared his throat. 'Carley, I just heard that you applied for the job that's opening up at the magazine.'

'Yes.'

'How come?'

'I want to write for a serious financial magazine, not just have a column that is essentially a financial filler in a general interest Sunday supplement. Reporting for *Wall Street Weekly* is my goal. How do you know I applied?'

'The big boss, Will Kirby, asked about you.'

'What did you tell him?'

'I said you had brains and you'd be a big step up from the guy who's leaving.'

Half an hour later Sam dropped me off in front of my place. I live in the second-floor apartment of a converted brownstone on East 37th Street in Manhattan. I ignored the elevator, which deserves to be ignored, and walked up the single flight. It was a relief to unlock my door and go inside. I was down in the dumps for very good reasons. The financial situation of those investors had gotten to me, but it was more than that. Many of them had made the investment for the same reason I had, because they wanted to stop the progress of an illness in someone they loved. It was too late for me, but I know that buying that stock as a tribute to Patrick was also my way of trying to cure the hole in my heart that was even bigger than the one that had killed my little son.

My apartment is furnished with chattels my parents had in the house in Ridgewood, New Jersey, where I was raised. Because I'm an only child, I had my choice of everything when they moved to Boca Raton. I reupholstered the couch in a sturdy blue fabric to pick up the blue in the antique Persian I'd found at a garage sale. The tables and lamps and easy chair were around when I was the smallest but fastest kid on the varsity basketball team at Immaculate Heart Academy.

I keep a picture of the team on the wall in the bedroom, and in it I hold the basketball. I look at the picture and see that in many ways I haven't changed. The short dark hair and the blue eyes I inherited from my father are still the same. I never did have that spurt of growth my mother assured me I'd experience. I was just over five feet four inches then, and I'm five feet four inches now. Alas, the victorious smile isn't around anymore, not the way it was in that picture, when I thought the world was my oyster. Writing the column may have something to do with that. I'm always in touch with real people with real financial problems.

But I knew there was another reason for feeling drained and down tonight.

Nick. Nicholas Spencer. No matter how overwhelming the apparent evidence, I simply could not accept what they were saying about him.

Was there another answer for the failure of the vaccine, the disappearance of the money, the plane crash? Or was it something in me that let me be conned by smooth-talking phonies who don't give a damn about anyone but themselves? Like I was by Greg, the Mr. Wrong I married nearly eleven years ago.

When Patrick died after living only four days, Greg didn't have to tell me that he was relieved. I could see it. It meant that he wouldn't be saddled with a child who needed constant care.

We didn't really talk about it. There wasn't much to say. He told me that the job he was offered in California was too good to pass up.

I said, 'Don't let me keep you.'

And that was that.

All these thoughts did nothing but depress me further, so I went to bed early, determined to clear my head and make a fresh start the next day.

I was awakened at seven in the morning by a phone call from Sam. 'Carley, turn on the television. There's a news bulletin. Lynn Spencer went up to her house in Bedford last night. Somebody torched it. The fire department managed to get her out, but she inhaled a lot of smoke. She's in St. Ann's Hospital in serious condition.'

As Sam hung up, I grabbed the remote from the bedside table. The phone rang just as I clicked the TV on. It was the office of St. Ann's Hospital. 'Ms. DeCarlo, your stepsister, Lynn Spencer, is a patient here. She very much wants to see you. Will you be able to visit her today?' The woman's voice became urgent. 'She's terribly upset and in quite a bit of pain. It's very important to her that you come.'

# Chapter 2

On the forty-minute drive to St. Ann's Hospital I kept tuned to the CBS station to catch anything new that was being said about the fire. According to the reports, Lynn Spencer had driven to her home in Bedford around eleven o'clock last night. The house-keepers, a couple, Manuel and Rosa Gomez, live in a separate residence on the estate. They apparently were not expecting her to be there that evening and were not aware that she was in the main house.

What made Lynn decide to go to Bedford last night? I wondered as I decided to risk the Cross Bronx Expressway, the fastest way to get from the east side of Manhattan to Westchester County if there isn't an accident to snarl traffic. The problem is there usually is an accident, causing the Cross Bronx to be called the worst roadway in the country.

The Spencers' New York apartment is on Fifth Avenue, near the building in which Jackie Kennedy had lived. I thought of my nine hundred square feet of domain and the $25,000 I'd lost, the money that was to be a deposit on a co-op. I thought of the guy at the meeting yesterday whose child was dying and who was going to lose his home because he'd invested in Gen-stone. I wondered if Lynn felt a shred of guilt going back to that opulent apartment after the meeting. I wondered if she was planning to talk about that to me.

April had returned to being April. When I walked the three blocks to the garage where I park my car, I sniffed the air and appreciated being alive. The sun was shining and the sky was intensely blue. The few clouds overhead were like puffs of white cushions, drifting around up there almost as an afterthought. That's the way my interior designer friend, Eve, tells me she uses throw pillows when she decorates a room. The pillows should look casual, an afterthought when everything else is in place.

The thermometer on the dashboard registered 62 degrees. It would be a terrific day for a drive to the country if the reason for the drive wasn't the one I had. Still, I was curious. I was on my way to visit a stepsister who was virtually a stranger and who, for some unknown reason, had sent for me instead of one of her celebrity friends when she was rushed to the hospital.

I actually got across the Cross Bronx in about fifteen minutes, a near record, and turned north toward the Hutchinson River Parkway. The newscaster began updating the story about Lynn. At 3:15 A.M. the fire alarm in the Bedford mansion had gone off. When the firefighters got there a few minutes later, the entire downstairs of the house was engulfed in flames. Rosa Gomez assured them there was no one inside. Fortunately, one of the firemen recognized the Fiat in the garage as the car Lynn always drove and asked Rosa how long it had been there. At her shocked response, they put a ladder up to the bedroom she pointed out, broke a window, and got in. They found a dazed and disoriented Lynn trying to grope her way through the dense smoke. By then she was suffering from smoke inhalation. Her feet were blistered from the heat of the floor, and her hands suffered second-degree burns because she had been feeling along the wall searching for the door. The hospital reported that her condition had been upgraded from guarded to stable.

A preliminary report indicated that the fire was arson. Gasoline had been sprayed over the front porch that ran the entire front of the residence. When ignited, it resulted in a fireball that within seconds engulfed the downstairs floor in flames.

Who would set the house on fire? I wondered. Did anyone know or suspect that Lynn was there? My mind immediately raced to the stockholders' meeting and the man who had shouted at her. He had specifically referred to her Bedford mansion. I was sure that when the police heard about him, he'd be paid a visit.

Lynn was in a cubicle in a special care section of St. Ann's Hospital. There were oxygen tubes in her nostrils, and her arms were bandaged. Her complexion, however, wasn't nearly as pale as it had been yesterday when I saw her at the stockholders' meeting. Then I remembered that smoke inhalation can give the skin a pinkish glow.

Her blond hair was brushed back and seemed limp, even ragged. I wondered if they'd had to cut off some of it in the emergency room. Her palms were bandaged, but the tops of her fingers were bare. I was ashamed that for a moment I wondered if the solitaire diamond she'd been flashing at the meeting was somewhere in the burned-out house.

Her eyes were closed, and I wasn't sure if she was asleep. I looked at the nurse who had brought me to her. 'She was awake a minute ago,' she said quietly. 'Talk to her.'

'Lynn,' I said uncertainly.

She opened her eyes. 'Carley.' She tried to smile. 'Thank you for coming.'

I nodded. I'm not usually tongue-tied, but I simply didn't know what to say to her. I was sincerely thankful that she hadn't been severely burned or suffocated in the fire, but I couldn't imagine why I was playing next of kin. If there's one thing I'm sure of in this world, it's that Lynn Hamilton Spencer has as little regard for me as I have for her.

'Carley . . .' Her voice rose in pitch, and realizing it, she closed her lips. 'Carley,' she began again, her tone quieter, 'I had no idea that Nick was taking money from the company. I still can't believe it. I don't know anything about the business part of his life. Carley, he owned the house in Bedford and the apartment in New York before we were married.'

Her lips were cracked and dry. She lifted her right hand. I knew she intended to reach for the water glass, and I picked it up and held it for her. The nurse had left as soon as Lynn opened her eyes. I wasn't sure if I should push the button that would raise the bed. Instead, I slipped my arm around her neck and supported her while she sipped.

She drank only a little, then leaned back and closed her

eyes as though that brief effort had drained her. It was then that I felt a wrench of genuine pity for her. There was something hurt and broken about her. The exquisitely dressed and coiffed Lynn I had met in Boca Raton was light-years from this vulnerable woman who needed help in drinking a few drops of water.

I laid her back on the pillow, and tears slid down her cheeks. 'Carley,' she said, her voice tired and spent, 'I've lost everything. Nick is dead. I've been asked to resign from the PR firm. I introduced Nick to a lot of new customers. More than half of them invested heavily in the company. The same thing happened in Southhampton at the club. People who were my friends for years are furious that because of me they met Nick, and now have lost lots of money.'

I thought of how Sam had described Nick as a snake oil salesman.

'The lawyers for the stockholders are going to file suit against me.' In her urgency, Lynn had begun speaking rapidly. She put her hand on my arm and then winced and bit her lip. I'm sure the contact sent a shot of pain through her blistered palm. 'I have some money in my personal bank account,' she said, 'and that's it. Soon I won't have a home. I don't have a job anymore. Carley, I need your help.'

How could I possibly help her? I wondered. I didn't know what to say, so I just looked at her.

'If Nick did take that money, my only hope is that people will believe I'm an innocent victim, too. Carley, there's talk of indicting me. Please don't let that happen. People respect you. They'll listen to you. Make them understand that if there was deception, I had no part in it.'

'Do you believe Nick is dead?' It was a question I had to ask.

'Yes, I do. I know that Nick absolutely believed in the legitimacy of Gen-stone. He was on his way to a business meeting in Puerto Rico, and he got caught in a freak storm.

Now her voice was becoming strained and her eyes filled with tears. 'Nick liked you, Carley. He liked you so much. He admired you. He told me about your baby. Nick's son, Jack, just turned ten. His grandparents live in Greenwich. Now they won't even let me see him. They never liked me because I looked like their daughter, and I'm alive and she's dead. I miss Jack. I want to be able to at least visit him.'

That I could understand. 'Lynn, I'm sorry, truly sorry.'

'Carley, I need more than your sympathy. I need you to help people realize that I was not part of any scheme to defraud them. Nick said he could tell that you were a stand-up person. Will you be a stand-up person for me?' She closed her eyes. 'And for him,' she whispered. 'He liked you a lot.'

# Chapter 3

Ned sat in the hospital lobby, a newspaper open in front of him. He had come up the walk closely behind a woman carrying flowers, and he hoped that anyone watching would believe they were together. Once inside, he'd taken a seat in the lobby.

He slouched down so that the newspaper shielded his face. Everything was happening so fast. He needed to think.

Yesterday he had almost lunged at Spencer's wife when she grabbed the microphone at the stockholders' meeting to say that she was sure it was all an accounting mistake. He was lucky the other guy had started shouting at her.

But then when they were outside the hotel and he saw her get into a shiny limousine, rage had exploded inside him.

He had immediately hailed a cab and had given the driver the address of her New York apartment, that swanky building across the street from Central Park. He'd arrived just as the doorman was holding open the door for her to go inside.

As he paid off the cab and got out, he imagined Lynn Spencer going up in the elevator to the swanky place that had been bought with the money she and her husband stole from him.

He'd resisted the urge to rush after her and started walking down Fifth Avenue. All along the way he saw contempt in the eyes of the people coming toward him. They knew he didn't belong on Fifth Avenue. He belonged in a world where people bought only the things they absolutely needed, paying for them with credit cards and then making only the smallest monthly payment they could get away with.

On TV Spencer had talked about how anyone who had invested in IBM or Xerox fifty years ago became millionaires. 'You'll not only be helping others by buying Gen-stone, but you'll make a fortune.' Liar! Liar! Liar! – the word exploded in Ned's mind.

From Fifth Avenue he walked to where he could get the bus home to Yonkers. The house there was an old two-story frame. He and Annie had rented the bottom floor twenty years ago when they were first married.

The living room was a cluttered mess. He'd cut out all the articles about the plane crash and the no-good vaccine, and scattered them on the coffee table. The rest of the papers he'd tossed on the floor. When he arrived home, he read the articles again, every one of them.

When it grew dark, he didn't bother about supper. He wasn't hungry much anymore. At ten o'clock he got out a blanket and pillow and lay down on the couch. He no longer went into the bedroom. It made him miss Annie too much.

After the funeral the minister had given him a Bible.

'I've marked some passages for you to read, Ned,' he'd said. 'They may help.'

He wasn't interested in the Psalms, but just thumbing through he'd found something in the Book of Ezekiel. 'You have disheartened the upright man with lies when I did not wish him grieved.' It felt as if the prophet was talking about Spencer and him. It showed that God was mad at people who hurt other people, and he wanted them punished.

Ned had fallen asleep, but woke up a little after midnight with a vivid image of the Bedford mansion filling his mind. On Sunday afternoons he had driven Annie past it several times after he bought the stock. She'd been very upset because he had sold the house in Greenwood Lake that his mother left him and used the money to buy Gen-stone stock. She wasn't as convinced as he was that the stock would make them rich.

'That was our retirement home,' she would yell at him. Sometimes she would cry. 'I don't want a mansion. I loved that house. I worked so hard on it and made it so pretty, and you never even talked to me about selling it. Ned, how could you do that to me?'

'Mr. Spencer told me I wasn't only helping people by buying his stock, but someday I'd have a house like this.'

Even that hadn't convinced Annie. Then two weeks ago, when Spencer's plane crashed and word got out that the vaccine had problems, she went crazy. 'I'm on my feet eight hours a day at the hospital. You let that crook talk you into buying that phony stock, and now I guess I'm supposed to keep working for the rest of my life.' She was crying so hard she could hardly talk. 'You just can't get it right, Ned. You keep losing jobs because of that lousy temper of yours. And then when you finally do have something, you let yourself be talked out of it.' She had grabbed the car keys and rushed out. The tires had screeched as she shot the car back into the street.

The next instant kept replaying in Ned's mind. The image of the garbage truck that was backing up. The squeal of brakes. The sight of the car flipping up and slamming over. The gas tank exploding and the flames engulfing the car.

Annie. Gone.

They had met at this hospital over twenty years ago, when he was a patient here. He'd gotten into a fight with another guy at a bar and ended up with a concussion. Annie had brought his trays in and scolded him about giving in to his temper. She was spunky, small, and bossy in a cute way. They were the same age, thirty-eight. They had started going out together; then she moved in with him.

He came here this morning because it made him feel closer to Annie. He could imagine that at any minute she'd come trotting down the hall and say she was sorry to be late, that one of the other girls hadn't shown up and she'd stayed through the dinner hour.

But he knew that was a fantasy. She'd never be here again.

With an abrupt snapping motion, Ned crumpled the newspaper, stood up, walked to a nearby trash receptacle, and shoved the paper inside. He started toward the door, but one of the doctors who was crossing the lobby called to him. 'Ned, I haven't seen you since the accident. I'm so sorry about Annie. She was a wonderful person.'

'Thank you.' Then he remembered the doctor's name. 'Thank you, Dr. Ryan.'

'Is there anything I can do for you?'

'No.' He had to say something. Dr. Ryan's eyes were curious, looking him over. Dr. Ryan might know that at Annie's insistence he used to come here to Dr. Greene for psychiatric counseling. But Dr. Greene had pissed him off when he said, 'Don't you think you should have discussed selling the house with Annie before you sold it?'

The burn on his hand really hurt. When he tossed the match into the gasoline, the fire had flashed back and caught his hand. That was his excuse to be here. He held up his hand for Dr. Ryan to see. 'I got burned last night when I was cooking dinner. I'm not much of a cook. But the emergency room's crowded. I gotta get to work. Anyhow, it's not that bad.'

Dr. Ryan looked at it. 'It's serious enough, Ned. That could get infected.' He pulled a prescription pad out of his pocket and scrawled on the top sheet. 'Get this ointment and keep putting it on. Have your hand checked in a day or two.'

Ned thanked him and turned away. He didn't want to run into anyone else. He started toward the door again, but stopped. Cameras were being set up around the main exit.

He put on his dark glasses before he got into the revolving door behind a young woman. Then he realized that the cameras were there for her.

He stepped aside quickly and slipped behind the people who had been about to enter the hospital but waited when they saw the cameras. The idle ones. The curious.

The woman being interviewed was dark-haired, in her late twenties, attractive. She looked familiar. Then he remembered where he'd seen her. She'd been at the shareholders' meeting yesterday. She'd been asking questions of people as they left the auditorium.

She had tried to talk to him, but he'd brushed past her. He didn't like people asking him questions.

One of the reporters held a mike up to her. 'Ms. DeCarlo, Lynn Spencer is your sister – is that right?'

'My *step*sister.'

'How is she?'

'She's obviously in pain. She had a terrible experience. She nearly lost her life in that fire.'

'Does she have any idea who might have set the fire? Has she received any threats?'

'We didn't talk about that.'

'Do you think it was someone who lost money by investing in Gen-stone, Ms. DeCarlo?'

'I can't speculate on that. I can say that anyone who would deliberately incinerate a home, taking the chance that someone may be inside sleeping, is either psychotic or evil.'

Ned's eyes narrowed as rage filled him. Annie had died trapped in a burning car. If he hadn't sold the house in Greenwood Lake, they would have been there on that day two weeks ago when she was killed. She'd have been on her knees planting her flowers instead of rushing out of the Yonkers house, crying so hard that she hadn't paid attention to the traffic when she backed out the car.

For a brief moment he locked eyes with the woman being interviewed. DeCarlo was her name, and she was Lynn Spencer's sister. I'll show you who's crazy, he thought. Too bad your sister wasn't trapped in the fire the way my wife was trapped in the car. Too bad you weren't in the house with her. I'll get them, Annie, he promised. I'll get back at them for you.

# Chapter 4

I drove home not even remotely pleased with my performance during that unexpected news conference. I liked it much better when I was asking the questions. However, I realized that like it or not, I was now going to be perceived as Lynn's spokesperson and defender. It was not a role I wanted, nor was it an honest one. I was still not at all convinced that she was a naive and trusting wife who never sensed that her husband was a con man.

But *was* he? When his plane crashed, he supposedly had been on his way to a business meeting. When he got in that plane, did he still believe in Gen-stone? Did he go to his death believing in it?

This time the Cross Bronx Expressway ran true to form. An accident had it backed up for two miles, giving plenty of quiet time to think. Maybe too much time, because I realized that despite everything that had been disclosed about Nick Spencer and his company in the past few weeks, there was still something missing, something wrong. It was too pat. Nick's plane crashes. The vaccine is declared faulty if not worthless. And millions of dollars are missing.

Was the accident rigged, and was Nick now sunning himself in Brazil as Sam suggested? Or did his plane crash in that storm with him in the cockpit? And if so, where was all that money, $25,000 of which was mine?

*'He liked you, Carley,'* Lynn had said.

Well, I liked him, too. That's why I would like to believe that there was another explanation.

I drove past the accident that had reduced the Cross-Bronx to a one-lane road. A trailer truck had overturned. Broken crates of oranges and grapefruits had been shoved to the side to open the single lane. The cabin of the truck seemed intact. I hoped the driver was all right.

I turned onto the Harlem River Drive. I was anxious to get home. I wanted to go over next Sunday's column before I e-mailed it to the office. I wanted to call Lynn's father and reassure him that she was going to be all right. I wanted to see if there were any messages on the answering machine, specifically from the editor of *Wall Street Weekly*. God, how I'd love to get a job writing for that magazine, I thought.

The rest of the drive went quickly enough. The trouble was that in my mind I kept seeing the sincerity in Nick Spencer's eyes when he talked about the vaccine. I kept remembering my reaction to him: What a terrific guy.

Was I dead wrong, stupid, and naive, everything a reporter should not be? Or was there perhaps another answer? As I pulled into the garage, I realized what else was bothering me. My gut was talking to me again. It was telling me that Lynn was much more interested in clearing her own name than she was in learning the truth about whether or not her husband was still alive.

There was a message on my answering machine, and it was the one I wanted. Would I please call Will Kirby at *Wall Street Weekly*.

Will Kirby is editor in chief there. My fingers raced as they pushed the numbers. I'd met Kirby a few times at big gatherings, but we'd never really talked. When his secretary put me through and he got on the phone, my first thought was that his voice matched his body. He's a large-framed man in his mid-fifties, and his voice is deep and hearty. It has a nice, warm tone to it, even though he is known as a no-nonsense guy.

He didn't waste time chatting with me. 'Carley, can you come in and see me tomorrow morning?'

You bet I can, I thought. 'That would be fine, Mr. Kirby.'

'Ten o'clock okay with you?'

'Absolutely.'

'Fine. See you then.'

Click.

I had been screened by two people at the magazine already, so this was definitely going to be a make-or-break interview. My mind flew to my closet. A pantsuit was probably a better choice for the interview than a skirt. The gray stripe that I'd bought during a sale in Escada at the end of last summer would be great. But if it turned cold, the way it was yesterday, that would be too light. In which case, the dark blue would be a better choice.

I hadn't felt this combination of being both apprehensive and eager for a long time. I knew that even though I loved writing the column, it just wasn't enough to keep me busy. If it was a daily column, it might have been different, but a weekly supplement that has a lot of lead time isn't much of a challenge once you learn the ropes. Even though I was getting occasional freelance assignments writing profiles of people in the financial world for various magazines, it still wasn't enough.

I called down to Boca. Mom had moved into Robert's apartment after they were married because it had a great view of the ocean and was larger than hers. What I didn't like about it was that now when I visited, I slept in 'Lynn's room.'

Not that she ever really stayed there. She and Nick took a suite at the Boca Raton Resort when they visited. But Mom's changing apartments meant that when I flew down for a weekend, I was acutely aware that Lynn had furnished that room for herself before she married Nick. It was *her* bed I was sleeping in, *her* pale pink sheets and lace-edged pillowcases I was using, *her* expensive monogrammed towel I wrapped around me after I showered.

I had liked it a lot better when I slept on the convertible couch in Mom's old apartment. The plus factor, of course, was that Mom was happy and I sincerely liked Robert Hamilton. He is a quiet, pleasant man with none of the arrogance Lynn displayed at that first meeting. Mom told me that Lynn had been trying to set him up with one of the wealthy widows in nearby Palm Beach, but he wasn't interested.

I picked up the receiver, touched number one, and the automatic dial did its job. Robert answered. Of course he was terribly worried about Lynn, and I was happy to be able to reassure him that she really would be fine and out of the hospital in a few days.

Allowing for the fact that he'd been concerned about his

daughter, I still felt that something else was wrong. Then he came out with it. 'Carley, you met Nick. I can't believe he was a fraud. My God, he talked me into putting almost all my savings in Gen-stone. He wouldn't have done that to his wife's father if he knew it was a scam, would he?'

At the interview the next morning, I sat across the desk from Will Kirby, my heart sinking when he said, 'I understand you're Lynn Spencer's stepsister.'

'Yes, I am.'

'I saw you on the news last night outside the hospital. Frankly, I was worried that it might be impossible for you to do the assignment I had in mind, but Sam tells me you're not very close to her.'

'No, I'm not. Frankly, I was surprised that she wanted me to go up to see her yesterday. But she did have a reason. She wants people to understand that whatever Nick Spencer did, she had no part in it.'

I told him that Nick had persuaded Lynn's father to put most of his savings in Gen-stone.

'He'd have to be a real skunk to deliberately cheat his own father-in-law,' Kirby agreed.

Then he told me that the job was mine and my first assignment was to do an in-depth profile on Nicholas Spencer. I had submitted samples of the profiles I'd done previously, and he liked them. 'You'll be part of a team. Don Carter will handle the business angle. Ken Page is our medical expert. You'll do the personal background. Then the three of you will put the story together,' he told me. 'Don is setting up appointments at Gen-stone with the chairman and a couple of the directors. You should go along on them.'

There were a couple of copies of my column on Kirby's desk. He pointed to them. 'By the way, I don't see any conflict if you want to keep writing the column. Now go introduce yourself to Carter and Dr. Page, and then stop by Personnel to fill out the usual forms.'

Interview over, he reached for the phone, but as I got up from the chair, he smiled briefly. 'Glad to have you with us, Carley,' he said, then added, 'Plan to drive to wherever in Connecticut Spencer came from. I liked the job you did on your sample profiles, getting hometown people to talk about your subject.'

'It's Caspien,' I said, 'a little town near Bridgeport.' I thought of the stories I'd read about Nick Spencer working side by side with his doctor father in the lab in their home. I hoped that when I got to Caspien I'd at least be able to confirm that that was true. And then I wondered why I simply couldn't believe that he was dead.

The answer wasn't hard to figure out. Lynn had seemed more concerned about her own image than about Nicholas Spencer because she was not a grieving widow. Either she knew he wasn't dead, or she didn't give a damn that he was. I intended to find out which was true.

# Chapter 5

I could tell that I would enjoy working with Ken Page and Don Carter. Ken is a big dark-haired guy with a bulldog chin. I met him first and was beginning to wonder if the men at *Wall Street Weekly* had to satisfy a minimum height and weight requirement. But then Don Carter arrived; he's a small, neat package of a man with light brown hair and intense hazel eyes. I judged both of them to be around forty.

I had barely said hello to Ken when he excused himself and ran out to catch Carter whom he spotted passing in the hallway. I took the moment to get a good look at the degrees on the wall and was impressed. Ken is a medical doctor and also has a doctorate in molecular biology.

He came back with Don behind him. They had confirmed appointments at Gen-stone for eleven o'clock the next day. The meeting would be in Pleasantville, which was the main headquarters for the company.

'They have plush offices in the Chrysler Building,' Don told me, 'but the real work gets done in Pleasantville.'

We would be seeing Charles Wallingford, the chairman of the board of directors, and Dr. Milo Celtavini, the research scientist in charge of the Gen-stone laboratory. Since both Ken and Don lived in Westchester County, we decided that I'd drive up and meet them there.

Bless Sam Michaelson. Obviously he had talked me up. There's no question that when you work on a top-priority team project, you want to be sure you can function smoothly as a unit. Thanks to Sam I had the feeling that there wouldn't be much of a 'wait and see' for me with these guys. In essence I was getting another 'welcome aboard.'

As soon as I left the building, I called Sam on my cell phone and invited him and his wife to a celebratory dinner at Il Mulino in the Village. Then I hurried home, planning to make a sandwich and a cup of tea and have lunch at the computer. I'd received a new stack of questions from readers of the column and needed to sort them out. When you get mail for a column like mine, questions tend to be repetitious. That means, of course, that a lot of people are interested in the same thing, which is an indication of which questions I should try to answer.

Occasionally I'll make up my own inquiries when I want my readers to have specific information. It's important that people who are financially inexperienced be kept up to date on such subjects as refinancing mortgages when the rates are rock-bottom low, or avoiding the snare of some 'interest-free' loans.

When I do that, I use the initials of my friends in the query letters and make the city one where they have a connection. My best friend is Gwen Harkins. Her father was raised in Idaho. Last week the lead question in my column was about what to consider before applying for a reverse mortgage. I signed the inquiry from G.H. of Boise, Idaho.

Arriving home, I realized I'd have to put aside plans to work on the column for a while. There was a message on the answering machine from the U.S. Attorney's Office. Jason Knowles, an investigator, urgently needed to talk to me. He left his number and I returned the call.

I spent the next forty minutes wondering what information I might have that would be useful for an investigator from the attorney general's office to have immediately. Then, when the buzzer from the vestibule sounded, I picked up the intercom phone, confirmed it was Mr. Knowles, warned him to take the staircase, and released the lock.

A few minutes later he was at my door, a silver-haired man with a manner that was both courteous and direct. I invited him in and he sat on the couch. I chose the straight-backed chair opposite the couch and waited for him to speak.

He thanked me for seeing him on such short notice, then got down to business: 'Ms. DeCarlo, you were at the Genstone stockholders' meeting on Monday.'

It was a statement, not a question. I nodded.

'We understand that many people who attended that meeting expressed strong resentment toward management and that one man in particular was enraged by the statement made by Lynn Spencer.'

'That's true.' I was sure the next verification would be that I was Lynn's stepsister. I was wrong.

'We understand that you were in the end seat of a row

reserved for media and that you were next to the man who shouted at Mrs. Spencer.'

'That's right.'

'We also understand that you spoke to a number of disgruntled stockholders after the meeting and took down their names.'

'Yes, I did.'

'By any chance did the man who talked about losing his house because of investing in Gen-stone talk to you?'

'No, he did not.'

'Do you have the names of the stockholders who talked to you?'

'Yes, I do.' I felt that Jason Knowles was waiting for an explanation. 'As you may or may not know, I write a financial advice column that is directed to the unsophisticated consumer or investor. I also do occasional freelance articles for magazines. At that meeting it occurred to me that I might want to do an in-depth article illustrating the way the collapse of Gen-stone has destroyed the future of so many little investors.'

'I do know that, and that's why I'm here. We'd like to have the names of the people who spoke to you.'

I looked at him. It appeared to be a reasonable request, but I guess I had every journalist's instant reaction about being asked to reveal sources.

It was as though Jason Knowles could read my mind. 'Ms. DeCarlo, I'm sure you can understand why I'm making that request. Your sister, Lynn Spencer – '

I interrupted him: 'Stepsister.'

He nodded. 'Stepsister. Your stepsister could have been killed when her home burned down the other night. We have no idea at this point whether the person who set the fire knew she was in the house. But it also seems reasonable that one of those angry – and even financially desperate – stockholders might have set it.'

'You do realize that there are hundreds of other people, both stockholders and employees, who might have been responsible for setting the fire?' I pointed out.

'We are aware of that. By any chance did you get the name of the man who had the outburst?'

'No.' I thought of how that poor guy had gone from anger to hopeless tears. 'He didn't set the fire. I'm sure of it.'

Jason Knowles's eyebrows raised. 'You're sure he didn't set it. Why?'

I realized how stupid it would be to say, 'I just know he didn't.' Instead I said, 'That man was desperate, but in a different way. He's heartbroken with worry. He said his daughter is dying and he's going to lose his home.'

It was obvious that Jason Knowles was disappointed when I couldn't identify the man who was so upset at the meeting, but he wasn't through with me. 'You *do* have the names of the people who spoke to you, Ms. DeCarlo?'

I hesitated.

'Ms. DeCarlo, I saw your interview at the hospital. You very properly condemned as evil or psychotic anyone who would set fire to a home.'

He was right. I agreed to give him the names and phone numbers I had jotted down at the meeting.

Again he seemed to read my mind. 'Ms. DeCarlo, when we call these people, we intend to simply tell them that we are speaking to everyone who attended the stockholders' meeting, which I assure you is true. Many of those present had returned the postcard sent by the company indicating that they planned to be there. Anyone who returned that card will be visited. The problem is that not everyone who attended bothered to return the card.'

'I see.'

'How did you find your stepsister, Ms. DeCarlo?'

I hoped my moment of hesitation did not register on this quietly observant man. 'You saw the interview,' I said. 'I found Lynn in pain and bewildered by all that has happened. She told me she had no idea that her husband was doing anything illegal. She swears that to the best of her knowledge, he was absolutely committed to the belief that Gen-stone's vaccine was a miracle drug.'

'Does she think the plane crash was staged?' Jason Knowles shot the question at me.

'Absolutely not.' And now, as I echoed Lynn, I wondered if I sounded either convinced or convincing. 'She insists she wants and needs to learn the absolute truth.'

# Chapter 6

At eleven o'clock the next morning I drove into the visitors' parking lot of Gen-stone in Pleasantville, New York. Pleasantville is a lovely Westchester town that was put on the map years ago when *Reader's Digest* opened its international headquarters there.

Gen-stone is about half a mile from the *Digest* property. It was another beautiful April day. As I walked along the path to the building, a line from a poem I loved as a child ran through my head: 'Oh, to be in England now that April's there.' The name of the famous poet simply wouldn't jump into my mind. I figured I'd probably wake up at three in the morning and there it would be.

There was a security guard standing outside the main entrance. Even so, I had to press a button and announce myself before the receptionist admitted me.

I was a good fifteen minutes early, which pleased me. It's so much better to be able to settle down and get your breath before a meeting rather than go in late, flustered and apologizing. I told the receptionist I was waiting for my associates and took a seat.

Last night after dinner I did some Internet homework on the two men we'd be seeing, Charles Wallingford and Dr. Milo Celtavini. I learned that Charles Wallingford had been the sixth member of his family to head the Wallingford chain of upscale furniture stores. Started by his great-great-great grandfather, the original hole-in-the-wall store on Delancey Street had grown, moved to Fifth Avenue, and expanded until Wallingford's became a household name.

The onslaught of discount furniture chains and a downturn in the economy weren't handled well by Charles when he took over the reins of the company. He'd added a much cheaper line of furniture to their stock, thereby changing the image of Wallingford's, closed a number of stores, reconfigured the remaining ones, and finally accepted a buyout from a British company. That was about ten years ago.

Two years later Wallingford met Nicholas Spencer who at the time was struggling to open a new company, Gen-stone. Wallingford invested a considerable sum in Gen-stone and accepted the job as chairman of the board.

I wondered if he wished he had stuck with furniture.

Dr. Milo Celtavini went to college and graduate school in Italy, did research work in immunobiology most of his life there, and then accepted an invitation to join the research team at Sloan-Kettering in New York. After a short time he left to take over the laboratory at Gen-stone because he was convinced they were on the path to a potentially revolutionary achievement in medicine.

Ken and Don came in as I was folding my notes. The

receptionist took their names, and a few minutes later we were escorted into Charles Wallingford's office.

He was sitting behind an eighteenth-century mahogany desk. The Persian carpet at his feet had faded just enough to give a soft glow to the red and blue and gold tones in its pattern. A leather couch and several matching chairs formed a seating group to the left of the door. The walls were paneled in a butternut shade of walnut. The narrow draperies were a deep shade of blue, framing rather than covering the windows. As a result, the room was filled with natural light, and the beautiful outside gardens served as living artwork. It was the room of a man with impeccable taste.

That verified the impression I'd had of Wallingford at the stockholders' meeting on Monday. Even though he was clearly under great strain, he had conducted himself with dignity when the derisive shouts were hurled at him. Now he got up from behind his desk to greet us with a courteous smile.

After we had introduced ourselves, he said, 'I think you'll be more comfortable there,' indicating the seating area. I sat on the couch, and Don Carter sat next to me. Ken took one of the chairs, and Wallingford perched on the edge of the seat of the other one, his elbows resting lightly on the arms, the fingertips of his hands touching.

As the business expert of our group, Don thanked Wallingford for agreeing to be interviewed and then began to ask some pretty tough questions, including how so much money could have gone missing without Wallingford and the board of directors getting some kind of warning.

According to Wallingford, it boiled down to the fact

that after Garner Pharmaceuticals contracted to invest in Gen-stone, they became alarmed at the continuing disappointments in the results of the ongoing experiments. Spencer had been looting the revenues of their medical-products division for years. Realizing the FDA would never approve the vaccine and he could no longer stave off discovery of his theft, he probably decided to disappear.

'Obviously fate took a hand,' Wallingford said. 'On his way to Puerto Rico, Nick's plane crashed in that sudden storm.'

'Mr. Wallingford, do you think that you were invited by Nicholas Spencer to join him in the company and be chairman of the board because of your investment expertise or your business acumen?' Don asked.

'I guess the answer is that Nick invited me for both those reasons.'

'If I may say, sir, not everyone was impressed by your handling of your previous business.' Don began reading excerpts of some articles from business publications which seemed to suggest that Wallingford had pretty much made a mess of the family company.

Wallingford countered by saying that retail sales of furniture had been diminishing steadily, labor and delivery problems had escalated, and if he had waited, the company would surely have ended up in bankruptcy. He pointed to one of the articles Carter was holding. 'I can cite a dozen other articles written by that guy that show how much of a guru he is,' he said sarcastically.

Wallingford seemed unperturbed by the implication that he'd been wrong in his handling of the family business. From my own research I had learned that he was forty-nine years old, had two grown sons, and had been divorced for ten years. It was only when Carter asked if it was true that he was estranged from his sons that his jaw hardened. 'Much to my regret, there have been some difficulties,' he said. 'And to prevent any misunderstanding, I will tell you the reason for them. My sons did not want me to sell the company. They were quite unrealistic about its potential future. Neither did they want me to invest most of the proceeds of the sale in this company. Unfortunately, it turns out they were right about that.'

He explained how he had gotten together with Nicholas Spencer. 'It was known that I was looking around for a good investment opportunity. A merger and acquisitions company suggested that I consider making a modest investment in Gen-stone. I met Nick Spencer and was greatly impressed by him, a not uncommon reaction as you may know. He asked me to speak to several top microbiologists, all of whom had impeccable credentials and all of whom told me that, in their opinion, he was onto something in his search for the vaccine that would both prevent cancer and limit its spread.

'I recognized the possibilities of what Gen-stone could become. Then Nick asked me if I would consider joining him as chairman of the board and co-chief executive officer. My function would be to run the company. His was to be head of research and the public face of the company.'

'Bring in other investors,' Don suggested.

Wallingford smiled grimly. 'He was good at that. My modest investment became an almost total commitment of my assets. Nick went to Italy and Switzerland regularly. He let it be known that his scientific knowledge rivaled or exceeded that of many molecular biologists.'

'Any truth at all to that?' Don asked.

Wallingford shook his head. 'He's smart, but not that smart.'

He certainly had fooled me, I thought, remembering how Nick Spencer exuded confidence when he told me about the vaccine he was developing.

I realized where Don Carter was going. He believed that Charles Wallingford had made a mess of his family business, but Nick Spencer had decided he was the perfect image for his company. He looked and sounded like the WASP he was, and he would be easily manipulated. Don's next question confirmed my analysis.

'Mr. Wallingford, wouldn't you say that your board of directors has a rather uneven mix?'

'I'm not sure I understand you.'

'They are all from extremely wealthy families, but not one of them has any real business experience.'

'They are people I knew well and they are on the boards of their own foundations.'

'Which doesn't necessarily prove they have the financial acumen to be on the board of a company such as this one.'

'You won't find a smarter or more honorable group of people anywhere,' Wallingford said. His tone was suddenly icy, and his face became flushed.

I really think he was on the verge of throwing us out, but then there was a knock at the door and Dr. Celtavini came in.

He was a relatively short, conservative-looking man in his late sixties, with a slight Italian accent. He told us that when he agreed to head the Gen-stone lab, he had strongly believed that a vaccine could be developed to prevent cancer. Initially he had some promising results in the offspring of mice with genetic cancer cells, but then problems developed. He had not been able to duplicate those early results. Exhaustive tests and much further work would be needed before any conclusions could safely be drawn.

'The breakthroughs will come in time,' he said. 'There are many workers in the field.'

'What is your opinion of Nicholas Spencer?' Ken Page asked.

Dr. Celtavini's face went gray. 'I put a spotless reputation of forty years in my field on the line when I came to Gen-stone. I am now considered involved in the downfall of this company. The answer to your question: I despise Nicholas Spencer.'

When Ken went back to the lab with Dr. Celtavini, Don and I took off. Don had an appointment with the Gen-stone auditors in Manhattan. I told him I'd meet him at the office later and that I was planning to drive in the morning to Caspien, the Connecticut town where Nicholas Spencer had grown up. We agreed that to put this cover story together while it was still hot news, we were going to have to move fast.

That fact didn't keep me from steering the car north rather than south. An overwhelming curiosity made me want to drive to Bedford and see for myself the extent of the fire that had almost taken Lynn's life.

# Chapter 7

Ned knew that Dr. Ryan had looked at him kind of funny when he ran into him in the hospital. That was why he was afraid to go back. But he had to go back. He had to go into the room where Lynn Spencer was a patient.

If he did that, maybe he wouldn't keep seeing Annie's face the way it had looked when the car was on fire and she couldn't get out. He needed to see that same look on Lynn Spencer's face.

The interview with her sister or stepsister, whatever she was, had been broadcast on the six o'clock and then the eleven o'clock news the day before yesterday. 'Lynn is in great pain,' she had said, her voice oh so sad. 'Be sorry for her' was what she meant. It's not her fault that your wife is dead. She and her husband just wanted to cheat you. That's all they meant to do.

Annie. When he did get to sleep, he always dreamt of her. Sometimes they were good dreams. They were in Greenwood Lake and it was fifteen years ago. They never went there while his mother was alive. Mama didn't like anyone to visit her. But when she died, the house became his, and Annie had been thrilled. 'I never had a home of my own. I'm going to fix it up so nice. Wait and see, Ned.'

And she *had* fixed it up nice. It was small, only four rooms, but over the years she had saved enough money to buy new cabinets for the kitchen and to hire a handyman to put them in. The next year she saved enough to have a new toilet and sink installed in the bathroom. She had made him soak off all the old wallpaper, and together they painted the place inside and out. They'd bought windows from that guy who advertised on CBS all the time about how cheap his windows were. And Annie had her garden, her beautiful garden.

He kept thinking about them working together, painting. He dreamed of Annie hanging the curtains and standing back and saying how pretty they looked.

He kept thinking about the weekends. They drove there every weekend from May until the end of October. They had only a couple of electric heaters to keep the place warm, and they cost too much to use in the winter. She had planned that when she was able to retire from the hospital, they'd put in central heat so that they could live there all year round.

He'd sold the house to their new neighbor last October. The neighbor wanted more property. He hadn't paid that much for it, because under the new town code it wasn't considered a building lot, but Ned hadn't cared. He knew that whatever he was able to put into Gen-stone would bring him a fortune. Nicholas Spencer had promised that when he talked to Ned about the vaccine. When Ned was working for the landscaper at the Bedford property, he had met Spencer.

He hadn't told Annie he was selling the house. He didn't want her to talk him out of it. Then one nice Saturday in February, when he was working, she'd decided to take a ride to Greenwood Lake, and the house was gone. She'd come home and pounded his chest with her fists, and even though he'd driven her to Bedford to see the kind of mansion he was going to buy for her, it hadn't helped calm her anger.

Ned was sorry that Nicholas Spencer was dead. I wish I could have killed him myself, he thought. If I hadn't listened to him, Annie would still be here with me.

Then last night when he couldn't sleep, he had a vision of Annie. She was telling him to go to the hospital and see Dr. Greene. 'You need medicine, Ned,' she was saying. 'Dr. Greene will give you medicine.'

If he made an appointment with Dr. Greene, he'd be able to go to the hospital, and nobody would think it was unusual to see him there. He'd find out where Lynn Spencer was and go into her room. And before he killed her, he'd tell her all about Annie.

# Chapter 8

I hadn't intended to visit Lynn that day, but after I passed the ruin that had been her home in Bedford, I realized that I was only ten minutes away from the hospital. I decided to stop in. I'll be honest: I'd seen pictures of that beautiful house, and now, witnessing the charred remains, it hit me how very fortunate Lynn had been to survive. There were two other cars in the garage that night. If that fireman hadn't noticed the red Fiat she usually drove and inquired about it, she would be dead now.

She had been lucky. Luckier than her husband, I thought as I drove into the hospital parking lot. I was sure I wouldn't have to worry about running into cameramen today. In this fast-paced world, Lynn's brush with death was already old news, only interesting if someone was arrested for setting the fire or if Lynn herself was found to be a co-conspirator in the looting of Gen-stone.

When I got my visitor's pass at the hospital, I was directed to the top floor. When I stepped out of the elevator, I realized it was for patients with big bucks. The hallway was carpeted, and the unoccupied room I passed could have been in a five-star hotel.

It occurred to me that I should have phoned ahead. My mental image had been of the Lynn I'd seen two days ago, with oxygen tubes in her nostrils, bandaged hands and feet – and pathetically grateful to see me.

The door of her room was partially open, and when I looked in, I hesitated before entering because she was talking on the phone. She was reclining on a divan at the window, and the change in her appearance was dramatic. The oxygen tubes were gone. The bandages on her palms were much smaller. A pale green satin robe had replaced the hospital-issue nightshirt she had been wearing on Tuesday. Her hair was no longer loose but once again was swept up in a French knot. I heard her say, 'I love you, too.'

She must have sensed my presence because she turned as she closed her cell phone. What did I see on her face? Surprise? Or for an instant did she look annoyed, even alarmed?

But then her smile was welcoming and her voice warm. 'Carley, how nice of you to come. I was just talking to Dad. I can't convince him that I'm really all right.'

I walked over to her, and realizing that I probably shouldn't touch her hand, I awkwardly patted her shoulder, and then sat on the loveseat facing her. There were flowers on the table next to her, flowers on the dresser, flowers on the night table. None of the arrangements were the kind you grab in the hospital lobby. Like everything else about Lynn, they were expensive.

I was angry at myself for immediately feeling a sense of

being off-balance with her, as though I was waiting for her to establish the mood. In our first meeting in Florida, she'd been condescending. Two days ago she'd been vulnerable. Today?

'Carley, I can't thank you enough for the way you spoke about me when they interviewed you the other day,' she said.

'I simply said that you were lucky to be alive and that you were in pain.'

'All I know is that I've had calls from friends who had stopped talking to me after they found out what Nick had done. They saw you, and I guess they realized that I'm a victim along with them.'

'Lynn, what do you think about your husband now?' It was a question I had to ask, the one I realized I had come here to ask.

Lynn looked past me. Her mouth tightened. She clasped her hands together, then winced and pulled them apart. 'Carley, it's all happened so fast. The plane crash. I couldn't believe Nick was gone. He was larger than life. You met him, and I think you sensed that. I believed in him. I thought of him as a man with a mission. He'd say things like, "Lynn, I'm going to beat the cancer cell, but that's just the beginning. When I see kids who were born deaf or blind or retarded or with spina bifida, and know how close we are to preventing such birth defects, I go crazy that we're not out there with this vaccine yet." '

I had met Nicholas Spencer only once, but I had seen him interviewed on television any number of times. Consciously or unconsciously, Lynn had caught something of the tenor of his voice, of that forceful passion that had made such an impression on me.

She shrugged. 'Now I can only wonder if everything about my life with him was a lie. Did he seek me out and then marry me because I gave him access to people he might not have known otherwise?'

'How did you meet him?' I asked.

'He came to the public relations firm where I work, about seven years ago. We handle only top-drawer clients. He wanted to start getting publicity for his firm and get the word out about the vaccine they were developing. Then he started asking me out. I knew I resembled his first wife. I don't know what it was. My own father lost his retirement money because he trusted Nick. If he deliberately cheated Dad as well as all those other people, the man I loved never even existed.'

She hesitated, then went on. 'Two members of the board came to see me yesterday. The more I learn, the more I believe that from beginning to end Nick was a fraud.'

I decided it was necessary to tell her that I would be writing an in-depth article on him for *Wall Street Weekly*. 'It will be a chips-fall-where-they-may article,' I said.

'The chips have already fallen.'

The phone at the bedside rang. I picked it up and handed it to her. She listened, sighed, and said, 'Yes, they can come up.' She handed the receiver back to me and said, 'Two people from the police department in Bedford want to talk to me about the fire. Don't let me keep you, Carley.'

I would love to have sat in on that meeting, but I had been dismissed. I replaced the phone on the receiver, picked up my purse, and then thought of something. 'Lynn, I'm going to Caspien tomorrow.'

'Caspien?'

'The town where Nick was raised. Would you know anyone you'd suggest I see there? I mean, did Nick ever mention any close friends?'

She considered my question for a moment, then shook her head. 'None that I can recall.' Suddenly she looked past me and gasped. I turned to see what had startled her.

There was a man standing in the doorway, one hand inside his jacket, the other in his pocket. He was balding and had a sallow complexion and sunken cheekbones. I wondered if he was ill. He stared at the two of us, then glanced down the corridor. 'Sorry. I guess I'm on the wrong floor,' and with that murmured apology, he was gone.

A moment later two uniformed police officers replaced him at the entrance to the room, and I left.

# Chapter 9

On the way home I heard on the radio that the police were questioning a suspect in the torching of the Bedford home of Nicholas Spencer, described, as always, as the missing or deceased chief executive of Gen-stone.

To my dismay I heard that the suspect was the man who had the emotional outburst at the shareholders' meeting on Monday afternoon at the Grand Hyatt Hotel in Manhattan. He was thirty-six-year-old Marty Bikorsky, a resident of White Plains, New York, who worked at a gasoline station in Mount Kisco, the neighboring town to Bedford. He had been treated at St. Ann's Hospital on Tuesday afternoon for a burn on his right hand.

Bikorsky claimed that the night of the fire he had worked until eleven o'clock, met with some friends for a couple of beers, and by twelve-thirty was home and in bed. Under questioning he admitted that at the bar he had sounded off about the Spencers' mansion in Bedford and how for two cents he'd torch it.

His wife corroborated the testimony about the time he had arrived home and gone to bed, but she also admitted that when she woke up at three o'clock, he was not there. She also said that she had not been surprised at his absence, because he was a restless sleeper, and sometimes in the middle of the night he would put a jacket over his pajamas and go out on the back porch to smoke. She went back to sleep and did not wake up until seven. At that time he was already in the kitchen and his hand was burned. He said it had happened when his hand touched the flame on the stove while he was cleaning up spilled cocoa.

I had told the investigator from the U.S. Attorney's Office, Jason Knowles, that I did not think the man I now knew was Marty Bikorsky had anything to do with the fire, that he was troubled rather than vindictive. I wondered if I was losing the instinct that is essential to anyone in the news business. Then I decided that no matter how it looked for Bikorsky, I still felt that way.

As I drove, I realized that something had been flickering in and out of my subconscious. Then it registered: It was the face of the man who had briefly stood at the door of Lynn's hospital room. I knew I'd seen him before. Tuesday, he'd been standing outside the hospital when I was interviewed.

Poor guy, I thought. He looks so defeated. I wondered if someone in his family was a patient in the hospital.

That evening I had dinner with Gwen Harkins at Neary's on East 57th Street. Growing up, she lived near me in Ridgewood. We went through grammar school and high school together. For college she went south to Georgetown, and I went north to Boston College, but we took semesters in London and Florence together. She was my maid of honor when I married the lemon of the century, and she was the one who kept making me go out with her after the baby died and the lemon took off for California.

Gwen is a tall, willowy redhead who usually wears high heels. When we're together, I'm sure we make an odd sight. I'm single courtesy of a decree that says that what God has put together, the State of New York can declare asunder. She's had a couple of guys she could have married, but neither one, she says, made her want to keep the cell phone pinned to her ear rather than miss his call. Her mother, like mine, assures her that someday she'll meet 'Mr. Right.' Gwen is a lawyer for one of the major drug companies, and when I called her and suggested dinner at Neary's, I had two reasons for wanting to see her.

The first, of course, is that we always have a good time together. The second is that I wanted to get her take on Gen-stone and what the people in the pharmaceutical industry were saying about it.

As usual, Neary's was bustling. It's a home away from home for many people. You never know which celebrity or politician might be at one of the corner tables.

Jimmy Neary joined us at the table for a moment, and as Gwen and I sipped red wine, I told him about my new job. 'Nick Spencer would drop by here from time to time,' he said. 'I'd have pegged him as a straight arrow. Shows you never can be sure.' He nodded toward two men standing at the bar. 'Those fellows lost money in Gen-stone, and I happen to know they can't afford it. Both of them have kids in college.'

Gwen ordered red snapper. I chose my favorite comfort food, a sliced steak sandwich and French fries. We settled back to talk.

'This dinner is on me, Gwen,' I said. 'I need to pick your brain. How was Nick Spencer able to get so much hype going on his vaccine if it's a sham?'

Gwen shrugged. She's a good lawyer, which means that she never answers a question directly. 'Carley, break-throughs in new drugs are happening practically every day. Compare it to transportation. Until the nineteenth century, people rode in carriages or stagecoaches or on horseback. The train and the automobile were the great inventions that moved the world faster. In the twentieth century we had prop planes, then jets, then supersonic aircraft, and then spaceships. That kind of acceleration and progress is happening in medical laboratories as well. Think about it. Aspirin was only discovered in the late 1890s. Before that they were bleeding people to relieve fever. Smallpox. That vaccine is only eighty years old, and wherever it was, it eradicated the disease. As recently as fifty years ago there was a polio epidemic. The Salk and then the Sabin vaccines took care of that. I could go on and on.'

'DNA?'

'Exactly. And don't forget that DNA has revolutionized the legal system as well as making it possible to predict hereditary diseases.'

I thought about the prisoners who were being released from death row because their DNA proved they hadn't committed the crime.

Gwen still had a full head of steam. 'Remember all the books where a child was kidnapped, and then thirty years later an adult showed up at the door and said, "I'm home, Mommy."' Today it isn't a case of whether or not somebody looks like somebody else. DNA testing makes the difference.'

Our dinners arrived. Gwen took a couple of bites, then went on. 'Carley, I don't know whether Nick Spencer was a charlatan or a genius. I understand some of the early results of his cancer vaccine as reported in medical journals seemed to be very encouraging, but face it: At the end of the day, they couldn't verify the results. Then, of course, Spencer disappears, and it turns out he looted the company.'

'Did you ever meet him?' I asked.

'In a big group at some of the medical seminars. A very impressive guy, but you know what, Carley? Knowing how much he stole from people who couldn't afford to lose it and, even worse, how he dashed the hopes of people desperate for the vaccine he touted, I can't feel a scintilla of sympathy for him. So his plane crashed. As far as I'm concerned, he got what he deserved.'

# Chapter 10

Connecticut is a beautiful state. My father's cousins lived there when I was growing up and when we visited them, I thought that all of the state was like Darien. But like every other state, Connecticut has its modest working-class towns, and the next morning when I got to Caspien, a hamlet ten miles from Bridgeport, that was what I found.

The trip didn't take that long, less than an hour and a half. I left my garage at nine o'clock and was passing the 'Welcome to Caspien' sign at ten-twenty. The sign was a wood carving illustrated with the image of a revolutionary soldier holding a musket.

I drove up and down through the streets to get the feel of the place. The majority of the houses were Cape Cods and split levels, the kind built in the mid-1950s. Many of them had been enlarged, and I could see where yet another generation had replaced the original owners, the veterans of World War II. Bicycles and skate boards were visible in carports or leaning near side doors. The large percentage of vehicles parked in the driveways or on the streets were SUVs or roomy sedans.

It was a family kind of town. Almost all the houses were well kept. As in every place where people dwell, there was a section where the houses were bigger, the lots larger. But there were no cookie-cutter mansions in Caspien. I decided that when people started to make it big, they set out the 'for sale' sign and moved to a more pricey enclave nearby, such as Greenwich or Westport or Darien.

I drove slowly down Main Street, the center of Caspien. Four blocks long, it had the usual mix of small-town business establishments: Gap, J. Crew, Pottery Barn, a furniture store, a post office, a beauty parlor, a pizza joint, a few restaurants, an insurance broker. I cruised through a couple of the intersecting blocks. On Elm Street I passed a funeral parlor and a shopping mall that included a supermarket, dry cleaner, liquor store, and movie house. On Hickory Street I found a diner and next to it a two-story building with a sign that read CASPIEN TOWN JOURNAL.

From my map I could see that the Spencer family home was located at 71 Winslow Terrace, an avenue that spiked off from the end of Main Street. At that address I found a roomy frame house with a porch, the kind of turn-of-the-century house I grew up in. There was a shingle outside that read PHILIP BRODERICK, M.D. I wondered if Dr. Broderick lived on the upstairs floor where the Spencer family had lived.

In an interview, Nicholas Spencer had painted a glowing picture of his childhood: 'I knew I couldn't interrupt my father when he had patients, but just knowing he was there downstairs, a minute away, made me feel so great.'

I intended to pay a visit to Dr. Philip Broderick, but not yet. Instead I drove back to the building that housed the *Caspien Town Journal*, parked at the curb, and went inside.

The heavyset woman at the reception desk was so absorbed in something on the Internet that she looked startled when the door opened. But her expression immediately became pleasant. She gave me a cheery 'good morning' and asked how she could help me. Wide rimless glasses magnified her light blue eyes.

I had decided that instead of announcing myself as a reporter for *Wall Street Weekly*, I would simply request recent back issues of the newspaper. Spencer's plane had crashed nearly three weeks ago. The scandal about the missing money and the vaccine was now two weeks old. My guess was that this hometown paper had probably covered both stories in depth.

The woman had an amazing lack of curiosity about what I was doing there. She disappeared down the hall and returned with copies of the last weeks' editions. I paid for them – a total of $3.00 – tucked them under my arm, and headed for the diner next door. Breakfast had been half an English muffin and a cup of instant coffee. I decided that a bagel and brewed coffee would make excellent 'elevenses' as my British friends call their mid-morning tea or coffee break.

The diner was small and cozy, one of those places with red checkered curtains and plates with pictures of hens and their chicks lining the wall behind the counter. Two men in their seventies were just getting up to leave. The waitress, a tiny bundle of energy, was whisking away their empty cups.

She looked up when the door opened. 'Take your pick of the tables,' she said, smiling. 'East, west, north, or south.' The name tag on her uniform read, 'Call me Milly.' I judged her to be about my mother's age, but unlike my mother, Milly had fiercely red hair.

I chose the rounded corner booth where I could spread out the papers. Before I'd settled, Milly was beside me, order pad in hand. Moments later the coffee and bagel were in front of me.

Spencer's plane had gone down on April 4. The oldest paper I'd bought was dated April 9. The front page had a picture of him. The headline read 'Nicholas Spencer Feared Dead.'

The story was an ode to the memory of a small-town boy who had made good. The picture was a recent one. It had been taken on February 15 when Spencer was awarded the first 'Distinguished Citizen Award' ever presented by the town. I did some arithmetic. February 15 to April 4. At the time of the award, he had forty-seven days left on this planet. I've often wondered if people get a sense that their time is running out. I think my father did. He went out for a walk that morning eight years ago, but my mother told me that at the door he hesitated, then came back and kissed the top of her head. Three blocks away he had a heart attack. The doctor said he was dead before he hit the ground.

Nicholas Spencer was smiling in this picture, but his eyes looked pensive, even worried.

The first four pages of the paper were all about him. There were pictures of him as an eight-year-old Little Leaguer. He'd been the pitcher on the Caspien Tigers. Another picture showed him at about age ten with his father in the laboratory of the family home. He'd been on the swim team in high school – that picture had him posing with a trophy. Another had him in a Shakespearean costume holding something that looked like an Oscar – he'd been voted best actor in the senior play.

The picture of him with his first wife on their wedding day twelve years ago made me gasp. Janet Barlowe Spencer of Greenwich had been a slender, delicately featured blonde. It's too much to say that she was a double for Lynn, but there's no question that there was a very strong resemblance. I wondered if their similarity had anything to do with his getting together with Lynn.

There were tributes to him from a half-dozen local people, including a lawyer who said they'd been best friends in high school, a teacher who raved about his thirst for knowledge, and a neighbor who said he always volunteered to run errands for her. I took out my notebook and jotted down their names. I guessed I'd be able to find their addresses in the phone book, if I decided to contact them.

The following week's issue of the newspaper covered the fact that the Gen-stone vaccine that Spencer's company had claimed would be the definitive cure for cancer was a failure. The article noted that the co-chief executive of Gen-stone had conceded they might have been too hasty in publicizing its early successes. The picture of Nick Spencer that accompanied the story appeared to be company issued.

The newspaper that came out five days ago had the same picture of Spencer but carried a different caption: 'Spencer Accused of Looting Millions.' They used the word 'alleged' throughout the article, but an editorial suggested that the appropriate award for the town to have offered him should have been another Oscar for best actor and not its first 'Distinguished Citizen Award.'

'Call me Millie' was offering me more coffee. I accepted and could see that her eyes were snapping with curiosity at the sight of the pictures of Spencer side by side on the table. I decided to give her an opening.

'Did you know Nicholas Spencer?' I asked.

She shook her head. 'No. He was gone by the time I came to town twenty years ago. But let me tell you, when those stories came out about him swindling his company and his vaccine being no good, a lot of people around here got mighty unhappy. Plenty of them bought stock in his company after he got the medal. In his speech he said it might be the most important discovery since the polio vaccine.'

His claims had been getting loftier, I thought. Had it been a case of rope in one more bunch of suckers before you disappear?

'The dinner was a sellout,' Milly said. 'I mean, Spencer's been on the cover of a couple of national magazines. People wanted to see him up close. He's the only thing resembling a celebrity this town ever produced. It was a fund-raiser, of course. I hear that after they heard his speech, the board of directors bought a lot of stock in Genstone for the hospital's portfolio. Now everybody's mad at everybody else for thinking up the award and getting him here for it. They won't be able to go ahead with the new children's wing of the hospital.'

The coffeepot was in her right hand, and she put her left hand on her hip. 'Let me tell you, in this town Spencer's name is *mud*.

'But God rest him,' she added reluctantly. Then she looked at me. 'Why are you so interested in Spencer? You a reporter or something?'

'Yes, I am,' I admitted.

'You're not the first nosing around about him. Someone from the FBI was in here asking questions about who his friends might be. I said he didn't have any left.'

On that note I paid my bill, gave Millie my card, saying, 'In case you ever want to get in touch with me,' and got back in the car. This time I drove to 71 Winslow Terrace.

# Chapter 11

Sometimes I get lucky. Dr. Philip Broderick did not have office hours on Thursday afternoon. When I arrived, it was a quarter of twelve and his last patient was leaving. I gave one of my brand-new *Wall Street Weekly* cards to his receptionist. Looking doubtful, she asked me to wait while she spoke to the doctor. Keeping my fingers crossed, I did just that.

When she returned, she said, 'The doctor will see you.' She sounded surprised, and frankly I was, too. While doing the freelance profiles I learned that when the subject is controversial, you have just as good a chance of getting an interview by ringing a doorbell as you have by phoning and trying to make an appointment. My theory is that some people still have an innate sense of courtesy and feel that if you take the trouble to come to them, you deserve to be tolerated if not welcomed. The rest of that theory is that some people worry that if they refuse you on their own doorstep, you might write something negative about them.

Anyhow, whatever this doctor's reasons, we were about to meet. He must have heard my footsteps because he got up from behind his desk as I entered his office. He was a lean, tall man in his mid-fifties, with an abundance of gray hair. His greeting was courteous but businesslike. 'Ms. DeCarlo, I'll start off by being very frank. I've only agreed to speak with you because I read and respect the magazine you represent. However, you must understand that you are not the first or the fifth or the tenth reporter to call or to drop in here.'

I wondered how many cover stories there were going to be on Nicholas Spencer. I only hoped that what I contributed to ours would at least give it something fresh or newsworthy. I did have one approach that I hoped might work. I quickly thanked the doctor for seeing me without notice, took the seat he'd indicated, and cut to the chase. 'Dr. Broderick, if you read our magazine regularly, you know that the editorial policy is to tell the absolute truth without sensationalism as the facts are revealed. I intend to do that for the magazine, but also on a personal level, three years ago my widowed mother remarried. My stepsister, whom I know only casually, is Nicholas Spencer's wife. She is in the hospital recovering from injuries she suffered when her home was deliberately set on fire the other night. She doesn't know what to believe about her husband, but she wants and needs to know the truth. Any help you can give will be greatly appreciated.'

'I read about the fire.'

I detected the note of sympathy I wanted from him, even while I hated myself for playing that card. 'Did you know Nicholas Spencer?' I asked.

'I knew his father, Dr. Edward Spencer, as a friend. I

shared his interest in microbiology and often came over to observe his experiments. For me it was a fascinating hobby. Nicholas Spencer had already graduated from college and moved to New York by the time I settled here.'

'When was the last time you saw Nicholas Spencer?'

'February 16, the day after the fund-raiser.'

'He stayed in town overnight?'

'No, he came back the morning after the fund-raiser. I did not expect to see him. Let me explain. This is the home where he grew up, but I assume you're aware of that.'

'Yes, I am.'

'Nick's father died suddenly of a heart attack twelve years ago, right around the time Nick was married. I immediately offered to buy the house. My wife always loved it, and I had outgrown my first office. At that time I planned to keep the laboratory and play around with some of the early experiments that Dr. Spencer had decided were going nowhere. I asked Nick if he would let me copy only those records. Instead he left them with me. He took all his father's later files, which he felt held promising research. As I'm sure you also know, his mother died of cancer as a young woman, and his father's lifelong goal was to find a cure for the disease.'

I remembered the intensity in Nick Spencer's face when he told me that story. 'Did you use Dr. Spencer's notes?' I asked.

'Not really.' Dr. Broderick shrugged. 'It was a case of the best laid plans of mice and men. I was always too busy, and then I needed the area the laboratory took up to create two new examination rooms. I stored the records in the attic just in case Spencer ever came for them. He never did, until the day after the fund-raiser.'

'That was only a month and a half before he died! Why do you think he came back for them then?' I asked.

Broderick hesitated. 'He didn't give any explanation, so of course I can't be sure. He was obviously unsettled. Tense would be a better word, I guess. But then I said that he'd made the trip for nothing, and he asked me what I meant.'

'What did you mean?'

'Last fall someone from his company came for the records, and, of course, I gave them to him.'

'How did Nick react when you told him that?' I asked, intrigued now.

'He asked me if I could give him the name or describe the person who was here. I could not remember the man's name, but I did describe him. He was well-dressed, had reddish brown hair, was of average height, and was about forty years old.'

'Did Nick recognize who it was?'

'I can't be sure, but he was visibly upset. Then he said, "I don't have as much time as I thought," and he left.'

'Do you know if he was visiting anyone else in town?'

'He must have been. An hour later, when I was on my way to the hospital, he passed me in his car.'

I had planned for my next stop to be the high school Nick had attended. I just wanted the usual background of what kind of kid he'd been. But after talking to Dr. Broderick, I changed my mind. I intended to drive straight to Gen-stone, find the guy with the reddish brown hair, and ask him a few questions.

If indeed he worked for Gen-stone, which somehow I seriously doubted.

# Chapter 12

After he left the hospital, Ned drove home and lay down on the couch. He had done his best, but he had failed Annie. He had the gasoline in a jar and had a long string in one pocket, the lighter in another. One single minute more, and he could have done to that room what he had done to the mansion.

Then he had heard the click of the elevator door, and he saw the Bedford cops. They knew who he was. He was sure they didn't get close enough to see his face, but he didn't want them to start wondering why he was in the hospital now that Annie was dead.

Of course he could have told them that he was there because he had an appointment with Dr. Greene. It would have been the truth – Dr. Greene had been busy, but he'd squeezed him in during his lunch hour. He was a nice man, even if he had agreed with Annie that he should have discussed the sale of the Greenwood Lake house with her.

He hadn't told Dr. Greene that he was angry. He had

just said how sad he was. He'd said, 'I miss Annie. I love her.'

Dr. Greene didn't know the real reason Annie had died, that she had rushed out of the house, into the car, and been hit by the garbage truck, all because she was so mad at him about the Gen-stone stock. He didn't know that Ned had worked for the landscaper who took care of the Bedford mansion that burned down, and that's why he knew his way around the grounds there.

Dr. Greene gave him pills to relax him, and some sleeping pills as well. Ned took two sleeping pills as soon as he got home from the hospital and fell asleep on the couch. He didn't wake up for fourteen hours, until eleven o'clock on Thursday morning.

That was when his landlady, Mrs. Morgan, rang the doorbell. Her mother had owned the house twenty years ago when he and Annie moved in, but Mrs. Morgan had taken it over last year.

Ned didn't like her. She was a big woman with the face of someone who wants a fight. He stood in the doorway, blocking the entrance, but he could tell that she was trying to peer past him, looking for trouble.

When she spoke, her voice didn't have its usual rough, loud sound: 'Ned, I thought you'd be up and out to work by now.'

He hadn't answered. It was none of her business that he'd been fired again.

'You know how sorry I am about Annie.'

'Yeah. Sure.' He was still so tired from the effects of the pills that it was hard to even mumble.

'Ned, there's a problem.' Now the sympathy tone changed, and she became Mrs. Big Business. 'Your lease is up the first of June. My son is getting married and needs your apartment. I'm sorry, but you know how it is. But as a concession to the memory of Annie, you can stay here for the month of May for free.'

An hour later he went for a drive to Greenwood Lake. Some of their old neighbors were outside, working on their lawns. He stopped in front of the property where their house had been. Now it was all lawn. Even the flowers Annie had planted with so much love were gone. Old Mrs. Schafley, who had lived on the other side of their house, was pruning the mimosa trees in her yard. She looked up, spotted him, and asked him to come in for a cup of tea.

She served homemade coffee cake and even remembered that he liked a lot of sugar in his tea. She sat down opposite him. 'You look terrible, Ned,' she said, her eyes filling up. 'Annie wouldn't be happy to see you looking so disheveled. She always made sure that you looked very nice.'

'I have to move,' he said. 'The landlady wants the apartment for her son.'

'Ned, where will you go?'

'I don't know.' Still struggling with the residual fatigue from the sleeping pills, Ned had a thought. 'Mrs. Schafley, could I rent your spare bedroom for a while until I can figure something out?'

He saw the instant refusal in her eyes. 'For Annie's sake,' he added. He knew Mrs. Schafley had loved Annie. But then she began to shake her head.

'Ned, it wouldn't work. You're not the neatest person. Annie was always picking up after you. This house is small, and we wouldn't end up good friends.'

'I thought you liked me.' Ned felt the anger rising in his throat.

'I *do* like you,' she said soothingly, 'but it's not the same when you live with someone.' She looked out the window. 'Oh, look, there's Harry Harnik.' She ran to the door and called to him to come over. 'Ned's paying a visit,' she yelled.

Harry Harnik was the neighbor who had offered to buy their house because he wanted to have a bigger yard. If Harry hadn't made that offer, he wouldn't have sold the house and put the money in that company. Now Annie was gone, her house was gone, and the landlady wanted to throw him out. Mrs. Schafley, who always acted so nice when Annie was around, wouldn't even rent him a room. And Harry Harnik was walking into the house, a sympathetic smile on his face.

'Ned, I didn't hear about Annie until it was over. I'm so sorry. She was a lovely person.'

'Lovely,' Mrs. Schafley agreed.

Harnik's offer to buy the property was the first step toward Annie's death. Mrs. Schafley had called him over just now because she didn't want to be alone with Ned. She's afraid of me, Ned thought. Even Harnik was looking at him funny. He's afraid of me, too, he decided.

The landlady, for all her bluster, had offered to let him stay in the apartment free for the month of May because she was afraid of him, too. Her son would never move in with her; they didn't get along. She just wants to get rid of me, Ned told himself.

Lynn Spencer had been afraid of him when he stood at the door of her room in the hospital. Her sister, the DeCarlo woman, had looked past him when she did the interview and hardly bothered to turn her head to see him yesterday. But he would change that. She'd learn to be afraid of him, too.

All the rage and pain that had been building up in him was shifting. He could feel it. It was turning into a feeling of power, the kind he had when, as a kid, he used to shoot BB pellets at squirrels in the woods. Harnik, Schafley, Lynn Spencer, her sister – they were all squirrels. That was the way to treat them, he thought, just like those squirrels.

Then he could drive away while they lay crumbled and bleeding, just the way he'd left the squirrels when he was a kid.

What was the song he used to sing in the car? 'A-hunting We Will Go.' That was it.

He began to laugh.

Harry Harnik and Mrs. Schafley were staring at him. 'Ned,' Mrs. Schafley said, 'have you been remembering to take your medicine since Annie died?'

Don't make them suspicious, he warned himself. He managed to stop laughing. 'Oh, yes,' he said. 'Annie would want me to take it. I was just laughing because I was remembering the day you got so mad, Harry, because I drove that old car home that I was going to fix.'

'It was two old cars, Ned. They made this block look pretty shabby, but Annie made you get rid of them.'

'I remember. That's why you bought the house, because you didn't want to see me bring home any more old cars that I like to fix. That's why when your wife wanted to phone Annie and make sure it was all right with her if you bought my property, you wouldn't let her call. And Mrs. Schafley, you knew Annie would be heartbroken if the house was gone. You didn't call her, either. You didn't help her save her house because you wanted me out of here.'

Guilt was written on both their faces, Harnik's blustery red face and Mrs. Schafley's wrinkled cheeks. Maybe they had loved Annie, but not enough that they hadn't conspired to take her home away from her.

Don't show them how you really feel, he warned himself again. Don't give yourself away. 'I'll be going,' he said. 'But I thought you should realize that I know what both of you were up to, and I hope you burn in hell for it.'

He turned his back to them and walked out of the house and down the path to the car. Just as he opened the door, he spotted a tulip pushing its way up near where the walk to their house had been. He could see Annie on her knees last year planting the bulbs.

He ran over, bent down, plucked the tulip, and held it up to heaven. It was his promise to Annie that he would avenge her. Lynn Spencer, Carley DeCarlo, his landlady Mrs. Morgan, Harry Harnik, Mrs. Schafley. What about Harnik's wife, Bess? As he got in the car and drove away, Ned considered, then added Bess Harnik to the list. She could have called Annie on her own and warned her about the impending sale of the house. She didn't deserve to live, either.

# Chapter 13

I wasn't sure if I'd be intruding on Dr. Ken Page's territory when I went back to the Pleasantville office of Gen-stone, but it was something I felt I had to do immediately. As I drove down I-95 from Connecticut to Westchester, I turned over in my mind the possibility that whoever had come to collect Dr. Spencer's records had been from an investigating firm, maybe even one hired by the company itself.

In his speech at the stockholders' meeting, Charles Wallingford had claimed, or at least insinuated, that the missing money and the problem with the vaccine were totally shocking and unexpected occurrences. But months before Spencer's plane crashed, somebody had collected those old records. Why?

'I haven't as much time as I thought.' That was what Nick Spencer said to Dr. Broderick. Not enough time for what? To cover his tracks? To secure a future in a new location with a new name, maybe a new face, and millions of dollars? Or was there some totally different reason? And why did my mind keep coming back to that possibility?

This time when I arrived at company headquarters, I asked for Dr. Celtavini and said it was urgent. His secretary asked me to wait. It was a good minute and a half before she said that Dr. Celtavini was busy, but his assistant, Dr. Kendall, would see me.

The laboratory building was behind and to the right of the executive office headquarters and reached by a long corridor. There, a guard examined my purse and sent me through a metal detector. I waited in a reception area until Dr. Kendall came for me.

She was serious-looking, aged anywhere from thirty-five to forty-five, and had a full head of straight, dark hair and a determined chin.

She brought me to her office. 'I met Dr. Page from your magazine yesterday,' she said. 'He spent a considerable amount of time with Dr. Celtavini and me. I would have thought that we had succeeded in answering all his questions.'

'There is one question that would not have occurred to Ken Page because it has to do with something I just learned this morning, Dr. Kendall,' I said. 'It is my understanding that Nicholas Spencer's initial interest in the vaccine was triggered by his father's research in his home laboratory.'

She nodded. 'That is what I've been told.'

'Dr. Spencer's earlier records were being kept for Nick Spencer by the doctor who bought his house in Caspien, Connecticut. Someone who purported to be from Genstone went up and got them last fall.'

'Why do you say "purported to be from Gen-stone"?'

I turned. Dr. Celtavini was at the door. 'The reason I say it is that Nick Spencer personally went to get those records and, according to Dr. Broderick who was holding them, was visibly upset to learn that they were gone.'

It was hard to judge the reaction on Dr. Celtavini's face. Surprise? Concern? Or was it something more than that, something more like sadness? I'd have given anything to be able to read his mind.

'Do you have the name of the person who took the records?' Dr. Kendall asked.

'Dr. Broderick does not remember his name. He described him as a well-dressed man with reddish brown hair who was about forty years old.'

They looked at each other. Dr. Celtavini shook his head. 'I don't know any such person connected with the laboratory. Perhaps Nick Spencer's secretary, Vivian Powers, could help you.'

I had a dozen questions I would have liked to ask Dr. Celtavini. My instinct told me that the man was at war with himself. Yesterday he had said that he despised Nick Spencer not only because of his duplicity but because his own reputation had been tarnished. There was no question in my mind that he was sincere about that, but I still felt something else was going on in his head. Then he addressed Dr. Kendall. 'Laura, if we were sending for records, wouldn't we be likely to use our own delivery people?'

'I think so, Doctor.'

'I do, too. Ms. DeCarlo, do you have Dr. Broderick's number? I'd like to talk with him.'

I gave it to him and left. I did stop at the reception desk

and confirmed that if Mr. Spencer wanted something of a business nature delivered to him, he would almost certainly use one of the three men employed for just that purpose. I also asked to see Vivian Powers, but she had taken the day off.

When I left Gen-stone, I was pretty sure of at least one thing: The guy with reddish brown hair who picked up Dr. Spencer's notes from Dr. Broderick was not authorized to take them.

The question was, where did those notes go? And what important information, if any, did they contain?'

# Chapter 14

I'm not sure when I started to fall in love with Casey Dillon. Maybe it was years ago. His full name is Kevin Curtis Dillon, but all his life he's been called Casey, just the way I, Marcia, have been known as Carley. He's an orthopedic surgeon in the Hospital for Special Surgery. Way back when we both lived in Ridgewood and I was a high school sophomore, he invited me to his senior prom. I had a crush on him that wouldn't go away, but then he went to college and didn't give me the time of day when he came home. Big shot, I remind him.

We bumped into each other about six months ago in the lobby of an off-Broadway theater. I had gone there on my own; he was there with a date. A month later he called me. Two weeks after that, he called me again. It's very clear that Dr. Dillon, a handsome thirty-six-year-old surgeon, is not longing for my company too often. Now he calls me regularly, but not that regularly.

I will say that, wary as I am of having my heart broken again, I love every moment I'm with Casey. I was absolutely shocked when I woke up in the middle of the night a couple of months ago and realized I'd been dreaming that he and I were shopping for the cocktail napkins we would have at our parties. In the dream I could even see our names written in curlicues across them: 'Casey and Carley.' How cute can you possibly get?

Most of our dates are planned ahead, but when I got home from my rather long day, there was a call on my answering machine: 'Carley, want to grab a bite?'

It sounded like a great idea to me. Casey lives on West 85th Street, and often we just meet at a midtown restaurant. I called him, left a message saying okay, made careful notes of the day's events, and then decided that a hot shower was in order.

The nozzle on my shower has been replaced twice, which hasn't helped. It still squirts, then gushes water; the temperature change is downright traumatizing, and I couldn't help reflecting on how nice it would be to soak in a warm and bubbly Jacuzzi. I had intended that when I bought my own apartment, I'd definitely bite the bullet and have one of those heavenly inventions installed. Now, thanks to my investment in Gen-stone, that Jacuzzi is a long way off.

Casey returned the call as I was drying my hair. We agreed that Chinese food at Shun Lee West was a splendid idea and that we'd meet there at eight o'clock and make it an early night. He had surgery scheduled in the morning, and I needed to get prepared for my nine o'clock meeting in the office with the guys.

I got to Shun Lee's promptly at eight. Casey looked settled in a booth as though he'd been there a while. I joke that he makes me feel late even when he could set his watch by me. We ordered wine, looked over the menu, debated, and agreed to share the shrimp tempura and spicy chicken. Then we got caught up on the last couple of weeks.

I told him about being hired by *Wall Street Weekly*, and he was properly impressed. Then I told him about the cover story on Nicholas Spencer and began to think out loud, something I tend to do when I'm with Casey.

'My problem,' I said as I bit into an egg roll, 'is that the level of anger I see directed at Spencer is so personal. Sure, it's the money, and for some it's only the money, but for many people, it's bigger than that. They have an absolute sense of betrayal.'

'They thought of him as a god who would put healing hands on them and make them or their sick child well,' Casey said. 'As a doctor I see the hero worship we get when we pull a very sick patient through a crisis. Spencer promised to free the whole world from the threat of cancer. When the vaccine failed, he may have gone over the edge.'

'What do you mean, "over the edge"?'

'Carley, for whatever reason, he took money. The vaccine failed. He's going to be disgraced and has nowhere to go except prison. I wonder how much insurance he was carrying. Has anyone checked that out?'

'I'm sure Don Carter, who's writing the business end of our story, will do that if he hasn't already. Then you think that Nick Spencer may have deliberately chosen to crash the plane?'

'He wouldn't be the first to take that way out.'

'No, I guess he wouldn't.'

'Carley, I can tell you that research laboratories are

hotbeds of gossip. I've talked to some of the guys I know. The word has been drifting around for some months that at Gen-stone the final results weren't holding up.'

'You think Spencer knew that?'

'If everyone else in the business did, I don't know how he'd miss hearing it as well. Let me give you a tip – pharmaceuticals are a multibillion-dollar business, and Gen-stone isn't the only one trying desperately to cure cancer. The company which finds the magic bullet will have a patent that's worth billions. Don't kid yourself. The other companies are cheering that Spencer's vaccine isn't proving out. There isn't one of them who isn't working frantically to be the winner. Money and the Nobel prize are pretty good incentives.'

'You're not exactly placing the medical profession in the best light, Doctor,' I said.

'I don't mean to place it in any one light. I'm telling it as it is. It's the same way with hospitals. We're in competition for patients. Patients bring in income. Income means hospitals can keep up with the latest equipment. How do you attract patients? By having top doctors on staff. Why do you think doctors who've made a name in their field are constantly being recruited? There's a tug of war over them, and always has been.

'I have friends in hospital research labs who tell me they're always on the watch for spies. Stealing information about new drugs and vaccines is going on all the time. And even without outright theft, the race to be the one to discover the latest wonder drug or vaccine goes on twenty-four/seven. That's what Nick Spencer was up against.'

I picked up on the word 'spies' and thought of the

stranger who had picked up the files from Dr. Broderick's office. I told Casey about him.

'Carley, you're saying that Nick Spencer took his father's files twelve years ago and that some unauthorized person went back for the remainder of them last fall. Doesn't that say to you that someone thought there might be value in them, and came to that conclusion before Spencer himself made that determination?'

' "I don't have as much time as I thought" – Casey, that was the last thing Spencer said to Dr. Broderick, and that was only six weeks before his plane crashed. I keep puzzling over that.'

'What do you think he meant?' Casey asked.

'I don't know. But how many people do you think he would have told about leaving his father's early notes in his old family home? I mean, when you move out and another family takes over, it's not as though they want to keep storage bins for you. This was a special set of circumstances. The doctor had hoped to work in his own lab as a hobby. But then he claims he used the space for examination rooms.'

Our entrees arrived, steaming and bubbly, looking and smelling heavenly. I realized that I had not eaten a single thing since the bagel and coffee in the diner. I also realized that after I met with Ken Page and Don Carter at the office the next morning, I was going to have to take another ride to Caspien.

I had been surprised that Dr. Broderick saw me so readily this morning. It was equally surprising that he so quickly volunteered that he'd been in possession of some of Dr. Spencer's records and that only months ago he had turned them over to a messenger, whose name he couldn't remember. Spencer had always credited his father's preliminary research as assisting in the development of Gen-stone. He had left those records behind at Broderick's request. They ought to have been treated with great care.

Maybe they had been, I thought. Maybe there was no red-headed man.

'Casey, you're a good thinking post for me,' I told him as I began to concentrate on the shrimp. 'Maybe you should have been a psychiatrist.'

'All doctors are psychiatrists, Carley. Some of them just haven't discovered that yet.'

# Chapter 15

It felt good to be at *Wall Street Weekly*, to have a cubicle of my own, a desk of my own, a computer of my own. Maybe there are some people who long only for the open road, but I'm not one of them. Not that I don't love to travel – I do. I have done profiles on famous or at least well-known people that have taken me to Europe and South America, even one to Australia, but after I've been away for a couple of weeks, I'm ready to go home.

Home for me is the great, marvelous, wonderful piece of real estate called Manhattan Island. East side, west side, all around the town. I love to walk through it on a quiet Sunday and feel the presence of the buildings that my great-grandparents saw when they arrived in New York, one from the Emerald Isle, the other from Tuscany.

All of the above ran through my head as I put a few personal items in my new desk and went over my notes for the meeting that would take place in Ken's office.

In the world of deadlines and breaking news, there's very little waste of time. Ken, Don, and I exchanged greetings and got down to business. Ken settled behind his desk. He was wearing a sweater and an open shirt and looked for all the world like a retired football player. 'You first, Don,' he said.

Don, small and neat, flipped though his notes. 'Spencer went with the Jackman Medical Supply Company fourteen years ago after getting an MBA at Cornell. At that time it was a struggling, privately owned family company. With his father-in-law's help, he ended up buying the Jackman family out. Eight years ago, when he founded Gen-stone, he folded the medical-supply business into it and went public to finance the research. That's the division he's been looting.

'He'd bought the house in Bedford and the New York apartment,' Don said. 'Bedford initially cost three million, but with renovations and the escalation of prices in the real estate market, it was worth a lot more when it was torched. The apartment was purchased for four million, and then some money went into it. It wasn't one of those astronomically priced penthouses or duplexes, which is what some of the articles about him painted it out to be. Incidentally, both house and apartment had mortgages that were eventually paid off.'

I remembered Lynn had told me that she had been living in his first wife's home and apartment.

'The looting of the medical-supplies division started years ago. A year-and-a-half ago he started borrowing against his own stock. Nobody knows why.'

'To keep this in sequence, I'll jump in here,' Ken said. 'That was at the time when, according to Dr. Celtavini, problems started to turn up in the laboratory. Subsequent generations of mice that were getting the vaccine were beginning to develop cancer cells. Spencer probably realized that the house of cards was about to fall and began to really loot the company. The feeling is that the meeting in Puerto Rico was just a step on his way to fleeing the country. Then his luck ran out.'

'He told the doctor who bought his father's house that he didn't have as much time as he thought,' I said. Then I told them about the records that Dr. Broderick claimed he had given to a man with reddish brown hair who said he was from Spencer's office.

'What I found hard to swallow,' I said, 'is that any doctor would hand over research files without checking to be sure the request was valid, or at least getting a signed receipt for them.'

'Any chance that someone in the company was getting suspicious of Spencer?' Don suggested.

'Not according to what was said at the stockholders' meeting,' I said. 'And it certainly was news to Dr. Celtavini that the files even existed. I think that if anyone might be interested in the early experiments of an amateur microbiologist, it would be someone like him.'

'Did Dr. Broderick tell anyone else about the records being collected?' Ken asked.

'He said something about talking to the investigators. Since he volunteered to tell me, I would say no.' I realized that I had not directly asked that question of Dr. Broderick.

'Probably the U.S. Attorney's Office was up to see him.' Don closed his notebook as he spoke. 'They're the ones trying to trace the money, but my guess is that it's in a numbered Swiss bank account.'

'Is that where they think he was planning to end up?' I asked.

'Hard to say. There are other places that welcome people with big bucks, no questions asked. Spencer liked Europe and spoke fluent French and German, so he wouldn't have a hard time adjusting wherever he chose to settle.'

I thought of what Nick said about his son, Jack: 'He means the world to me.' How did he reconcile abandoning his son by leaving this country and then not being able to return unless he wanted to end up in prison? I threw that issue on the table, but neither Don nor Ken saw it as a conflict.

'With the amount of money he took, the kid can hop on a private plane and visit Daddy anytime. I can give you a list of people who can't come back here but are real family men. Besides, how often would he have seen the kid if he was in the slammer?'

'There's still an unknown,' I pointed out. 'Lynn. If she's to be believed, she had no part in his scheme. Was he planning to leave her high and dry when he took off? Somehow I don't see her living a life in exile. She has wormed her way into being part of the chic crowd in New York. She claims she now has virtually no money.'

'What is no money to people like Lynn Spencer is probably a lot different from what the three of us consider no money,' Don said dryly as he stood up.

'One more thing,' I said quickly. 'That's exactly the point I'd like to touch on in this story. I've gone over the press coverage about corporate failures, and the emphasis always seems to be on how lavishly the guy who was taking the money was living, usually with planes and boats and a half-dozen homes. We don't have that kind of story. Whatever Nick Spencer did with the money isn't visible to us. Instead, I want to interview the little people, including the guy who has been indicted for setting the fire. Even if he's guilty, which I doubt, he was frantic because his little girl is dying of cancer and he's going to lose his home.'

'What makes you think he isn't guilty?' Don asked. 'It looks like a slam-dunk case to me.'

'I saw him at the stockholders' meeting. I was practically shoulder to shoulder with him when he had that outburst.'

'Which lasted how long?' Don raised one eyebrow, a trick I've always envied.

'For about two minutes, if that,' I admitted. 'But whether or not he set that fire, he's certainly an example of what's happening to the real victims as Gen-stone goes bankrupt.'

'Talk to some of them. See what you come up with,' Ken agreed. 'Okay, let's all get busy.'

I went back to my cubicle and went through the file I had on Spencer. After the crash, quotes had been given to newspapers by people close to him at Gen-stone. The one from Vivian Powers, his secretary of six years, had praised him to the skies. I put in a call to her at the Pleasantville office and kept my fingers crossed that she was at work.

She took my call. She sounded young, but told me firmly that she would not be able to agree to an interview either by phone or in person. I jumped in before she could hang up. 'I'm part of a team at *Wall Street Weekly* writing a cover story on Nicholas Spencer,' I said. 'I'll be honest. I'd like to put in something positive about him, but people are so angry about losing their money that it's going to be a very negative portrait. At the time of his death you spoke very kindly of him. I guess you've changed your mind, too.'

'I will never believe Nicholas Spencer took a dime for himself,' she said heatedly. Then her voice broke. 'He was a *wonderful* person,' she finished, almost in a whisper, 'and *that* is my quote.'

I had the sense that Vivian Powers was afraid of being overheard. 'Tomorrow is Saturday,' I said hastily. 'I could come to your home or meet you anywhere you want.'

'No, not tomorrow. I'll have to think about it.' There was a click in my ear and the line went dead. What did she mean that Spencer wouldn't take any money for himself? I wondered.

Maybe not tomorrow, but we're going to talk, Ms. Powers, I vowed. We are going to talk.

# Chapter 16

When Annie was alive, she wouldn't let him have a drink because she said it interfered with his medicine. But on the way home from Greenwood Lake yesterday, Ned had stopped at a liquor store and bought bottles of bourbon, scotch, and rye. He hadn't taken his medicine since Annie died, so maybe she wouldn't be mad at him for drinking now. 'I need to sleep, Annie,' he explained when he opened the first bottle. 'It will help me to sleep.'

It did help. He had fallen asleep sitting in the chair, but then something happened. Ned couldn't tell whether he was dreaming or remembering about the night of the fire. He was standing in that clump of trees with the can of gas when a shadow came from the side of the house and rushed down the driveway.

It was so windy, and the branches of the trees kept moving and swaying. He had thought at first that was what caused the shadow.... But now the shadow had become the figure of a man, and in his dream he sometimes thought he could even see a face.

Was it like his dreams about Annie, the ones that were so real he could even smell the peach body lotion she wore?

It had to be that, he decided. Because it was just a dream, wasn't it?

At five o'clock, just as the first light of dawn was pushing past the shade, Ned got up. His body ached from having fallen asleep in the chair, but even worse was the ache in his heart. He wanted Annie. He needed her – but she was gone. He went across the room and got his rifle. All these years he'd kept it hidden behind a pile of junk in their half of the garage. He sat down again, his hands wrapped tightly around the barrel.

The rifle would bring him to Annie. When he was finished with those people, the ones who had caused her to die, he would go to her. He would join her.

Then suddenly he flashed on last night. The face in the driveway at Bedford. Had he seen it or dreamed it?

He lay down and tried to fall asleep again, but he couldn't. The burn on his hand was getting messy, and it hurt a lot. He couldn't go to the emergency room of the hospital. He'd heard on the radio that the guy they arrested for the fire had a burn on his hand.

He was lucky he had met Dr. Ryan in the hospital lobby. If he had gone to the emergency room, someone might have reported him to the police. And they would have found out that last summer he had worked for the landscaper who took care of the grounds at the Bedford house. But he had lost the prescription Dr. Ryan gave him.

Maybe if he put butter on his hand it would feel better.

That's what his mother had done once when she burned her hand lighting a cigarette from the stove.

Could he ask Dr. Ryan for another prescription? Maybe he could phone him.

Or would that merely remind Dr. Ryan that hours after the fire in Bedford Ned had showed him a burned hand?

He couldn't make up his mind what to do.

# Chapter 17

I had cut out all the stories about Nick Spencer in the *Caspien Town Journal*. After I spoke to Vivian Powers, I went through them and found the picture of the dais at the Distinguished Citizen Award dinner on February 15, at which he'd been honored. The caption listed all the people who were sitting at the table with him.

They included the chairman of the board of directors of Caspien Hospital, the mayor of Caspien, a state senator, a clergyman, and several men and women who were undoubtedly prominent citizens in the area, the kind of people trotted out regularly for fund-raising dinners.

I jotted down their names and looked up their phone numbers. What I specifically wanted was to find the person in Caspien whom Nick Spencer had gone to see after he left Dr. Broderick the next morning. It was a slim possibility, but maybe, just maybe, it was one of those people on the dais with him. For the present I skipped calling the mayor, the state senator, or the chairman of the board of the hospital. Instead I hoped to get one of the women who'd been there.

According to Dr. Broderick, Spencer had returned unexpectedly to Caspien that morning and had been upset that his father's early records were missing. I always try to put myself in the shoes of someone I'm trying to understand. If I had been in Nick's shoes and had nothing to hide, I would have driven straight to my office and started an investigation.

Last night, after I got back home from dinner with Casey, I changed into my favorite nightshirt, got into bed, propped pillows against the headboard, and spread out on the bed all the articles in the voluminous file I had on Nick. I'm a pretty good speed reader, but no matter how many articles I read, I never saw a single reference to the fact that he had left the notes of his father's early experiments with Dr. Broderick in Caspien.

It stands to reason that kind of information would be known by only a very few people. But if Dr. Celtavini and Dr. Kendall were to be believed, they were not aware the old notes existed, and the man with the reddish brown hair was not a regular messenger for the company.

But why would someone outside the company know about Dr. Spencer's records, and, even more puzzling, why would he want them?

I made three phone calls and left messages. The only person I connected with was the Reverend Howell, the Presbyterian minister who had given the invocation at the fund-raiser. He was cordial but said he did not have much conversation with Nick Spencer that evening. 'I congratulated him on receiving the award, of course, Miss DeCarlo. Then, like everyone else, I was saddened and dismayed to learn of his alleged misdeeds and also to learn that the hospital suffered a heavy financial loss because of having invested so much of its portfolio in his company.'

'Reverend, at most of these dinners, between courses, people get up and move around,' I said. 'Did you happen to notice if Nicolas Spencer spoke to any one person in particular?'

'I did not, but I can make inquiries if you like.'

My investigation wasn't going very far. I called the hospital and was told that Lynn had checked out.

According to the morning papers, Marty Bikorsky had been indicted for arson and reckless endangerment and released on bail. He was listed in the White Plains phone book. I dialed his number. The answering machine was on, and I left a message. 'I'm Carley DeCarlo from *Wall Street Weekly*. I saw you at the stockholders' meeting, and you absolutely did not strike me as the kind of man who would set fire to someone's home. I hope you will call me. If I can, I'd like to help you.'

My phone rang almost as soon as I hung up. 'I'm Marty Bikorsky.' His voice was both weary and strained. 'I don't think anyone can help me, but you're welcome to try.'

An hour and a half later I was parking in front of his house, a well-kept older split-level. An American flag flew from a pole on the lawn. The capricious April weather was continuing to play games. Yesterday the temperature had hit 70 degrees. Today it was down to 58 and windy. I could have used a sweater under my light spring jacket.

Bikorsky must have been watching for me, because the door opened before I could ring the bell. I looked into his face, and my instant reaction was to think, That poor guy. The expression in his eyes was so defeated and tired that I ached for him. But he made a conscious effort to square his slumping shoulders and managed to muster a faint smile.

'Come in, Ms. DeCarlo. I'm Marty Bikorsky.' He started to extend his hand but then pulled it back. It was heavily bandaged. I knew he'd claimed that he burned it on the stove.

The narrow entrance vestibule led straight back to the kitchen. The living room was directly to the right of the door. He said, 'My wife made fresh coffee. If you'd like some, we could sit at the table.'

'That would be very nice.'

I followed him back into the kitchen where a woman with her back to us was taking a coffee cake out of the oven. 'Rhoda, this is Ms. DeCarlo.'

'Please call me Carley,' I said. 'Actually it's Marcia, but in school the kids started calling me Carley, and it stuck.'

Rhoda Bikorsky was about my age, a couple of inches taller than I am, a shapely size twelve with long dark blond hair and brilliant blue eyes. Her cheeks were flushed, and I wondered if she had natural high color or if the emotional upheaval in her life was taking a toll on her health.

Like her husband, she was dressed in jeans and a sweatshirt. She smiled briefly, said, 'I wish someone had figured out a nickname for Rhoda,' and shook hands. The kitchen was spotless and cozy. The table and chairs were Early American style, and the brick-patterned floor covering was the kind we had had in our kitchen when I was a kid.

At Rhoda's invitation I went to the table and sat down,

said, 'Yes, thank you,' to the coffee, and willingly reached for a slice of the cake. From where I was sitting, I could look out a bay window into a small backyard. An outdoor gym with a swing and a seesaw gave evidence of the presence of a child in the family.

Rhoda Bikorsky saw what I was observing. 'Marty built that set himself for Maggie.' She sat down across from me. 'Carley, I'm going to be straight with you. You don't know us. You're a reporter. You're here because you told Marty you'd like to help us. I have a very simple question for *you:* Why would you want to help us?'

'I was at the stockholders' meeting. My reaction to your husband's outburst was that he was a distraught father, not a vengeful man.'

Her face softened. 'Then you know more about him than the arson squad does. If I had known what they were fishing for, I never would have talked about the way Marty has insomnia and gets up in the middle of the night to go outside for a cigarette.'

'You're always after me to give them up,' Bikorsky said wryly. 'I should have listened to you, Rhod.'

'From what I've read, you went directly from the stockholders' meeting to work at the service station. Is that right?' I asked.

He nodded. 'My hours were three to eleven this week. I was late, but one of the guys was covering for me. I was still so charged up that I went out after work for a couple of beers before I came home.'

'Is it true that in the bar you said something about setting a torch to the Spencer house?'

He grimaced and shook his head. 'Look, I'm not going to tell you I wasn't upset at losing all that money. I'm still upset about it. This is our home, and we have to list it for sale. But I'd no more burn someone's house down than I'd set fire to *this* house. I'm all talk.'

'You can say that again!' Rhoda Bikorsky squeezed her husband's arm, then put her hand under his chin. 'This is going to get straightened out, Marty.'

He was telling the truth. I was sure of it. All the evidence against him was circumstantial. 'You went out for a cigarette around two o'clock Tuesday morning?'

'That's right. It's a lousy habit, but when I wake up and know I can't get back to sleep, a couple of cigarettes calm me down.'

I happened to glance out the window and noticed how windy it had become. It reminded me of something. 'Wait a minute,' I said. 'Monday night into Tuesday morning was blustery and cold. Did you just sit outside?'

He hesitated. 'No, I sat in the car.'

'In the garage?'

'It was in the driveway. I turned the engine on.'

He and Rhoda exchanged glances. She was giving him a clear warning not to say anymore. The phone rang. I could tell he was glad to have an excuse to leave the table. When he came back, his face was grim. 'Carley, that was my lawyer. He hit the ceiling that I let you come up. He told me I can't say another word.'

'Daddy, are you mad?'

A security blanket trailing behind her, a little girl about four years old had come into the kitchen. She had her mother's long blond hair and blue eyes, but her complexion was chalky. Everything about her seemed so fragile that I could only think of the exquisite porcelain dolls I'd seen once in a doll museum.

Bikorsky bent down and picked her up. 'I'm not mad, baby. Did you have a nice nap?'

'Uh-huh.'

He turned to me. 'Carley, this is our Maggie.'

'Daddy, you're supposed to say that I'm your *treasure*, Maggie.'

He pretended to be horrified. 'How could I forget? Carley, this is our *treasure*, Maggie, and Maggie, this is Carley.'

I took the small hand she extended. 'I'm very pleased to meet you, Carley,' she said. Her smile was wistful.

I hoped the tears wouldn't well in my eyes. It was obvious that she was very, very sick. 'Hello, Maggie. I'm very pleased to meet you, too.'

'Why don't I make some cocoa for you while Mommy says good-bye to Carley?' Marty suggested.

She patted his bandaged hand. 'Promise you won't burn your hand again when you make the cocoa, Daddy?'

'I promise, Princess.' He looked at me. 'You can print that if you want, Carley.'

'I intend to,' I said quietly.

Rhoda walked me to the door. 'Maggie has a brain tumor. You know what the doctors told us three months ago? They said take her home and enjoy her. Don't put her through any chemo or radiation, and don't let yourself be talked into any crazy treatments by charlatans, because they won't work. They said that Maggie won't be here next Christmas.' The color in her cheeks deepened. 'Carley, I'm going to tell you something. When you're storming heaven morning, noon, and night the way Marty and I are, praying that God will spare your only child, you don't piss Him off by burning down someone else's home.'

She bit her lip to stifle a sob. 'I talked Marty into getting that second mortgage. Last year I went to the hospice at St. Ann's to see a friend who was dying. Nicholas Spencer was a volunteer there. That's where I met him. He told me about the vaccine he was developing and that he was sure it would cure cancer. That's when I persuaded Marty to put all our money into his company.'

'You met Nicholas Spencer at a hospice? He was a volunteer at a hospice?' I was so astonished, I felt as though I was babbling.

'Yes. Then only last month when we found out about Maggie, I went to see him there again. He said that his vaccine wasn't ready, that he couldn't help her. It's so hard to believe that anyone so convincing could deceive, could risk . . .' She shook her head and clasped her hand over her mouth, then sobbed. 'My little girl is going to die!'

'Mommy.'

'I'm coming, Baby.' Rhoda dabbed impatiently at the tears that were now flowing down her cheeks.

I opened the door. 'I was in Marty's corner instinctively,' I said. 'Now that I've met you, if there's a way to help, I'll find it.' I clasped her hand and left her.

On the way back to New York, I called and checked my messages. The one I received sent a chill through me. 'Hi, Ms. DeCarlo, this is Milly. I waited on you in the diner in Caspien yesterday. I know you were going to see Dr. Broderick yesterday, and I thought you'd want to know that while he was jogging this morning, he was run over by a hit-and-run driver and isn't expected to live.'

# Chapter 18

I think I made it home on automatic pilot. All I could think about was the accident that had left Dr. Broderick comatized and in critical condition. Was it an accident? I couldn't keep from wondering.

Yesterday I had gone straight from talking to Dr. Broderick to the Gen-stone office and began asking questions to find out who had sent for those records. I spoke to Dr. Celtavini and Dr. Kendall. I inquired at the reception desk about other possible messenger services and described the man with reddish brown hair as Dr. Broderick had described him to me. Now this morning, only hours later, Dr. Broderick had been attacked by someone in a car. I deliberately use the word 'attacked' rather than hit.

I called the diner in Caspien from the car and spoke to Milly. She told me that the accident had happened around 6:00 a.m. in the county park near his home.

'From what I hear the police think the guy must have been drunk or something,' she said. 'He had to go way over to the side of the road to hit the doctor. Isn't that awful? Say a prayer for him, Carley.'

I certainly would.

When I got home, I changed into a comfortable light sweater, slacks, and sneakers. At five o'clock I poured a glass of wine and got out some cheese and crackers, put my feet up on the hassock, and let myself think about the day.

Seeing Maggie who had only a few months to live brought back vivid memories of Patrick. I wondered if, given a choice, it would have been worse to have had Patrick for four years and then lose him? Was it easier to let him go after only a few days rather than having him become the soul and center of my life, as Maggie was to Rhoda and Marty Bikorsky? If only . . . If only . . . If only . . . If only the chromosomes that formed Patrick's heart had not been flawed. If only the cancer cells that had invaded Maggie's brain could have been destroyed.

Of course, positing 'if only' questions is pointless because there are no answers. It didn't happen that way, so we'll never know. Patrick would be ten now. In my mind and heart I can see him as he would have looked if he had lived. He'd have dark hair, of course. Greg, his father, has dark hair. He'd probably be tall for his age. Greg is tall, and judging by my parents and grandparents, I must have a recessive gene for tallness. He'd have blue eyes. Mine are blue, Greg's are a kind of smoky blue. I'd like to think that his features would be more like mine because I look like my dad, and he was the nicest man – as well as one of the nicest looking – anyone could ever know.

It's funny. My baby who lived only a few days remains

so real to me, while Greg, with whom I went to graduate
school for a year and was married to for a year, has
become so vague and unimportant. If anything, the only
lasting imprint I have of him is to wonder how I could
have been so foolish as to be unaware how superficial he
was from the start. You know that old poster. 'He ain't
heavy, he's my brother.' How about 'He ain't heavy, he's
my son.' Five pounds and four ounces of beautiful baby
boy, but with his wounded heart too heavy for his father
to carry.

I hope there is a second time around. I'd like to have a
family someday. I keep my fingers crossed that my eyes
will be open, that I won't make another mistake. That
worries me about myself. I'm too quick to judge people. I
instinctively liked and felt sorry for Marty Bikorsky.
That's why I went to see him. That's why I believe he's
innocent of setting that fire.

Then I began to think about Nicholas Spencer. Two
years ago when I met him, I instinctively liked and
admired him. Now I'm only seeing the tip of the iceberg
of what he has done to people's lives, not only by
destroying their financial security with his inflated stock,
but destroying their hope that his vaccine would prevent
and cure cancer in the people they love who are dying.

Unless there is another answer.

The man with the reddish brown hair who had taken
Dr. Spencer's records is part of that answer. I am sure of it.
Was it possible that Dr. Broderick was attacked because he
could identify him?

After a while I went out, walked to the Village, and had
linguini with clam sauce and a salad at an unpretentious
little cafe. It helped with the headache I was getting, but

unfortunately did nothing for the heartache. I felt weighted down with guilt that my visit may have cost Dr. Broderick his life. But later, when I went home, I did get to sleep.

I awoke feeling better. I love Sunday morning, reading the Sunday papers in bed while I sip a cup of coffee. But then I flipped on the radio to catch the nine o'clock news and heard the bulletin. Earlier that morning some kids in Puerto Rico, fishing from a boat near where wreckage of Nicholas Spencer's plane had been found, hooked a charred and bloodstained strip of a man's blue sports shirt. The newscaster said that missing financier Nicholas Spencer, who was alleged to have looted millions of dollars from his medical research company, had been wearing a blue sports shirt when he left Westchester County Airport several weeks prior. The remnant was being tested and would be compared with similar shirts from Paul Stuart, the Madison Avenue haberdasher where Spencer shopped. Divers would go down again to look for the body, concentrating on that location.

I called Lynn at her apartment and could tell immediately that I had woken her up. Her voice sounded sleepy and annoyed, but it changed quickly when she realized it was me. I told her about the news bulletin, and for a long moment she said nothing, then she whispered, 'Carley, I was so sure they'd find him alive, that this was all a nightmare and I'd wake up and find him still here with me.'

'Are you alone?' I asked.

'Of course,' she said indignantly. 'What kind of person do you think – ?'

I interrupted. 'Lynn, I meant do you have a housekeeper or anyone staying there to help you while you're recovering?' This time it was my voice that was sharp. Why in the name of God would she think that I would insinuate she had a guy around?

'Oh, Carley, I'm sorry,' she said. 'My housekeeper is usually off on Sunday, but she's coming in a little later.'

'Would you like company?'

'Yes, I would.'

We agreed that I'd come up around eleven. I was just leaving when Casey phoned. 'Have you heard the latest about Spencer, Carley?'

'Yes, I have.'

'That should pretty much stop all the speculation that he's still alive.'

'I guess so.' Nicholas Spencer's face filled my mind. Why had I expected that he would suddenly reappear and straighten everything out, that it had all been a terrible mistake. 'I'm on my way to see Lynn now.'

'I'm on the run, too. Don't let me hold you up. Talk to you later, Carley.'

I suppose I had a mental image of sitting quietly with Lynn, but that wasn't what happened. When I got there, I found Charles Wallingford at her side and two men who turned out to be attorneys for Gen-stone also in the living room with her.

Lynn was dressed in beautifully cut beige slacks and a pastel print blouse. Her blond hair was brushed back from her face. Her makeup was light but artfully applied. The bandages on her hands had been reduced to a single wide piece of gauze taped to each of her palms. She was wearing transparent step-in slippers, and I could see the padding protecting her blistered feet.

I kissed her cheek somewhat awkwardly, received a frosty greeting from Wallingford, and when I introduced myself, a polite acknowledgment from the lawyers, both serious-looking, conservatively dressed men.

'Carley,' Lynn said, apologetically, 'we're just going over the statement we're preparing for the media. It won't take long. We're sure we'll be getting a lot of calls.'

Charles Wallingford and I exchanged glances. I could read his mind. What was I doing observing them while they prepared a statement for the media? I *was* the media. 'Lynn,' I protested, 'I shouldn't be here. I'll come another time.'

'Carley, I want you here.' For an instant Lynn's ice-queen composure broke. 'No matter what went wrong that Nick couldn't face, when he started the company, I'm sure he believed in the vaccine and believed that he was giving people a chance to be part of its financial success story. I want people to understand I wasn't part of a scheme to defraud anybody. But I also want people to understand that initially, at least, Nick didn't set out to defraud. This isn't about doing a good PR job. Trust me.'

I still wasn't happy to be included in this planning session, but reluctantly retreated to a chair near the window and looked around the room. The walls were a sunny yellow, the ceilings and molding white. The two couches were slipcovered in a yellow and green and white print. There were matching needlepoint-covered chairs facing each other beside the fireplace. The tall English desk and occasional tables were finely polished antiques. The windows to the left offered a view of

Central Park. It was a warm day, and the trees were starting to bloom. The park was filled with people, walking and jogging or just sitting on the benches enjoying the day.

I realized that the room had been decorated to give it an indoor-outdoor feeling. It was vibrant and springlike and somehow less formal than I'd expected from Lynn. In fact, the apartment was not at all what I expected in the sense that while it was certainly spacious, it was more like a comfortable family home than a CEO's showplace.

Then I remembered that Lynn had said it had been bought by Nick and his first wife, and that she had wanted to sell it and move. Lynn and Nick had been married only four years. Was it possible that Lynn had not redecorated it to her own taste because it was not where she wanted to stay? I'd have given odds that was the answer.

A few moments later the doorbell chimed. I saw the housekeeper pass the living room to answer it, but I don't think Lynn heard it at all. She and Charles Wallingford were intensely comparing notes, and then she began to read aloud: 'From what we understand, it would seem that the scrap of clothing found early this morning two miles from Puerto Rico was from the shirt my husband was wearing when he flew out of Westchester Airport. In these three weeks I have clung to the hope that somehow he survived the crash and would return to defend himself against the allegations being lodged against him. He passionately believed that he was on his way to finding a vaccine that would both prevent and cure cancer. I am certain that any money he withdrew, even without authorization, would have been used for that purpose and that purpose only.'

'Lynn, I'm sorry, but I have to tell you the response to that statement is going to be, "Who do you think you're kidding?" ' The tone of voice was gentle, but Lynn's cheeks flamed, and she dropped the sheet of paper she'd been holding.

'Adrian!' she said.

If you were in the financial world, the newcomer needed no introduction, as the television hosts used to say when announcing their celebrity guests. I recognized him immediately. He was Adrian Nagel Garner, the sole owner of Garner Pharmaceutical Company, and a world-class philanthropist. He was not very tall, in his mid-fifties, with graying hair and plain features – the sort of unassuming man you probably wouldn't notice in a crowd. Nobody knew how rich he was. He never allowed personal publicity, but, of course, word gets around. People spoke in awe about his home in Connecticut, which contained a splendid library, an eighty-seat theater, a recording studio, and a sports bar, just to name a few of the amenities. Twice divorced and with grown children, he was currently said to be linked romantically with a British blueblood.

It was his company that had planned to pay $1 billion for the right to distribute Gen-stone's vaccine if it was approved. I knew one of his executives had been elected to serve on the Gen-stone board, but he had not been in evidence at the stockholders' meeting. I am sure that the last thing Adrian Nagel Garner wanted was for his company to be linked any further in the public mind to the disgraced Gen-stone. Frankly, I was shocked to see him in Lynn's living room.

It was evident that his visit was a total surprise to her as well. She seemed uncertain what to expect. 'Adrian, what a nice surprise,' she said. She was almost stammering.

'I'm on my way upstairs to have lunch with the Parkinsons. When I realized this was your building as well, I had to stop off. I heard the news this morning.'

He glanced at Wallingford. 'Charles.' There was a distinct coolness in his greeting there. He nodded to the lawyers, then glanced at me.

'Adrian, this is my stepsister, Carley DeCarlo,' Lynn said. She still sounded rather flustered. 'Carley is working on a cover story about Nick for *Wall Street Weekly*.'

He remained silent and looked at me quizzically. I was angry at myself for not leaving the minute I saw Wallingford and the lawyers here. 'I stopped in to see Lynn for the same reason you did, Mr. Garner,' I said crisply, 'to tell her how sorry I am that it seems definite Nick did not get out of the plane alive.'

'Then we don't agree, Ms. DeCarlo,' Adrian Garner said sharply. 'I don't think it seems definite at all. For every one person who believes that this piece of shirting material is proof of his death, there'll be ten others who'll say Nick left it in the area of the wreckage with the hope that it would be found. The shareholders and employees are angry and bitter enough already, and I think you will agree that Lynn has already been sufficiently victimized by that anger. Short of Nick Spencer's body being found, she should not say anything that might be interpreted as an attempt to convince people of that fact. I believe the dignified and appropriate response would be for her to simply say, "I don't know what to think." '

He turned to her. 'Lynn, you must do what you think appropriate, of course. I wish you well, and I wanted you to know that.'

With a nod to the rest of us, one of the wealthiest and most powerful men in the country departed.

Wallingford waited until we heard the click of the outside door, then said heatedly, 'I find Adrian Garner pretty damn high-handed.'

'But he may be right,' Lynn said. 'In fact, Charles, I think he is.'

Wallingford shrugged. 'There's nothing "right" about this whole mess,' he said, then looked chagrined. 'Lynn, I'm sorry, but you know what I mean.'

'Yes, I do.'

'The hardest part is that I loved Nick,' Wallingford said. 'I worked with him for eight years and considered it a privilege. It's still so unbelievable.' He shook his head and looked at the lawyers; then he shrugged. 'Lynn, I'll keep you posted on anything we hear.'

She stood up, and from the immediate grimace she unconsciously made, I could tell that being on her feet was painful.

It was obvious that she was exhausted, but at her urging I stayed long enough to have a Bloody Mary with her. We fell back on our tenuous family relationship as a subject of conversation. I told her I'd spoken to her father on Tuesday when I returned from the hospital to report on her condition and that I called my mother Wednesday to tell her about my new job.

'I spoke to Dad the day I went into the hospital and again the next morning,' Lynn said. 'Then I told him I was going to leave the phone off so I could rest, and I'd call him over the weekend. I'll do it this afternoon, after I put my feet up for a while.'

I stood up and put down the empty glass. 'We'll stay in touch.'

It was such a beautiful day that I decided to walk the two miles home. Walking clears my head, and it seemed to me I had a lot going on in it. The last two minutes with Lynn were getting special attention. When I went to visit her in the hospital the second time, she'd been on the phone. As she was hanging up she said, 'I love you, too.' Then she saw me and volunteered that she'd been speaking to her father.

Was she mistaken about the day she talked to him? Or was there someone else on the phone? It could have been a girlfriend. I think nothing of saying 'Love you' when I'm talking with some of my pals. But there are a lot of ways to say, 'I love you, too,' and Lynn's voice had sounded mighty warm in a sexy way.

I was shocked at the next possibility that ran through my mind: Had Mrs. Nicholas Spencer been having a cozy chat with her missing husband?

# Chapter 19

Carley DeCarlo. He *had* to find out where she lived. She was Lynn Spencer's stepsister, but that was all he knew about her. Even so, Ned felt as though he recognized her name, that Annie had talked about her. But why? And how would Annie ever have met her? Maybe she'd been a patient in the hospital. That was possible, he decided.

Now that he had his plan and he'd cleaned and loaded his rifle, Ned was feeling calmer. Mrs. Morgan would be first. She would be easy – she always locked her door, but he'd go upstairs and say he had a present for her. He would do it soon. Before he shot her, he wanted to tell her face-to-face that she shouldn't have lied to him about wanting his apartment for her son.

He'd drive to Greenwood Lake while it was still dark. There he'd visit Mrs. Schafley and the Harniks. It would be easier than shooting squirrels, because they'd all be in bed. The Harniks always left their bedroom window open. He could push it up and lean over the windowsill before they even knew what was happening. And he wouldn't have to go inside Mrs. Schafley's house. He could just stand at the bedroom window and shine a flashlight on her face. When she woke up, he'd shine it on his face so she could see him and know what he was going to do. Then he'd shoot her.

He was sure that when the police started to investigate, they would come looking for him. Mrs. Schafley had probably told everyone in Greenwood Lake about his wanting to rent a room from her. 'Can you imagine the nerve of him?' That was the way she would put it. That was the way she always started when she was complaining about someone. 'Can you imagine the nerve of him?' she'd asked Annie when the kid who mowed her lawn tried to raise his price. 'Can you imagine the nerve of him?' when the guy who delivered her newspaper asked if she'd forgotten to give him a tip at Christmas.

Was that what she would be thinking in that second before he killed her? Can you imagine the nerve of him, killing me?

He knew where Lynn Spencer lived. But he'd have to find out where her stepsister lived. Carley DeCarlo. Why did that name sound so familiar? Had he heard Annie talk about her? Or did she read about her? 'That's it,' Ned whispered. 'Carley DeCarlo had a column in that part of the Sunday paper Annie loved to read.'

Today was Sunday.

He went into the bedroom. The candlewick spread that Annie had liked so much was still on the bed. He hadn't touched it. He could still see her as she was that last morning, her hands tugging so that both sides of the spread were exactly even, then tucking the extra material at the top under the pillows.

He spotted the Sunday supplement that Annie had left folded on her night table. He picked it up and opened it. Slowly he turned the pages. Then he saw her name and picture: Carley DeCarlo. She wrote an advice column about money. Annie had sent a question to her once, and for a long time afterwards looked to see if it was used in the column. It wasn't, but she still liked the column and sometimes would read it to him. 'Ned, she agrees with me. She says you waste a lot of money if you put charges on your credit card and pay only the minimum every month.'

Last year Annie had been mad at him for charging a new set of tools. He'd bought an old car at the junkyard and wanted to fix it up. He had told her it didn't matter that the tools cost a lot of money, he could take a long time to pay them off. Then she read him that column.

Ned stared at Carley DeCarlo's picture. A thought came to him. He'd like to upset her and make her nervous. From the time in February when she found out that the house in Greenwood Lake was gone until the day when the truck hit her car, Annie had been worried and nervous. The whole time, she also cried a lot. 'If the vaccine is no good, we have nothing, Ned, nothing,' she'd said over and over again.

In the weeks before she died, Annie had been suffering. Ned wanted Carley DeCarlo to suffer, too, to be worried and upset. And he knew just how to do it. He would e-mail a warning to her: 'Prepare yourself for Judgment Day.'

He had to get out of the house. He'd take the bus downtown, he decided, and walk past Lynn Spencer's apartment house, the fancy one on Fifth Avenue. Just knowing that she might be inside made him feel almost as if he already had her in his sights.

An hour later Ned was standing across the street from the entrance to Lynn Spencer's building. He'd been there less than a minute when the doorman opened the door and Carley DeCarlo came out. At first he thought that he was dreaming, just as he had dreamed about the man coming out of the house in Bedford before he set the fire.

Even so, he started to follow her. She walked a long way, all the way to 37th Street, and then crossed east. Finally she walked up the steps of one of those town houses, and he was sure that meant she was home.

Now I know where she lives, Ned thought, and when I decide it's time, it will be just like the Harniks and Mrs. Schafley. Shooting her won't be any harder than shooting squirrels.

# Chapter 20

'It was scary to see how on target Adrian Garner was yesterday,' I told Don and Ken the next morning. The three of us had been at our desks early, and by a quarter of nine were gathered in Ken's office with our second cups of coffee.

Garner's prediction that people would immediately conclude the piece of charred and bloodstained shirt was merely part of Spencer's elaborate escape plan had come true. The tabloids were having a field day with the story.

Lynn's picture was on the front page of the *New York Post*, and on page three of *The Daily News*. They looked as if they had been taken at the door of her building last evening. In both she managed to look simultaneously stunning and vulnerable. There were tears in her eyes. Her left hand was open, showing the medical padding on her burned palm. The other hand was clasping the arm of her housekeeper. The *Post*'s headline was WIFE NOT SURE IF SPENCER SANK OR SWAM, while *The News* had WIFE SOBS, 'I DON'T KNOW WHAT TO THINK.'

Earlier, I had checked with the hospital and learned that Dr. Broderick's condition remained critical. I decided to tell Ken and Don about him now, and about my suspicions as well.

'You think Broderick's accident may have had something to do with your talking to him about those records?' Ken asked. In the few days I'd known him, I'd come to realize that when Ken was weighing the pros and cons of a situation, he sometimes took off his glasses and dangled them from his right hand. He was doing that now. The stubble on his chin and cheeks indicated that he had decided to start growing a beard or that he had been in a rush this morning. He was wearing a red shirt, but somehow when I looked at him, the mental picture I got was of him in a white doctor's coat with a prescription pad protruding from his pocket and a stethoscope around his neck. No matter what he wears, and with or without stubble on his face, Ken has the look of the doctor about him.

'You could be right,' he continued. 'We all know that the pharmaceutical business is as competitive as it gets. The company that's the first to market a drug to prevent or cure cancer will be worth billions.'

'Ken, why bother to steal the early records of a guy who wasn't even a biologist?' Don objected.

'Nicholas Spencer always credited his father's later research with being the basis for the vaccine he was developing. Maybe somebody got the idea that there might be something valuable in the early records,' Ken theorized.

That made sense to me. 'Dr. Broderick was the direct link between the records and the man who picked them up,' I said. 'Could those records possibly be valuable enough that someone would kill him, rather than risk his being able to identify the man with reddish brown hair? Wouldn't that suggest that whoever he is, that guy's someone who might be traceable. He might even be from Gen-stone, or at least know someone from Gen-stone who was close enough to Nick Spencer to be aware of Broderick and the records.'

'Something we may be missing is that Nick Spencer may have sent someone to collect those records himself and then pretended to be surprised that they were gone,' Don said slowly.

I stared at him. 'Why would he do that?' I asked.

'Carley, Spencer is – or was – a con man with just enough knowledge of microbiology to raise start-up money, make a guy like Wallingford – who managed to run his own family company into the toilet – chairman, let him fill a board of directors with guys who couldn't manage their way out of a turnstile, and then claim he's on the verge of proving he has the definitive cure for cancer. He got away with it for eight years. He's lived relatively modestly for a guy in his position. You know why? Because he knew it wouldn't work, and he was stashing away a fortune for his retirement when his pyramid club collapsed. But an added bonus would be for Spencer to create the illusion that somebody stole valuable data and that he was the victim of some kind of scheme. I say that his claiming he didn't know about the records having been taken was done for the benefit of people like us who'll be writing about him.'

'And almost killing Dr. Broderick is part of that scenario?' I asked.

'I bet it will turn out to be a coincidence. I'm sure all the service stations and repair shops in that area in Connecticut have been alerted to report any suspiciously damaged cars to the police. They'll find some guy who was on his way home from an all-night bender or some kid with a lead foot on the gas pedal.'

'That may happen if whoever ran down Dr. Broderick was from that area,' I said. 'Somehow, though, I don't think he was.' I got up. 'And now I'm going to see if I can't get Nick Spencer's secretary to agree to talk to me, and then I'm going to visit the hospice where Spencer was a volunteer.'

I was told that Vivian Powers had taken the day off again. I called her home, and when she heard who I was, she said, 'I don't want to talk about Nicholas Spencer,' and hung up. There was only one course left to me – I had to ring her doorbell.

Before I left the office, I checked my e-mail. There were at least one hundred questions for my column, all fairly routine, but then there were two other e-mails that jolted me. The first one read, *'Prepare yourself for Judgment Day.'*

It isn't a threat, I told myself. It's probably from some religious nut, a doomsday kind of message. I shrugged it off, perhaps because the other message really took my breath away: *'Who was the man in Lynn Spencer's mansion a minute before it caught fire?'*

Who could have seen someone leave the house before the fire started? Wouldn't it have to be the person who actually set it? And if so, why would he write to *me*? Then a thought came to me: The housekeeping couple hadn't expected Lynn to be there that night, but had they seen someone else leaving the house? If so, why hadn't they come forward? I could think of one reason: They might be in this country illegally and don't want to be deported.

I now had three stops to make in Westchester County.

I elected to make the first one to the home of Vivian and Joel Powers in Briarcliff Manor, one of the towns that borders Pleasantville. Using my road map I found their house, a charming two-story stone dwelling that must have been over one hundred years old. A realtor's sign was on the front lawn. The house was for sale.

Mentally keeping my fingers crossed as I had when I arrived unannounced on Dr. Broderick's doorstep, I rang the bell and waited. There was a peephole in the heavy old door, and I sensed that I was being observed. Then the door was opened, the safety chain clearly in sight.

The woman who answered the door was a dark-haired beauty in her late twenties. She was wearing no makeup and needed none. Her brown eyes were enhanced by long lashes. Her high cheekbones and perfectly shaped nose and mouth made me wonder if she had ever been a model. She certainly had the looks it took to be one.

'I'm Carley DeCarlo,' I said. 'Are you Vivian Powers?'

'Yes, I am, and I already told you that I would not be interviewed,' she responded.

I was sure she was on the verge of closing the door, so I said hurriedly, 'I'm trying to write a fair and balanced story about Nicholas Spencer. I don't accept the fact that there isn't a lot more to his disappearance than what is being reported in the media. When we spoke on Saturday, I got the sense that you're very defensive of him.'

'I am. Good-bye, Ms. DeCarlo. Please don't come back.'

I was taking a chance, but I plunged ahead. 'Ms. Powers,

on Friday I went up to Caspien, the town where Nick Spencer grew up. I spoke to a Dr. Broderick who bought the Spencer home and who was holding some of Dr. Spencer's early records. He's in the hospital right now, a hit-and-run victim, and probably won't make it. I believe that his talking to me about Dr. Spencer's research may have had something to do with his so-called accident.'

I held my breath, but then I saw a startled look come into her eyes. A moment later her hand moved to unfasten the safety latch. 'Come in,' she said.

The interior of the house was in the process of being dismantled. Rolled-up carpets, stacks of boxes clearly marked to show their contents, empty table tops, and bare walls and windows attested to the fact that Vivian Powers was on the verge of moving. I noticed she was wearing a wedding ring, and I wondered where her husband was.

She led me to a small enclosed sun porch that was still intact, with lamps on the tables and a small rug on the wide plank floor. The furniture was wicker with brightly colored chintz seat cushions and backrests. She sat on the loveseat, which left the matching chair for me. I was thankful that I'd persevered and had driven up and forced my way in today. Real estate wisdom is that a house shows much better when there are people living in it. Which made me ask, what was her rush to get out? I intended to make it my business to see how long this place had been on the market. I bet myself that it had not been listed before the plane crash.

'This has been my retreat since the packers started.'

'When are you leaving?' I asked.

'Friday.'

'Are you staying local?' I asked, trying to sound casual.

'No. My parents live in Boston. I'll live with them until I find my own place. I'll put the furniture in storage for the present.'

I was beginning to believe that Joel Powers was not part of his wife's future plans. 'Could I ask you just a few questions?'

'I wouldn't have let you in if I hadn't decided to let you ask me a few questions,' she said. 'But first I have a few of my own.'

'I'll answer them if I can.'

'What made you go to see Dr. Broderick?'

'I went solely to get background on the home where Nicholas Spencer was raised and anything Dr. Broderick might know about Dr. Spencer's laboratory which had been in that house.'

'Were you aware that he had been holding Dr. Spencer's early records?'

'No. Dr. Broderick volunteered that information. He obviously was troubled when he realized that Nicholas Spencer had not sent for the records. Did Spencer tell you they were missing?'

'Yes, he did.' She hesitated. 'Something happened at that award dinner in February, and it related to a letter Nick received around Thanksgiving. In it the writer said she wanted to tell him about a secret she had shared with his father, and she stated that his father had cured her daughter of multiple sclerosis. She even put in her phone number. At the time Nick tossed the letter over to me to give the standard reply. He said, "This is as nutty as they get. That's totally impossible".'

'But the letter was answered?'

'All his mail was answered. People wrote in all the time,

begging to be used in an experiment, willing to sign anything for a chance to get the cancer vaccine he was working on. Sometimes people wrote that they'd been cured of some ailment and wanted him to test their homespun remedies and distribute them. We had a couple of form letter responses.'

'Did you keep copies of these letters?'

'No, just a list of names of people who got them. Neither of us remembered that woman's name. There are two employees who deal with that kind of mail. But then something happened at the award dinner. Nick was very excited the next morning and said he had to go right back to Caspien. He said he'd learned something terribly important. He said that his gut had told him to take seriously that letter from the woman who wrote about his father curing her daughter.'

'Then he rushed back to Caspien to collect his father's early records and found that they had disappeared. This happened around Thanksgiving, at about the same time the letter came into the office,' I said.

'That's right.'

'Let me get this straight, Vivian. You think there was a connection between that letter and the fact that his father's early records were taken from Dr. Broderick a few days later?'

'I'm sure there was, and Nick was different after that day.'

'Did he ever say who he went to see after he left Dr. Broderick?'

'No, he didn't.'

'Can you check his calendar for that day. The award dinner was on February 15, so it would be February 16. Maybe he jotted down a name or number.'

She shook her head. 'He didn't write it down that morning, and he never put anything on his calendar after that day – I mean, anything about appointments outside the office.'

'Suppose you had to reach him, how would you do it?'

'I called his cell phone. Let me correct that. There were some events already scheduled, like medical seminars, dinners, board meetings – those kinds of things. But Nick was out of the office a lot those last four or five weeks. When the U.S. attorney's people came to the office, they told us that they'd learned he'd been to Europe twice. But he didn't use the company plane, and no one at the office knew his plans, not even me.'

'The authorities seem to think he was either making arrangements for face-changing plastic surgery, or he was setting up his future residence. What do you think, Vivian?'

'I think there was something terribly wrong, and he knew it. I think he was afraid that his phone was tapped. I was there when he called Dr. Broderick, and looking back at it, I wonder why he didn't just say that he wanted his father's records. All he did was ask if he could stop in.'

It was obvious to me that Vivian Powers wanted desperately to believe that Nick Spencer had been the victim of a conspiracy.

'Vivian,' I asked, 'do you think he seriously expected the vaccine to work? Or did he always know it was flawed?'

'No. He was driven by his need to find a cure for cancer. He lost both his wife and his mother to that terrible disease. In fact, I met him in a hospice two years ago when my husband was a patient there. Nick was a volunteer.'

'You met Nick Spencer at the hospice?'

'Yes. St. Ann's. It was just a few days before Joel died. I had given up my job to take care of him. I'd been assistant to the president of a brokerage firm. Nick stopped in Joel's room and talked with us. Then a few weeks after Joel died I got a phone call from him. He told me that if I ever wanted to work for Gen-stone, to come see him. He'd find a place for me. Six months later I took him up on that. I never expected to be hired to work for him personally, but my timing was good. His assistant was pregnant and planning to stay home for a couple of years, so I got the job. It was a godsend for me.'

'How did he get along with other people in the office?'

She smiled. 'Fine. He really liked Charles Wallingford. He joked about him to me sometimes. Said if he hears once more about his family tree, he'll have it cut down. I don't think he liked Adrian Garner, though. He said he was overbearing, but it was worth putting up with that because of all the money Garner could bring to the table.'

Then I heard again the passionate tone I first noticed when I called her on Saturday. 'Nick Spencer was a dedicated man. He'd have carried Garner's boots if that was necessary to get his company to market the vaccine and make it available all over the world.'

'But if he realized that the vaccine didn't work, and if he'd been taking out money that he couldn't replace, then what?'

'Then I admit that he could have snapped. He was nervous, and he was worried. He also told me about something that happened only a week before the plane crash, something that could have led to a fatal accident. He was driving home from New York to Bedford late at night, and the accelerator froze in his car.'

'Did you ever tell anyone else about that?'

'No. He made light of it. He said that he was lucky because there was very little traffic and he was able to maneuver the car until he turned off the engine and it stopped on its own. It was an old car, one that he loved, but he said it was clearly time to get rid of it.' She hesitated. 'Carley, now I wonder if it's at all possible that somebody did something to jam the accelerator. The incident with the car was only a week before his plane went down.'

I tried to keep my expression neutral and merely nodded thoughtfully. I didn't want her to see that I absolutely agreed with her. There was something else I needed to find out. 'What do you know about his relationship with Lynn?'

'Nothing. Gregarious as he seemed to be, Nick was a very private person.'

I saw the genuine grief in her eyes. 'You were very fond of him, weren't you?'

She nodded. 'Anyone who had the chance to be with Nick Spencer regularly would have been very fond of him. He was so special. He was the heart and soul of that company. It's going to go bankrupt. People there are either being fired or are leaving, and all of them blame him and hate him. Well, I believe that he may be a victim, too.'

I left a few minutes later, having made Vivian promise to stay in touch with me. She waited while I walked down the path and waved to me as I got in my car.

My mind was churning. I was certain there was a connection between Dr. Broderick being hit by the car and Nicholas Spencer's jammed accelerator and the plane crash. Three accidents? No way. Then I allowed the question that had always been in the back of my mind to come front and center: Had Nicholas Spencer been murdered?

But when I was talking to the housekeeping couple at the Bedford property, another scenario cropped up, and this one changed my thinking entirely.

# Chapter 21

'Last night I dreamt I went to Manderley again.' I couldn't help thinking of the haunting opening lines of Daphne du Maurier's novel *Rebecca*, as I turned off the road in Bedford, stopped at the gate of the Spencer estate, and announced myself.

For the second time today I was making an uninvited visit. When a Hispanic-accented voice politely asked who I was, I replied that I was Mrs. Spencer's stepsister. There was a moment's pause, and then I was directed to drive around the site of the fire and to stay to the right.

I drove in slowly, giving myself a chance to admire the beautiful well-tended grounds that surrounded the ruined building. There was a pool in the back and a pool house on a terrace above it. To the left I could see what looked like an English garden. Somehow, though, I couldn't visualize Lynn on her knees, digging in the soil. I wondered if Nick and his first wife had been the ones to oversee the landscaping, or perhaps a previous owner had undertaken the task.

The house where Manuel and Rosa Gomez lived was a quaint limestone cottage with a sloping tile roof. A screen of evergreens shielded the cottage from the view of the mansion, giving privacy to both places. It was easy to see why the housekeepers had not been aware of Lynn's return last week. Late at night she could have punched in the code to unlock the gate and driven into the garage without their knowledge. It did seem odd to me that there were no security cameras on the premises, but I knew the house had been alarmed.

I parked, went up to the porch, and rang the bell. Manuel Gomez answered the door and invited me in. He was a wiry man, about five feet eight inches in height, with dark hair and a lean, intelligent face. I stepped into the vestibule and thanked him for seeing me without notice.

'You almost missed us, Miss DeCarlo,' he said stiffly. 'As your sister requested, we will be gone by one o'clock. We have already removed our personal belongings. My wife has purchased the groceries Mrs. Spencer ordered and is presently checking upstairs one last time. Would you care to inspect the house now?'

'You're leaving! But why?' I think he realized that my astonishment was genuine.

'Mrs. Spencer says she has no need of full-time help, and she intends to use this cottage for herself until she decides whether or not to rebuild.'

'But the fire was only a week ago,' I protested. 'Do you have a new situation to go to so quickly?'

'No, we do not. We will take a short vacation in Puerto Rico and visit with our relatives. Then we will stay with our daughter until we find another position.'

I could understand that Lynn might want to be able to stay in Bedford – I was sure she must have friends here – but to put these people out with so little notice seemed almost inhumane to me.

He realized I was still standing in the vestibule. 'I am sorry, Miss DeCarlo,' he said. 'Please come into the living room.'

As I followed him, I quickly glanced around. There was a rather steep staircase leading to the upstairs from the foyer. To the left there was what seemed to be a study with bookcases and a television set. The living room was a generous size, with creamy rough plaster walls, a fireplace, and leaded pane windows. It was comfortably furnished with a tapestry-patterned fabric covering the roomy couch and chairs. The ambience was that of an English country home.

It was spotlessly clean, and there were fresh flowers in a bowl on the coffee table.

'Please sit down,' Gomez said. He remained standing.

'Mr. Gomez, how long have you worked here?' I asked.

'Since Mr. and Mrs. Spencer – I mean the *first* Mrs. Spencer – were married twelve years ago.'

Twelve years, and less than a week's notice! Good God, I thought. I was dying to ask how much severance pay Lynn had given them, but I didn't have the nerve – at least not yet.

'Mr. Gomez,' I said, 'I haven't come here to inspect the house. I came because I wanted to talk to you and your wife. I'm a journalist, and I'm helping to write a story for my magazine, *Wall Street Weekly*, about Nicholas Spencer. Mrs. Spencer is aware I'm doing the story. I know people are saying some pretty vicious things about Nicholas, but

I intend to be scrupulously fair. May I ask some questions of you about him?'

'Let me get my wife,' he said quietly. 'She is upstairs.'

While I waited, I took a quick look through the archway at the back of the room. It led to a dining area, and beyond that was the kitchen. I wondered if this originally was intended to be a guest house rather than housing for employees. It had an expensive feel to it.

I heard footsteps on the stairs and settled back in the seat where Gomez had left me. Then I got up to meet Rosa Gomez, a pretty, slightly plump woman whose swollen eyes were a dead giveaway that she had been crying.

'Let's all sit down,' I suggested, and immediately felt like a fool. After all, this had been their home.

It wasn't hard to get them talking about Nicholas and Janet Spencer. 'They were so happy together,' Rosa Gomez said, her face lighting as she spoke. 'And when Jack was born, you would think he was the only child in the world. It is so impossible to think that both his parents are gone. They were such wonderful people.'

The tears that were glistening in her eyes began to overflow. Impatiently she brushed them away with the back of her hand.

They told me that the Spencers had bought the house a few months after they were married, and they had been hired shortly after. 'We lived in the house at that time,' Rosa said. 'There was a very nice apartment on the other side of the kitchen. But when Mr. Spencer remarried, your sister – '

'Stepsister,' I wanted to shout. Instead I said, 'I must interrupt you, Mrs. Gomez, and explain that Mrs. Spencer's father and my mother were married two years ago in

Florida. We are technically stepsisters, but we are not close. I'm here as a journalist, not as a relative.'

So much for being Lynn's advocate, but I needed to hear the truth from these people, not polite, carefully phrased answers.

Manuel Gomez looked at his wife, then at me. 'Mrs. Lynn Spencer did not want us living in the house. She preferred, as many people do, that the help have separate quarters. She suggested to Mr. Spencer that there were five guest bedrooms in the house, and they were more than sufficient for any guests they might wish to accommodate. He was quite agreeable to the idea of our moving into the cottage, and we were delighted to have this wonderful home to ourselves. Jack, of course, was living with his grandparents.'

'Did Nicholas Spencer stay close to his son?' I asked.

'Absolutely,' Manuel said promptly. 'But he did travel a great deal and did not want to leave Jack with a nanny.'

'And after his father's second marriage, Jack did not want to live with Mrs. Lynn Spencer,' Rosa said firmly. 'He told me once that he didn't think she liked him.'

'He told you that!'

'Yes, he did. Don't forget we were here when he was born. He was comfortable with us. To him, we were family. But he and his dad . . .' She smiled reminiscently and shook her head. 'They were pals. This is such a tragedy for that little boy. First his mother, then his father. I have spoken to Jack's grandmother. She tells me that he is sure his father is alive.'

'What makes him think that?' I asked quickly.

'Mr. Nicholas did some stunt flying when he was in college. Jack clings to the hope that somehow he was able to escape from the plane before it crashed.'

From the mouths of babes? I wondered. I listened while Manuel and Rosa vied with each other to tell anecdotes about the early years they had spent with Nick and Janet and Jack, and then I moved on to the questions I needed to ask. 'Rosa, Manuel, I received an e-mail from someone who claimed that a man had left the mansion only a minute before it caught fire. Do either of you know anything about that?'

They both looked startled. 'We don't have e-mail, and if we had seen someone leave the mansion before the fire, we would have told the police,' Manuel said emphatically. 'Do you think the person who started the fire sent it?'

'It could be,' I said. 'There are sick people who do that sort of thing all the time. Why it would have been sent to me instead of the police, though, I don't know.'

'I feel guilty that we did not think to check the garage for Mrs. Spencer's car,' Manuel said. 'She doesn't usually come home so very late, but it does happen.'

'How often did they use the house?' I asked. 'I mean, every weekend, during the week, or infrequently?'

'The first Mrs. Spencer loved the house. At that time they came up every weekend, and before Jack was in school, she would often stay for a week or two if Mr. Spencer was traveling. Mrs. Lynn Spencer wanted to sell this house *and* their apartment. She told Mr. Spencer that she wanted to start out fresh and not live with another's woman's taste. They used to argue about that.'

'Rosa, I don't think you should discuss Mrs. Spencer,' Manuel warned.

She shrugged. 'I am saying what is true. This house did not satisfy her. Mr. Spencer asked her to wait until the vaccine was approved before becoming involved with a building project. I understand in the last months there were problems with the vaccine, and he was terribly worried. He traveled a lot. When he was home, he would often go up to Greenwich and be with Jack.'

'I know Jack lives with his grandparents, but when Mr. Spencer was home, did Jack stay here on weekends?'

Rosa shrugged. 'Not so much. Jack was always very quiet around Mrs. Spencer. She is not one who naturally understands children. Jack was five when his mother died. Mrs. Lynn Spencer looks somewhat like her, but, of course, she isn't her. That makes it harder, and I think it upset him.'

'Would you say that Lynn and Mr. Spencer were very close?' I knew I was pushing the envelope with my questions, but I had to get a handle on their relationship.

'When they were first married four years ago, I would say yes,' Rosa said slowly, 'at least for a little while. But unless I am wrong, that feeling did not last. Frequently she would come up with her guests, and he would be away or in Greenwich with Jack.'

'You said that Mrs. Spencer didn't make it a habit to come up here late at night, but that it did happen occasionally. Did she usually call you first?'

'Sometimes she would phone ahead and say she wanted to have a snack or cold supper waiting for her. Other times we would get a call from the mansion in the morning to say that she was here and she would say what time she wanted breakfast. Otherwise we would always go over at nine o'clock and begin to work. It was a big house and needed to be kept up constantly, whether or not it was being occupied.'

I knew it was time to go. I could sense that Manuel and

Rosa Gomez did not want to prolong the painful moment of leaving this house. And yet I felt that I hadn't scratched the surface of the lives of the people who had lived here.

'I was surprised to see that there are no security cameras on the property,' I said.

'The Spencers always had a Labrador, and he was a good watchdog. But he went with Jack to Greenwich, and Mrs. Lynn Spencer did not want another dog,' Manuel told me. 'She said she was allergic to animals.'

That doesn't make sense, I thought. In the Boca Raton apartment, her father has pictures of her growing up with dogs and horses.

'Where was the dog kept?' I asked.

'It was outside at night unless the weather was very cold.'

'Would it bark at an intruder?'

They both smiled. 'Oh, yes,' Manuel said. 'Mrs. Spencer said besides her allergies, Shep was too noisy.'

Too noisy because he announced *her* nocturnal arrivals or because he alerted everyone to the nocturnal arrivals of *other* visitors? I wondered.

I stood up. 'You've been very kind to give me this time now. I only wish that everything had worked out better for everyone.'

'I pray,' Rosa told me. 'I pray that Jack is right and that Mr. Spencer is still alive. I pray that his vaccine will work in the end and that the trouble about the money will go away.' Tears welled in her eyes again and began to flow down her cheeks. 'And then I ask for a miracle. Jack's mother can't come back, but I pray that Mr. Spencer and that beautiful girl who works with him will get together.'

'Rosa, be quiet,' Manuel commanded.

'No, I won't,' she said defiantly. 'What harm can it do to say it now?' She looked at me. 'Just a few days before his plane crashed, Mr. Spencer came home one afternoon from work to pick up a briefcase he'd forgotten. The girl was with him. Her name is Vivian Powers. It was so clear that they were in love, and I was so glad for him. So much has gone wrong in his life. Mrs. Lynn Spencer is not a kind person. If Mr. Spencer *is* dead, I'm glad that at the end he knew someone loved him very much.'

I gave them my card and left, trying to absorb the ramifications of what I had just heard.

Vivian had quit her job, sold her home, and put her furniture in storage. She had talked about starting a new chapter in her life. But as I drove home, I would have bet dollars to doughnuts that that chapter wouldn't open in Boston. And what about her account of the discarded letter from someone who claimed that Dr. Spencer had miraculously cured her daughter? Were the letter, the missing records, and the story about the jammed accelerator all part of an elaborate plot to create the illusion that Nick Spencer was the victim of a sinister plot?

I thought of the *Post* headline: WIFE SOBS, 'I DON'T KNOW WHAT TO THINK.'

I could offer a new headline: STEPSISTER-IN-LAW DOESN'T KNOW WHAT TO THINK, EITHER.

# Chapter 22

The halls of the hospice wing of St. Ann's Hospital were softly carpeted, and the reception area was comfortable, with a windowed wall that looked out over a pond. There was an air of serenity and peace about the place, totally unlike the hospital's center building and the other wing where I'd visited Lynn.

The patients here arrived with the knowledge that they would not leave. They came to be relieved of their suffering, as much as was humanly possible, and to have a peaceful death surrounded by their loved ones and by dedicated people who would also be there to comfort those they were leaving behind.

The receptionist was surprised that I asked to see the director without an appointment, but she agreed, and there's no question that mentioning *Wall Street Weekly* will open doors. I was promptly escorted to the office of Dr. Katherine Clintworth, an attractive woman in her early fifties who wore her sandy hair long and straight. Her eyes were her dominant feature – they were winter blue, the color of water on a sunny January day. She was dressed in a casual knit jacket and matching slacks.

By now my apology for unscheduled visits followed by my explanation that I was contributing to a cover story for *Wall Street Weekly* was well practiced. She dismissed it with a gesture of her hand.

'I'll be happy to answer your questions about Nicholas Spencer,' she said. 'I admired him very much. As you can well understand, nothing would please us more than to have no need for hospices because cancer has been obliterated.'

'How long was Nicholas Spencer a volunteer here?' I asked.

'Since his wife Janet died over five years ago. Our staff could have taken care of her at home, but because she had a five-year-old child, she thought it better to come to us for those last ten days. Nick was very grateful for the help we were able to give, not only to Janet but to him, his son, and Janet's parents as well. A few weeks later he came back and offered his services to us.'

'It must have been pretty hard to schedule him, given how much he had to travel,' I suggested.

'He gave us a list of his available dates a couple of weeks ahead of time. We were always able to work around it. People liked Nick very much.'

'Then he was still a volunteer at the time of the plane crash?'

She hesitated. 'No. Actually he hadn't been here for about a month.'

'Was there a reason for that?'

'I suggested that he needed to take time off. He seemed to be under tremendous pressure in the weeks before then.'

I could see that she was weighing her words carefully. 'What *kind* of pressure?' I asked.

'He seemed nervous and high-strung. I told him that working on the vaccine all day and then coming here and working with patients who were begging him to try it on them was too heavy a psychological burden for him to carry.'

'Did he agree?'

'If he didn't agree, I would say that at least he understood. He went home that night and I never saw him again.'

The implication of what she was *not* saying hit me like a ton of bricks. 'Dr. Clintworth, *did* Nicholas Spencer ever test his vaccine on a patient?'

'That would have been illegal,' she replied firmly.

'That's not what I asked. Dr. Clintworth, I'm investigating the possibility that Nicholas Spencer may have met with foul play. Please be honest with me.'

She hesitated, then answered. 'I am convinced that he gave the vaccine to one person here. In fact, I'm positive he did, even though that patient won't admit it. There is someone else who I believe received it, but that, too, has been emphatically denied.'

'What happened to the person you're certain received the vaccine?'

'He's gone home.'

'He's *cured*?'

'No, but I understand he has had a spontaneous remission. The progression of the disease has slowed dramatically, which does happen, but only rarely.'

'Are you following up on his progress or lack of it?'

'As I said, he has not admitted that he received the vaccine from Nicholas Spencer, if indeed he did.'

'Will you tell me who he is?'

'I can't do that. It would be a violation of his privacy.'

I fished for another card and gave it to her. 'Would you mind asking that patient to contact me?'

'I will, but I'm very sure you won't hear from him.'

'What about the other patient?' I asked.

'That one is only a suspicion on my part, and I cannot confirm it. And now, Ms. DeCarlo, I have a meeting to attend. If you want something from me to quote about Nicholas Spencer, this is my statement: "He was a good man, and driven by a noble purpose. If he somehow got lost along the way, I am sure it was not for self-serving reasons".'

# Chapter 23

His hand was throbbing so much that Ned couldn't think of anything but the pain. He tried soaking it in ice water and putting butter on it, but neither helped. Then, at ten of ten, Monday night, just before closing time, he went to the hole-in-the-wall drugstore near where he lived and headed to the section where over-the-counter burn medications were displayed. He picked out a couple that sounded as if they might do the job.

Old Mr. Brown, the owner, was just locking up the pharmacy. The only other employee there was Peg, the cashier, a nosy woman who loved to gossip. Ned didn't want her to see how bad his hand looked, so he put the ointments in one of the little baskets that were stacked at the entrance, hooked it over his left arm, and had his money ready in his left hand. The right one he kept in his pocket. The bandage on it was messy even though he had already changed it twice that day.

There were a couple of people on line ahead of him, and as he waited, he shifted from one foot to the other. Damn hand, he thought. It wouldn't have been burned, and Annie wouldn't be dead, if he hadn't sold the house in Greenwood Lake and put all their money in that phony Gen-stone company, he told himself. When he wasn't thinking about Annie and picturing those last minutes – her crying and hitting his chest with her fists, then running from the house, followed by the sound of the car smashing into the garbage truck – he thought of the people he hated, and what he would do to them. The Harniks and Mrs. Schafley and Mrs. Morgan and Lynn Spencer and Carley DeCarlo.

His fingers hadn't hurt much when the fire caught him, but now they were so swollen that the slightest pressure hurt them. Unless they got better, he wouldn't be able to hold his rifle straight or even pull the trigger.

Ned watched as the man ahead of him picked up his package. As soon as the man moved, he put his basket and a twenty-dollar bill down on the counter and looked away as Peg totaled his items.

He thought about how he knew he should go to the emergency room and get a doctor to look at the burn, but he was afraid to do that. He could hear what the doctor might ask him: 'What happened? Why did you let this go so long?' These were questions he didn't want to deal with.

If he told them Dr. Ryan at St. Ann's had treated it, they might ask why he hadn't gone to have him look at it again when it wasn't getting better. Maybe he should go to an urgent care place somewhere, like in Queens or New Jersey or Connecticut, he decided.

'Hey, Ned, wake up.'

He looked back at the cashier. He had never liked Peg. Her eyes were too close together; she had heavy black brows and black hair with gray roots – she made him think of a squirrel. She was annoyed just because he hadn't noticed that she'd taken his ointments and put them in a bag and had his change ready. She was holding out his change in one hand and the bag in the other, and she was frowning.

He reached for the bag with his left hand and, without thinking, pulled his right hand out of his pocket and held it out for the change, then watched as Peg stared at the bandage.

'My God, Ned. What were you doing, playing with matches? That hand's a mess,' she said. 'You should see a doctor.'

Ned cursed himself for letting her see it. 'I burned it cooking,' he said, sullenly. 'I never had to cook before Annie died. I went to the doctor in the hospital where Annie used to work. He said to come back in a week. It's gonna be a week tomorrow.'

Immediately he realized what he had done. He had told Peg that he saw a doctor last Tuesday, and that was something he hadn't meant to say. He knew that Annie used to talk to Peg when she bought stuff at the drugstore. She said Peg wasn't really nosy; she was just curious in a friendly kind of way. Annie, who had been raised in a small town near Albany, said that there was a lady in the drugstore there who knew everybody's business and that Peg reminded her of that woman.

What else had Annie told Peg? About losing the Greenwood Lake house? About all the money he'd put in Gen-stone? About how he would drive Annie past Spencer's mansion in Bedford and promise her that she would have a home like that someday?

Peg was staring at him. 'Why don't you show your hand to Mr. Brown?' she asked. 'He might have something better than this stuff to give you.'

He stared back at her. 'I said I'm seeing the doctor in the morning.'

Peg had a funny look on her face. It reminded him of the way the Harniks and Mrs. Schafley had looked at him. It was a look of fear. Peg was afraid of him. Was she afraid of him because she was thinking about all the things that Annie had told her about the house and the money and driving past the Spencer mansion, and because she had put it all together and figured out that he was the one who set the fire?

She looked flustered. 'Oh, that's good that you're seeing a doctor tomorrow.' Then she said, 'I miss Annie coming in, Ned. I know how much you must miss her.' She looked past him. 'Ned, sorry, but I have to take care of Garret.'

Ned realized there was a young fellow standing behind him. 'Sure, sure you do, Peg,' he said, and moved aside.

He had to go. He couldn't just stand there. But something had to be done.

He went outside and got into the car, immediately reaching into the backseat and taking the rifle from under the blanket on the floor. Then he waited. From where he was parked he had a clear view of the interior of the store. As soon as that guy Garret left, Peg emptied the cash register and gave the receipts to Mr. Brown. Then she rushed around, turning out the lights in the rest of the store.

If she was going to call the cops, she apparently was going to wait until she got home to do it. Maybe she'd talk it over with her husband first, he thought.

Mr. Brown and Peg came out of the store together. Mr. Brown said good night and walked around the corner. Peg started walking quickly the other way, toward the bus stop down the block. Ned saw that the bus was coming. He watched her run to catch it, but she reached it too late. She was standing alone at the bus stop when he drove up, stopped, and opened the door. 'I'll drive you home, Peg,' he offered.

He saw the look on her face again, only this time she was really scared. 'Oh, that's all right, Ned. I'll just wait. It won't be long.' She looked around, but there was no one nearby.

He threw open the door, jumped out of the car, and grabbed her. His hand hurt when he slapped it on her mouth to keep her from screaming, but he managed to hold on. With his left hand he twisted her arm, dragged her into the car, and shoved her on the floor of the front seat. He locked the car doors as he took off.

'Ned, what's the matter? Please, Ned, what are you doing?' she wailed. She was on the floor of the car, holding her head where it had hit the dashboard.

He held the rifle in one hand, pointing it down at her.

'I don't want you to tell anyone that I was playing with matches.'

'Ned, why would I tell anyone?' She was starting to cry.

He headed toward the picnic area in the county park.

Forty minutes later he was home. It had hurt his finger and hand when he pulled the trigger, but he hadn't missed. He'd been right. It was just like shooting squirrels.

# Chapter 24

I'd stopped at the office after leaving the hospice, but both Don and Ken were out. I made some notes of things to discuss with them in the morning. Two heads are better than one, and three are better than two – not always true, of course, but it's definitely applicable when you include these two knowledgeable guys in the equation.

There were a number of questions I wanted to discuss with them. Was Vivian Powers planning to join Nicholas Spencer somewhere? Were Dr. Spencer's early records really missing, or were they mentioned merely as a smoke screen to cast doubt on Spencer's guilt? Was someone else in the mansion that night, only minutes before it was set on fire? And finally, and breathtaking in significance, did Nick Spencer test the vaccine on a terminally ill patient who later was able to leave the hospice?

I was determined to learn the name of that patient.

Why would he not shout to the skies that he was in remission? I wondered. Was it because the patient wanted to see if the remission would last or because he didn't want to be the subject of an intense media frenzy? I could only imagine the headlines if news leaked out that the Gen-stone vaccine worked after all.

And who was the other patient Dr. Clintworth was sure had been given the vaccine? Was there some way I could persuade her to give me that patient's name?

Nicholas Spencer had been on a championship swim team in high school. His son was clinging to the hope that he was alive because he had been a stunt flyer while he was in college. It wasn't too great a leap to imagine that with that kind of background he might have been able to stage his own death a few miles from shore and then swim to safety.

I longed to be able to talk over all these points with the guys while they were still fresh in my head. But I made copious notes, and then, since it was nearly six o'clock and it certainly had been an eventful day, I went home.

There were a half-dozen messages on my answering machine – friends suggesting we get together, a call from Casey instructing me to call back by seven if I was in the mood for pasta at Il Tinello. I was, I decided, and tried to figure out if I should be flattered to be called twice for dinner within seven days or if I should consider myself a 'she'll-do-in-a-pinch' date because he had run through the people who required more notice.

Be that as it may, I stopped the answering machine and called Casey on his cell phone. We had our usual brief telephone conversation.

His abrupt 'Dr. Dillon.'

'Casey, it's me.'

'Pasta tonight good for you?'

'Fine.'

'Eight o'clock at Il Tinello?'

'Uh-huh.'

'Great.' Click.

I asked him once if his bedside manner was as rapid-fire as his phone personality, but he assured me that wasn't the case. 'Do you know how much time people can waste on the phone?' he'd asked. 'I've made a study of it.'

I was curious. 'Where did you do the study?'

'At home, twenty years ago. My sister, Trish. A couple of times when we were in high school, I clocked her on the phone. One time she spent an hour and fifteen minutes telling her best friend how worried she was that she wasn't prepared for the test she was having the next day. Another time she spent fifty minutes telling another friend that she wasn't half finished with a science project that was due in two days.'

'Nonetheless, she managed to muddle through reasonably well,' I'd reminded him during that conversation. Trish had become a pediatric surgeon and now lived in Virginia.

Smiling at the memory, and slightly concerned that I was so ready to fall in with Casey's plans, I pushed the button on the answering machine to hear the final message.

The caller's voice was low and distressed. She did not identify herself, but I recognized her – Vivian Powers. 'Carley, it's four o'clock. Sometimes I brought work home. I was clearing out my desk. I think I know who took the records from Dr. Broderick. Call me, please.'

I had written my home number on the back of my card, but my cell phone was printed on the card. I wish she had tried to reach me on that. By four o'clock I had been on my way back to the city. I'd have turned around and gone straight to see her. I grabbed my notebook out of my purse, found her phone number, and called.

The answering machine picked up on the fifth ring, which said to me that Vivian had been home until fairly recently. The way most answering machines work is that they give you four or five rings to get to the phone if you're home, but after one message is recorded, they pick up on the second ring.

I carefully worded my response to her: 'I was glad to hear from you, Vivian. It's a quarter of seven. I'll be here until seven-thirty and then back around nine-thirty. Call me, please.'

I wasn't even sure myself why I didn't leave my name. If Vivian had caller ID, my number would have been been recorded on her phone screen. But just in case she happened to check the machine while someone else was with her, it seemed a more discreet way to go.

A quick shower before going out for the evening always helps to relieve the tensions that build up when I'm working. The shower I have in my minuscule bathroom is a combination tub-shower setup, a little cramped, but it does the job. As I played games with the hot and cold knobs, I thought of something I'd read about Queen Elizabeth I: 'The queen takes a bath once a month whether she needs it or not.' She might not have had so many people beheaded if she'd been able to relax in a hot shower at the end of the day, I decided.

I prefer pantsuits for daytime wear, but at night it does feel good to put on a silk blouse, slacks, and heels. I feel satisfyingly taller when I'm dressed like that. The temperature outside had started to drop by the time I came in, but instead of a coat, I grabbed a woolen scarf my mother had bought me on a trip to Ireland. It is a deep cranberry shade, and I love it.

I glanced in the mirror and decided I didn't look half bad. My grin turned into a frown, though, as I thought how I didn't like the fact that I was dressing up so carefully for Casey, and that I was so pleased he'd called me so soon after the last date.

I left the apartment in plenty of time but absolutely could not get a cab. Sometimes I think that all the cab-drivers in New York City send a signal out to each other and put their 'out of service' signs on simultaneously when they see me standing out in the street looking for one of them.

As a result, I was late – fifteen minutes late. Mario, the owner, took me to the table where Casey was settled and held out my chair. Casey looked serious, and I thought, Good God, he's not going to make a big deal of this, is he? He stood up, brushed a kiss against the side of my cheek, and asked, 'Are you okay?'

I realized that he was so used to my being on time that he'd been worried about me, which pleased me too much. A good-looking, smart, successful, unattached doctor like Dr. Kevin Curtis Dillon is bound to be in great demand among the many unattached women in New York City, and I worry that my role is to be the comfortable friend. It's a bittersweet situation. I kept a diary when I was in high school. Six months ago, when I bumped into Casey in the theater, I dug it out. It was embarrassing to read how rapturous I'd been about going to the prom with him, but it was worse to read the subsequent entries of bitter disappointment when he never called after that.

I reminded myself to throw away that diary.

'I'm fine,' I said. 'Just a major case of taxicabitis.'

He didn't look all that relieved. Something was clearly troubling him. 'Something's wrong, Casey. What is it?' I asked.

He waited until the wine he'd ordered had been poured, then said, 'It's been a tough day, Carley. Surgery can do just so much, and it's so damn frustrating to know that no matter what you do, you can only help a little. I operated on a kid who hit a truck with his motorcycle. He's lucky he still has a foot, but he'll have only limited movement in it.'

Casey's eyes were dark with pain. I thought of Nick Spencer who wanted so desperately to save the lives of people suffering with cancer. Had he gone beyond the limits of safety trying to prove he could do it? I couldn't get that question out of my mind.

Instinctively, I put my hand over Casey's. He looked at me and seemed to relax. 'You're very easy to be with, Carley,' he said. 'Thanks for coming on such short notice.'

'My pleasure.'

'Even though you were late.' The moment of intimacy was gone.

'Taxicabitis.'

'What's going on with the Spencer story?'

Over Portobello mushrooms, watercress salad, and linguine with white clam sauce, I told him about my encounters with Vivian Powers, Rosa and Manuel Gomez, and Dr. Clintworth at the hospice.

He frowned at the suggestion that Nicholas Spencer was experimenting on patients at the hospice. 'If true, that's not only illegal but also morally wrong,' he said emphatically. 'Look up the case histories of some of these drugs that seemed to be miraculous but didn't prove out. Thalidomide is a classic example. It was approved in Europe forty years ago to relieve nausea in pregnant women. Fortunately at the time Dr. Frances Kelsey of the FDA put the kibosh on approving it. Today, especially in Germany, there are people in their forties with horrendous genetic deformities, such as flippers instead of arms, because their mothers thought the drug was safe.'

'But haven't I read that thalidomide is proving to be valuable in the treatment of other problems?' I asked.

'That's absolutely true. But it isn't being given to pregnant women. New drugs have to be tested over an extended period of time, Carley, before we start handing them out.'

'Casey, suppose your choice is to be dead in a few months or to be alive and risk terrible side effects. Which would you choose?'

'Fortunately, it's a question that I haven't faced myself, Carley. I do know that as a doctor I wouldn't violate my oath and turn anyone into a guinea pig.'

But Nicholas Spencer was not a doctor, I thought. His mindset was different. And in the hospice he was dealing with people who were terminally ill, who had no alternative except to be a guinea pig or die.

Over espresso, Casey invited me to go with him to a cocktail party in Greenwich on Sunday afternoon. 'You'll like these people,' he said, 'and they'll like you.'

I accepted, of course. When we left the restaurant, I wanted him to put me in a cab, but this time he insisted on riding with me. I offered to fix him the after-dinner drink we'd both refused at the restaurant, but he had the cab wait while he saw me to the door of my apartment. 'It occurred to me that you really should be in a place with a doorman,' he said. 'This business of letting yourself in with a key isn't safe anymore. Someone could push in behind you.'

I was astonished. 'Whatever put that in your mind?'

He looked at me soberly. Casey is about six feet two. Even when I'm wearing heels, he towers over me. 'I don't know, Carley,' he said. 'I just wonder if you're not getting into something bigger than you realize with this Spencer investigation.'

I didn't know how prophetic those words were. It was nearly ten-thirty when I entered my apartment. I looked at the answering machine but saw no blinking light. Vivian Powers had not called back.

I tried her number again, but there was no answer, so I left another message.

The next morning the phone rang just as I was leaving for work. It was someone from the police department in Briarcliff Manor. A neighbor walking his dog that morning had noticed that the door of Vivian Powers's home was ajar. He rang the bell and on receiving no answer had walked inside. The house was empty. A table and lamp were knocked over and the lights were on. The police had been called. They had checked the answering machine and found my messages. Did I have any knowledge of where Vivian Powers might be or if she was in some kind of trouble?

# Chapter 25

Ken and Don listened with sober concentration when I told them about my meetings in Westchester and the call I'd received that morning from the police in Briarcliff Manor.

'Gut reaction, Carley?' Ken asked. 'Is this an elaborate performance to convince everyone that something else was going on? The housekeeping couple tell you that it was obvious Nick Spencer and Vivian Powers were lovebirds. Is it possible you were getting too close to the truth? Do you think she was planning to go to Boston for a while, live with Mommy and Daddy, then start a new life in Australia or Timbuktu or Monaco once the heat was off?'

'Absolutely possible,' I said. 'In fact, if that's the way it is, I have to tell you that I think leaving the door open and a table and chair knocked over was a bit much.' Having said that, I hesitated.

'What is it?' Ken asked.

'Looking back, I think she was frightened. When Vivian

opened the door for me, she kept the safety chain on for a couple of minutes before she let me in.'

'You were there around eleven-thirty?' Ken asked.

'Yes.'

'Did she give any indication of why she was frightened?'

'Not directly, but she did say that the accelerator on Spencer's car had jammed only a week before his plane crashed. She had begun to think neither one was an accident.'

I got up. 'I'm going to drive up there,' I said. 'And then I'm going back to Caspien. Unless this is a total charade, the fact that Vivian Powers called me to say that she thought she knew the identity of the reddish-haired man may mean that she had become a threat to someone.'

Ken nodded. 'Go ahead. And I have a few connections. There aren't that many people who went into St. Ann's Hospice to die and then later walked out. It certainly shouldn't be that hard to identify this guy.'

I was still new on the job. Ken was the senior on this cover story. Even so, I had to say it: 'Ken, when you find him, I'd like to be along when you talk to him.'

Ken considered for a moment, then nodded. 'Fair enough.'

I have a pretty good sense of direction. This time I didn't need my road map to find my way to Vivian's house. There was a lone cop stationed at the door, and he looked at me suspiciously. I explained that I had seen Vivian Powers the day before and had received a phone call from her.

'Let me check,' he said. He went into the house and came back quickly. 'Detective Shapiro said it's okay for you to go in.'

Detective Shapiro turned out to be a soft-spoken, scholarly-looking man with a receding hairline and keen hazel eyes. He was quick to explain that the investigation was just beginning. Vivian Powers's parents had been contacted, and in view of the circumstances had given permission for entry to her home. The fact that the front door was open, the lamp and table overturned, and her car still in the driveway had left them gravely worried that she had been the victim of foul play.

'You were here yesterday, Miss DeCarlo?' Shapiro confirmed.

'Yes.'

'I realize that with the dismantling of the house and the mover's boxes, it's hard to be sure. But do you see anything different about the premises than when you were here yesterday?'

We were in the living room. I looked around, remembering that it had been the same jumble of packed boxes and bare tables that I was looking at now. But then I realized there *was* something different. There was a box on the coffee table that had not been there yesterday.

I pointed to it. 'That box,' I said. 'She either may have been packing it or going through it after I left, but it wasn't here before.'

Detective Shapiro walked over to it and pulled out the file that was on top. 'She worked for Gen-stone, didn't she?' he asked.

I found myself giving him only the information I was absolutely sure of and saying nothing of my suspicions. I could imagine the look on the detective's face if I told him, 'Vivian Powers may have staged this disappearance because she's meeting Nicholas Spencer, whose plane crashed and is presumed dead.' Or would it make more sense to him if I said, 'I am beginning to wonder if Nicholas Spencer was in fact the victim of foul play, that a doctor in Caspien was the victim of a hit-and-run driver because of laboratory records he was holding, and that Vivian Powers disappeared because she was able to identify the man who collected those records.'

Instead, I limited myself to saying that I had interviewed Vivian Powers because I was cowriting a cover story on her boss, Nicholas Spencer.

'She called you after you left, Miss DeCarlo?'

I guessed that Detective Shapiro was aware he was not getting the full story.

'Yes. I had discussed with Vivian the fact that some records of lab experiments belonging to Nicholas Spencer were missing. As far as she knew, the man who picked them up, saying he had been sent by Spencer, was not authorized to do so. From the brief message she left on my machine, I got the impression she might be able to identify that person.'

The detective was still holding the Gen-stone file folder, but it was empty. 'Is it possible she made that connection when she was going through this file?'

'I don't know, but I certainly think it's possible.'

'Now the file is empty, and she's missing. What does that say to you, Miss DeCarlo?'

'I think there is the possibility that she may have been the victim of foul play.'

He gave me a sharp look. 'On the drive from the city, did you happen to have your car radio on, Miss DeCarlo?'

'No, I did not,' I said. I didn't tell Detective Shapiro that when I'm working on an investigative story such as this, I treasure quiet time in the car to think and to weigh the possible alternative scenarios with which I've been presented.

'Then you didn't hear the report of a rumor that Nick Spencer has been spotted in Zurich, observed there by a man who had seen him a number of times at stockholders' meetings?'

It took me a long minute to digest that question. 'Are you saying that you think the man who claims to have seen him is credible?'

'No, only that it's a new angle in the case. Naturally, they'll check out the story thoroughly.'

'If that story checks out, I wouldn't worry too much about Vivian Powers,' I said. 'If it is true, my guess is that she's on her way to meet him right now, if she isn't there already.'

'They were involved?' Shapiro asked quickly.

'Nicholas Spencer's housekeeping couple believed they were, which could mean that the so-called missing records are nothing but part of an elaborate cover-up.

'Didn't I hear that the front door was open?' I asked Shapiro.

He nodded. 'Which is why leaving that door open may have been an effort to draw notice to her absence,' he said. 'I'll be honest, Miss DeCarlo. There's something phony about this setup, and I think you've told me what it is. I bet that right now she's winging her way to Spencer, wherever he is.'

# Chapter 26

**M**illy greeted me like an old friend when I arrived at the diner, just in time for a late lunch. 'I've been telling everyone about how you're writing a story on Nick Spencer,' she said, beaming. 'How about today's news, that he's living it up in Switzerland? Two days ago those kids fished out the shirt he was supposed to be wearing, and everybody thought that meant he was dead. Tomorrow it'll be something else. I always said that anybody smart enough to steal that kind of money would figure out how to live long enough to spend it.'

'You may have a point, Milly,' I said. 'How's the chicken salad today?'

'Awesome.'

Now there's a recommendation, I thought, as I ordered the salad and coffee. Because it was the tail end of lunch time, the diner was busy. I heard the name Nicholas Spencer mentioned several times from different tables, but couldn't hear what was being said about him.

When Milly came back with the salad, I asked her what she had heard about Dr. Broderick's condition.

'He's doing a *little* better,' she said, dragging out the word so it sounded like 'l-e-e-e-tle.' 'I mean, he's still really critical, but I heard that he tried to talk to his wife. Isn't that good?'

'Yes, it is good. I'm very glad.' As I ate the salad, which indeed was awesomely filled with celery but somewhat short on chicken, my mind was leaping ahead. If Dr. Broderick recovered, would he be able to identify the person who had run him down, or would he have no memory at all of the accident?

By the time I'd had a second cup of coffee, the diner was rapidly emptying. I waited until I saw that Milly was finished clearing the other tables, then beckoned her over. I had brought along the photo taken the night Nick Spencer was honored, and I showed it to her.

'Milly, do you know these people?'

She adjusted her glasses and studied the group assembled on the dais. 'Sure.' She began to point. 'That's Delia Gordon and her husband, Ralph. She's nice; he's kind of a stiff. That's Jackie Schlosser. She's real nice. That's Reverend Howell, the Presbyterian minister. And there's the crook, of course. Hope they get him. That's the chairman of the board of the hospital. He has egg on his face since he persuaded the board to invest so much in Gen-stone. From what I hear, he'll be out of a job by the next board election, if not sooner. A lot of people think he should resign. I bet he does if they prove Nick Spencer is alive. On the other hand, if they arrest him, then maybe they can find out where he hid the money. That's Dora Whitman and her husband, Nils. Both their families go way back in this town. Real money. I mean live-in help and everything. Everybody likes the fact that the family never shook the dust of Caspien off their feet, but I hear they have a fabulous summer home in Martha's Vineyard, too. Oh, and at the end on the right is Kay Fess. She's head of the volunteers at the hospital.'

I made notes, trying to keep up with Milly's rapid-fire commentary. When she was finished, I said, 'Milly, I want to talk to some of those people, but Reverend Howell is the only one I've been able to reach so far. The others either have unlisted phone numbers or haven't returned my call. Any suggestions on how I can get to them?'

'Don't let on I told you, but Kay Fess is probably at the reception desk in the hospital right now. Even if she didn't call you back, she's easy to get to know.'

'Milly, you're a doll,' I said. I finished my coffee, paid the check, left a generous tip, and after consulting my map, drove the four blocks to the hospital.

I guess I expected to find a local community hospital, but Caspien Hospital was an obviously growing institution, with several smaller buildings adjacent to the main structure and a new area cordoned off and marked with a sign that read SITE OF FUTURE PEDIATRIC CENTER.

This, I was sure, was the planned construction now on hold thanks to the hospital's investment in Gen-stone.

I parked and went into the lobby. There were two women at the reception desk, but I was able to tell which was Kay Fess immediately. Deeply suntanned although it was only April, with short graying hair, dark brown eyes, granny glasses, an exqui-sitely shaped nose, and narrow lips, she had a very 'in charge' air about her. I seriously doubted that anyone slipped through without a visitor's pass on *her* watch. She was the one nearest to the roped-off entrance to the elevators, which suggested that she was the head honcho.

There were four or five people waiting for passes when I entered the lobby. I waited as she and her associate took care of them, and then I went up to speak to her. 'Miss Fess?' I said.

She was immediately on guard, as though suspecting I was going to ask to bring ten kids in to visit a patient.

'Miss Fess, I'm Carley DeCarlo with the *Wall Street Weekly*. I'd very much like to talk to you about the award dinner for Nicholas Spencer several months back. I understand that you were on the dais sitting quite close to him.'

'You phoned me the other day.'

'Yes, I did.'

The other woman at the reception desk was looking at us with curiosity, but then had to turn her attention to some newcomers.

'Miss DeCarlo, since I did not return your call, doesn't it suggest to you that I had no intention of talking to you?' Her tone was pleasant but firm.

'Miss Fess, I understand that you give a great deal of your time to the hospital. I'm also aware that the hospital has had to put construction of the pediatric center on hold because of the investment in Gen-stone. The reason I want to talk to you is that I believe the true story of Nicholas Spencer's disappearance has not come out, and if it does, then that money may be traceable.'

I saw the hesitation and doubt in her expression. 'Nicholas Spencer has been seen in Switzerland,' she said. 'I wonder if he's buying a chalet with money that would have saved the lives of children for generations to come.'

'What appeared to be definitive proof of his death was making headlines only two days ago,' I reminded her. 'Now this. The truth is, we still don't know the full story. Please, couldn't we talk for just a few minutes.'

Mid-afternoon was clearly not heavy-traffic visiting time at the hospital. Miss Fess turned to her coworker. 'Margie, I'll be right back.'

We sat in a corner of the lobby. She was clearly of a 'get-to-the-point' mind-set and was intent on keeping our discussion brief. I was not going to mention my suspicion that what had happened to Dr. Broderick might not have been an accident. What I *did* tell her was that I suspected Nicholas Spencer heard something at the award dinner that sent him rushing the next morning to collect his father's old research records from Dr. Broderick. Then I decided to go one step further: 'Miss Fess, Spencer was visibly upset to find out that someone else had already collected those records, saying that he was getting them for him. I think that if I can find out who gave him disturbing information at the dinner, as well as whom he visited after he left Dr. Broderick's office the next day, we might have some idea as to what *really* happened to him and to the missing money. Did you speak with Spencer at any length?'

She looked reflective. I had the feeling that Kay Fess was one of those people who missed nothing. 'The people on the dais gathered half an hour early in a private reception room for some picture taking; cocktails were served. Nicholas Spencer was the center of attention, of course,' she said.

'How would you judge his demeanor at the beginning of the evening? Did he seem relaxed?'

'He was cordial, pleasant – all the usual things you expect an honoree to be. He had presented his personal check for one hundred thousand dollars, earmarked for the building fund, to the chairman but did not want it announced at the dinner. He did say that when the vaccine was approved, he would be able to make a donation ten times larger.'

Her mouth tightened. 'He was quite a convincing con man.'

'But as far as you noticed, he didn't speak to anyone in particular at that time?'

'No, but I can tell you that just before dessert was served, he was chatting with Dora Whitman for at least ten minutes and seemed quite intent on what she was saying.'

'Have you any idea what they were talking about?'

'I was sitting to the right of Reverend Howell, and he had gotten up to greet some friends. Dora was on Reverend Howell's left, so I could hear her quite clearly. She was quoting someone who had praised Dr. Spencer, Nicholas's father. She told Nicholas that this woman claimed Dr. Spencer had cured her baby of a birth defect that otherwise would have destroyed her life.'

Immediately I knew that that was the connection I'd been trying to find. I also realized that I hadn't been able to contact the Whitmans because they had an unlisted number. 'Miss Fess, if you have Mrs. Whitman's phone number, would you please call her and ask if I might talk to her as soon as possible, even immediately if she's available.'

I watched the expression of doubt come into her eyes even as she began to shake her head. I didn't give her a chance to turn me down. 'Miss Fess, I'm a reporter. I'll find out where Mrs. Whitman lives, and one way or another, I'll get to speak to her. But the sooner I learn what she told Nicholas Spencer that night, the better chance there is that we'll know what really caused him to disappear and where the missing money is.'

She looked at me, and I could tell that I hadn't swayed her, that, if anything, I'd gotten her back up by reminding her that I was a reporter. I still didn't want to talk about Dr. Broderick as a possible victim, but I did play one more card: 'Miss Fess, I met with Vivian Powers, Nicholas Spencer's personal assistant, yesterday. She told me that something happened at the award dinner that upset or excited him terribly. Sometime late yesterday, hours after we spoke, that young woman disappeared, and I suspect she may have met with foul play. Clearly there is something going on; someone out there is desperate to keep information about these missing records from getting to the authorities. Now, will you please help me get in touch with Dora Whitman.'

She stood up. 'Please wait here while I call Dora,' she said. She went to the desk, and I watched her pick up the phone and tap in the number. Obviously she didn't have to look it up. She began to speak, and I held my breath as I watched her jot something down on a piece of note paper. There were more people coming into the lobby and making their way toward the reception desk. She beckoned to me, and I hurried over.

'Mrs. Whitman is home, but she's leaving for the City in an hour. I told her that you would come directly over, and she's waiting for you now. I've written down her address and phone number and directions to her house.'

I started to thank Miss Fess, but she was looking past me. 'Good afternoon, Mrs. Broderick,' she said solicitously. 'How is the doctor today? Still showing improvement, I hope?'

# Chapter 27

Now that Annie was dead, nobody ever came to see him. So on Tuesday morning when the doorbell rang, Ned decided to ignore it. He knew it had to be Mrs. Morgan. What did she want? he wondered. She had no right to bother him.

The doorbell rang again, then once more, only this time whoever was there kept jabbing it. He heard heavy steps coming down the stairs. That meant it wasn't Mrs. Morgan ringing the bell. Then he heard her voice and a man's voice. Now he'd have to go and see who was there; otherwise she might use her key to come in.

He remembered to put his right hand in his pocket. Even with the ointments he'd bought at the drugstore, his hand wasn't any better. He opened the door just enough to see who had been ringing his bell.

Two men were outside. They were holding up IDs for him to see. They were detectives. I have nothing to worry about, Ned told himself. Peg's husband had probably reported that she was missing, or maybe they'd found her body already. Doc Brown had probably told the police that he was one of the last people in the store last night. According to their IDs, the tall guy was Detective Pierce; the one who was black was Detective Carson.

Carson asked if they could talk to him for a few minutes. Ned knew he couldn't refuse – it would look funny. He could see that they were both looking at his right hand because it was in his pocket. He'd have to take it out. They might think he had a gun in it or something. The gauze he'd wrapped around the hand would keep them from seeing how bad the burn was. He pulled it out of his pocket slowly, trying not to show how much it hurt when it brushed against the lining. 'Sure, I'll talk to you,' he mumbled.

Detective Pierce thanked Mrs. Morgan for coming downstairs. Ned could see that she was dying to find out what was going on, and before he closed the door, he could see her trying to get a look into the apartment. He knew what she was thinking – that the place was a mess. She knew that Annie was always after him to pick up the papers and bring dishes into the kitchen and put them in the dishwasher and throw his dirty clothes in the hamper. Annie liked everything neat and clean. Now that she was gone, he didn't bother to tidy up anymore. He didn't eat much, either, but when he did, he just dumped the dishes in the sink and ran water over them if he needed a plate or cup.

He could tell that the detectives were taking in the room, noticing his pillow and blanket on the couch, the piles of newspapers on the floor, the box of cereal and the cereal bowl on the table next to the gauze and ointments and adhesive tape. The clothes he'd been wearing lately were heaped on a chair.

'Mind if we sit down?' Pierce asked.

'Sure.' Ned shoved the blanket aside and sat on the couch.

There was a chair on either side of the television set. They each picked up one and brought them nearer to the couch. Seated, they were too close to him for comfort. They were trying to make him feel trapped. Be careful what you say, he warned himself.

'Mr. Cooper, you were in Brown's drugstore last night just before it closed, weren't you?' Carson asked.

Ned could tell Carson was the boss. They were both looking at his hand. Talk about it, he told himself. Make them feel sorry for you. 'Yeah, I was there. My wife died last month. I never did any cooking. I burned my hand on the stove a couple of weeks ago, and it's still pretty sore. I went to Brown's last night to get some stuff to put on it.'

They'd expect him to ask why they were here, asking him questions. He looked at Carson. 'What's going on?'

'Did you know Mrs. Rice, the cashier at Brown's?'

'Peg? Sure. She's been at Brown's for twenty years. She's a nice lady. Very helpful.' They were being cagey. They weren't telling him anything about Peg. Did they think she was just missing, or had they found her body?

'According to Mr. Brown, you were the next-to-last person Mrs. Rice waited on last night. Is that right?'

'I guess so. I remember there was somebody behind me when I checked out. I don't know if anyone else came in after I left. I got in my car and came home.'

'Did you notice anyone hanging around outside when you left the drugstore?'

'No. As I said, I just got in my car and drove home.'

'Do you know who was behind you on the line in the drugstore?'

'No. I didn't pay attention to him. But Peg knew him. She called him . . . let me think. She called him "Garret." '

Ned saw the detectives look at each other. That's what they had come to find out. Brown hadn't known who the last customer had been. For now, they were going to concentrate on finding that guy.

They got up to go. 'We won't keep you any longer, Mr. Cooper,' Carson said. 'You've been very helpful.'

'That hand looks swollen,' Pierce said. 'I hope a doctor has seen it.'

'Yeah. Yeah. It's getting a lot better.'

They were looking at him funny. He knew it. But it was only after he had double-locked the door behind them that Ned realized they hadn't told him what had happened to Peg. They'd be sure to have noticed he let them go without finding out.

They were bound to be on their way back to Brown's to ask him about Garret. Ned waited ten minutes, then phoned the drugstore. Brown answered. 'Doc, this is Ned Cooper. I'm worried about Peg. There were two detectives here asking questions about her, but they never did tell me what was wrong. Did anything happen to her?'

'Wait a minute, Ned.'

He could tell Brown was covering the phone with his hand and talking to somebody. Then Detective Carson got on.

'Mr. Cooper, I'm sorry to tell you that Mrs. Rice has been the victim of a homicide.'

Ned was sure Carson's voice seemed friendlier now. He was right: They had noticed that he hadn't asked what happened to Peg. He told Carson how sorry he was and asked him to please tell Doc Brown how sorry he was, and

Carson said that if anything occurred to him, even if it didn't seem important, to call them.

'I'll do that,' Ned assured the detective. When he hung up, he walked over to the window. They'd be back; he was sure of it. But for now he was okay. The one thing he had to do was hide the rifle. It wasn't safe to leave it in the car or even behind all the junk in the garage. Where could he hide it? He needed a place where no one would look for it.

He looked down at the scrubby little patch of grass outside the house. It was muddy and messy and reminded him of Annie's grave. She was buried in his mother's plot, in the old cemetery in town. Hardly anyone used that cemetery anymore. It wasn't kept up, and all the graves looked neglected. When he had stopped there last week, Annie's grave was still so new that the ground hadn't settled. It was soft and muddy and looked as if she'd been thrown under a pile of dirt.

A pile of dirt . . . It was like an answer being given to him. He'd wrap the rifle and the bullets in plastic and an old blanket and bury them in Annie's grave until it was time to use them again. Then when it was all finished, he'd go back and lie down on the grave and be finished with it himself. 'Annie,' he called, the way he used to call to her when she was in the kitchen, 'Annie, I'll be with you soon, I promise.'

# Chapter 28

Ken and Don had both left the office by the time I was on my way back from Caspien, so I went straight home. I left messages for both of them, however, and they called me in the evening. We agreed to meet extra early in the morning, at eight o'clock, and talk with clear heads.

I worked on my column and was reminded again of the daily struggles 99 percent of the world has in trying to balance their expenses against their income. I went through the new batch of e-mail, hoping to hear something else from the guy who wrote about seeing someone leave Lynn's Bedford mansion before the fire, but there was nothing from him. Or from *her*, I added mentally.

I finished up the column and at twenty of eleven washed my face, put on my nightshirt and robe, called out for a small pizza, and poured myself a glass of wine. The timing could not have been better. The restaurant is only around the corner, on Third Avenue, and the pizza arrived just as the eleven o'clock news came on.

The lead story was about Nick Spencer. The press had connected the report of his possibly being seen in Switzerland with the disappearance of Vivian Powers. Their pictures were shown side by side, and the news angle was 'bizarre new twist to Spencer case.' The gist of the story was that Briarcliff Manor police doubted that Vivian Powers had been abducted.

I decided it was too late to call Lynn but reasoned that, if anything, this story strengthened her contention that she had no part in her husband's plans. But if somebody *did* leave the mansion only a few minutes before the fire, that opened up the distinct possibility that she had an agenda of her own, I decided.

I went to bed with conflicting emotions, and it took me a long time to fall asleep. If Vivian Powers was planning to join Nick Spencer only hours after I saw her, I can only say that she was one hell of an actress. I was glad I hadn't erased her phone message. I intended to keep it, and I intended to go back to Gen-stone and talk to some of the women who answered the mail.

The next morning at eight, Don and I were in Ken's office, clutching mugs brimming with fresh coffee. They looked at me expectantly.

'Chronological?' I suggested.

Ken nodded.

I told them about Vivian Powers's home, how the open door and overturned lamp and table had a phony, set-up look. Then added, 'But having said that, she sure sounded convincing when she phoned me to say she thought she knew who took Dr. Spencer's records from Dr. Broderick.'

I looked at them. 'And now I think I know why they

were taken and what they may have contained,' I said. 'It all came together yesterday.' I laid the picture of the dais at the award dinner on the desk and pointed to Dora Whitman. 'I visited her yesterday, and she told me that she had spoken to Nick Spencer at the dinner. She told him that she and her husband were on a cruise to South America early last November. They became friendly with a couple from Ohio who told them their niece lived in Caspien for a short time some thirteen years ago. She had a baby at Caspien Hospital, and it was diagnosed as having multiple sclerosis. She brought it to Dr. Spencer for the usual shots, and the day before the family moved back to Ohio, Dr. Spencer came to the house and gave the baby a shot of penicillin because it had a high fever.'

I took a sip of the coffee. The ramifications of what I had learned still stunned me. 'According to their story, a few weeks later Dr. Spencer called the mother in Ohio. He was in a terrible state. He said he realized that he'd given the baby an untested vaccine he'd been working on years earlier and that he bore full responsibility for any problems that might have developed.'

'He gave the baby an untested vaccine . . . an old vaccine he'd been working on? It's a wonder he didn't kill it,' Ken snapped.

'Wait until you hear the rest of it. The mother told him that the baby hadn't had any reaction to the shot. And what's unusual in this day and age was that she didn't go rushing to a lawyer with Dr. Spencer's admission. On the other hand, the baby showed no sign of developing a problem. A few months later her new pediatrician in Ohio said the baby had obviously been misdiagnosed, because it was developing normally and there was no sign of the disease. The girl is now thirteen years old and last fall was in a car accident. The MRI diagnostician remarked that if she didn't know it was impossible, she would have said that the result showed the faintest traces of sclerosis in a few cells, a very unusual indication. The mother decided to send to Caspien for the original X rays. They showed extensive sclerosis in both the brain and spinal cord.'

'The X rays were probably mixed up,' Ken said. 'That happens too often in hospitals.'

'I know, and no one in Ohio will believe that the X rays weren't mixed up, except the mother. She tried to write Dr. Spencer to let him know about it, but he had died years earlier, and the letter was returned.

'Dora Whitman told those people that Nicholas Spencer was Dr. Spencer's son and she was sure he'd like to hear from their niece. Mrs. Whitman suggested that their niece write to him at Gen-stone. Apparently she did write but never heard from him.'

'That's the story Mrs. Whitman told Spencer at the award dinner?' Don asked.

'Yes.'

'And the next day he rushed back to Caspien to get his father's early records but found that they were missing,' Ken said, jiggling his glasses. I wondered how often he had to replace the screw that held the frame together.

'Dora Whitman promised to give Spencer the address and phone number of the people who had told her about their niece. Of course she didn't have it at the dinner. He went to see her after he'd visited Dr. Broderick and learned that the records were gone. She said he was visibly upset. He phoned the Ohio couple from Whitman's home, got their niece's phone number, and spoke to her. Her name is Caroline Summers.

'Dora Whitman heard him ask Summers if she had a fax machine available. Apparently she did because he said he was going to go to Caspien Hospital to see if they had retained a set of her daughter's X rays, and if they had, he wanted to have her fax permission for him to pick them up.'

'So that's where he went after he saw Broderick?'

'Yes. I went back to Caspien Hospital after I left Mrs. Whitman. The clerk remembered that Nick Spencer had come in but couldn't help him. They had sent the only set of X rays to Caroline Summers.'

'Then the sequence of events seems to indicate that the Summers woman wrote that letter to Spencer sometime in November, after which someone rushed to collect his father's early records,' Don said.

I could see that he was drawing triangles and wondered what a psychologist would make of that kind of doodling. I knew what I made of it: A third person in the Gen-stone office had taken that letter seriously and had either taken action on it or passed it along to someone else.

'There's more. Nick Spencer flew to Ohio, met Caroline Summers and her daughter, examined her and took the X rays that had been taken at Caspien Hospital, and went with her to the hospital in Ohio, where the diagnostician claimed he could see traces of sclerosis cells. The MRI report was gone. Someone using Caroline Summers's name had picked it up the week after Thanksgiving. Nick asked Mrs. Summers not to talk about any of these revelations to anyone and said that he would get back in touch with her. Of course, he never did.'

'He has a mole somewhere in his company, and a little over a month later his plane crashes.' Ken put his glasses back on, a sign that we were going to wrap up soon. 'Now he's spotted in Switzerland, and his lady friend is missing.'

'No matter how you slice it, millions of dollars are also missing,' Don said.

'Carley, you say you spoke to Dr. Broderick's wife. Did you get any information from her?' Ken asked

'I spoke to her for only a moment. She knew I'd been to his office last week, and I guess he gave her a favorable impression of me. I said there were a few facts I'd like to check with her for the story, and she agreed to talk to me once her husband was out of danger. By then I can only hope that he'll be able to give some impression of what happened to him.'

'Broderick's accident, a plane crash, stolen records, stolen MRI report, a torched mansion, a missing secretary, a failed cancer vaccine, and a vaccine that may have cured multiple sclerosis thirteen years ago,' Don said as he got up. 'To think this started out as a con-man-on-the-run story.'

'I can tell you this right now,' Ken said, 'no shot of an old vaccine ever cured multiple sclerosis.'

My phone rang, and I ran to answer it. It was Lynn. In view of the reports that Nick had been seen in Switzerland, coupled with the shocking news that he was involved with his secretary, she wanted my help in preparing a statement for the media. Both Charles Wallingford and Adrian Garner were urging her to make one. 'Carley, even if the report about Nick doesn't turn out to be true, the fact that he was romantically linked with his assistant will effectively separate me from his activities in people's minds. They'll see me as an innocent wife. That's what we both want, isn't it?'

'We want the truth, Lynn,' I said, but I reluctantly agreed to meet her later for lunch at The Four Seasons.

# Chapter 29

The Four Seasons was, as always, serenely busy at one o'clock, the favored arrival time for at least half the lunch people. I recognized familiar faces, the kind who show up in the 'Style' section of the *Times* as well as in the political and business pages.

Julian and Alex, the co-owners, were both at the desk. I asked for Mrs. Spencer's table, and Alex said, 'Oh, the reservation is under the name of Mr. Garner. The others are all here. They're seated in the Pool Room.'

So this isn't to be a stepsisters-huddling-to-salvage-a-reputation session, I thought as I followed the escort down the marble corridor to the dining room. I wondered why Lynn hadn't told me that Wallingford and Garner were going to be at the luncheon. Maybe she thought that I would have backed out. Wrong, Lynn, I thought. I can't *wait* to get a real look at them, especially at Wallingford. But I needed to resist my reporter's instincts. I intended to be all ears and have very little to say.

We reached the Pool Room, so-called because it has a

large square pool in the center that is beautifully surrounded with trees that symbolize the season. This being spring, long, slender apple trees, with branches heavily laden with blossoms, were in evidence. It's a lighthearted, pretty room, and I'll bet as many high-powered deals are agreed on there with a shake of the hand as ever take place in boardrooms.

The escort left me with the captain, and I followed him across the room to the table. Even from a distance I could see that Lynn looked beautiful. She was wearing a black suit with white linen collar and cuffs. I couldn't see her feet, but the bandages were gone from her hands. On Sunday she had not been wearing jewelry, but today a wide gold wedding band was on the third finger of her left hand. As people were on their way to their own tables, they were stopping to greet her.

Was she acting, or was I so clinically disposed to dislike her that I found myself scornful of the brave smile and the girlish shake of the head when a man whom I recognized as being the CEO of a brokerage firm reached for her hand? 'It still hurts,' she explained to him as the captain pulled out the chair for me. I was glad that her head was turned away from me. It spared me the necessity of going through the motions of air-kissing her.

Adrian Garner and Charles Wallingford made the usual gesture of pushing back their chairs and attempting to stand as I arrived at the table. I made the usual protest, and we settled in our seats at the same time.

I must say both men were impressive. Wallingford was a genuinely handsome man, with the kind of refined features that happen when generations of bluebloods continue to mate. Aquiline nose, ice blue eyes, dark brown hair that was graying at the temples, a disciplined body and fine hands – he was the essence of the patrician. His dark gray suit with almost indiscernible narrow stripes looked like an Armani to me. The soft-red-and-gray-figured tie on a crisp white shirt completed the picture. I noticed several women looking at him appreciatively as they passed the table.

Adrian Garner might have been roughly the same age as Wallingford, but the resemblance stopped there. He was shorter by a couple of inches, and, as I had noticed on Sunday, neither his body nor his face displayed any of the refinement so apparent in Wallingford. His complexion was ruddy, as though he spent a lot of time outdoors. Today he wore glasses over his deep-set brown eyes, and his gaze was penetrating. I felt when he looked at me that he was able to read my mind. There was an air of power around the man that transcended his rather generic tan sports jacket and brown slacks, which looked as though he might have ordered them from a catalog.

He and Wallingford greeted me. They were drinking champagne, and at a nod from me, the waiter filled the glass at my place. Then I saw Garner shoot an irritated look at Lynn who was still talking with the brokerage guy. She must have sensed it because she wrapped up the conversation, turned to us, and acted thrilled to see me.

'Carley, it was so good of you to come on such short notice. You can imagine the roller coaster I'm on.'

'Yes, I can.'

'Isn't it a blessing that Adrian warned me about the statement I made on Sunday when we thought a piece of Nick's shirt had been found? And now, after hearing that

Nick may have been seen in Switzerland and that his assistant is missing, I just don't know what to think.'

'But that's not what you're going to say,' Wallingford said, his tone firm. He looked at me. 'All of this is confidential,' he began. 'We've been doing some investigating at the office. It was very clear to a number of the employees that Nicholas Spencer and Vivian Powers were emotionally involved. The feeling is that Vivian remained on the job these past weeks because she wanted to learn the progress of the investigation into the crash. The U.S. attorney's people are checking, of course, but we've hired our own fact-finding agency as well. Obviously it would have been a great comfort to Spencer if the consensus held that he is dead. But once he was seen in Europe, the game was over. He is now established as a fugitive, and it must be assumed that the Powers woman is one as well. There was no need for her to wait any longer once it was known that he survived the crash, and, of course, if she had lingered, the authorities would have questioned her.'

'The one good thing that woman has done for me is that people are no longer treating me as a pariah,' Lynn said. 'At least now they believe that I was as taken in by Nick as all the rest of them. When I think – '

'Ms. DeCarlo, when do you expect your story to be published?' Adrian Garner asked.

I wondered if I was the only one at the table irritated at the high-handed way he interrupted Lynn. I was sure Garner made a habit of doing that.

I deliberately gave him an 'if this, if that' answer, hoping to irritate him in turn. 'Mr. Garner, we sometimes deal with two opposing elements. One is the news aspect of a cover story, and of course Nicholas Spencer is big news. The other aspect is telling the story honestly and not having it become just a collection of the latest rumors. Do we have the full story of Nick Spencer yet? I don't think so. In fact, every day I become convinced that we haven't even scratched the surface of the story, so I can't answer your question.'

I could tell that I had managed to anger him, which pleased me no end. Adrian Nagel Garner may be a hugely successful business tycoon, but in my book that does not give him license to be rude.

I could see that we were drawing our battle lines. 'Miss DeCarlo – ' he began.

I interrupted him. 'My friends call me Carley.' He's not the only one who can interrupt people when they're talking, I thought.

'Carley, the four people at this table, as well as the investors and employees of Gen-stone, are all victims of Nicholas Spencer. Lynn tells me you invested twenty-five thousand dollars in the company yourself.'

'Yes, I did.' I thought of everything that I had heard about Garner's state-of-the-art mansion and decided to see if I could make him squirm. 'It was the money I was saving for a down-payment on a co-op apartment, Mr. Garner. I had dreamed about it for years: a building with an elevator that worked, a bathroom where the nozzle on the shower worked, maybe even an older building with a fireplace. I've always been big on fireplaces.'

I knew that Garner was a totally self-made man, but he wouldn't take my bait and say something like 'I know what it is to want a shower that works.' He ignored my humble dreams of a better place to live. 'Everyone who invested in Gen-stone has a personal history, a personal plan that has been shattered,' he said smoothly. 'My company went out on a limb by announcing plans to buy the distribution rights to the Gen-stone vaccine. We were not hurt financially because our commitment was contingent on FDA approval after the vaccine was tested. Nevertheless, my company has been seriously injured in the reservoir of good will that is an essential element in the future of any organization. People bought Gen-stone stock in part because of Garner Pharmaceutical's rock-solid reputation. Guilt by association is a very real psychological factor in the business community, Carley.'

He had almost called me Ms. DeCarlo but hesitated and said 'Carley' instead. I don't think I've ever heard a more contemptuous spitting out of my name, and I realized suddenly that Adrian Garner, for all his power and might, was afraid of me.

No, I thought, that's too strong. He *respects* the fact that I can help people understand that not only Lynn but also the Garner Pharmaceutical Company was a victim of Spencer's colossal scam, the cancer vaccine.

The three of them were looking at me, waiting for my response. I decided it was my turn to get a little information from them. I looked at Wallingford. 'Do you personally know the stockholder who claims he saw Nick Spencer in Switzerland?'

Garner raised his hand before Wallingford could answer. 'Perhaps we should order now.'

I realized the captain was standing to the side at our table. We accepted menus and made our selections. I absolutely love the crab cakes at The Four Seasons, and no matter how hard I look at the menu or listen to the specials, that dish and a green salad are almost inevitably my choice.

Not many people order steak tartare in this day and age. Raw beef combined with raw eggs is not considered the best way to live to a ripe old age. It interested me, therefore, that steak tartare was Adrian Garner's choice.

'The necessaries,' as Casey puts it, out of the way, I repeated my question to Wallingford: 'Do you know the stockholder who claims he saw Nick Spencer in Switzerland?'

He shrugged. '*Know* him? I've always been interested in the semantics of saying you *know* somebody. To me "know" means you really know about him, not just that you see him regularly at large gatherings such as stockholders' meetings or charity cocktail parties. The stockholder's name is Barry West. He's in mid-management in a department store and apparently has handled his own investments fairly well. He came to our meetings four or five times in the last eight years and always made it a point to talk to both Nick and me. Two years ago when Garner Pharmaceutical agreed to joint distribution of the vaccine after it was approved, Adrian put Lowell Drexel on our board to represent him. Barry West immediately attempted to ingratiate himself with Lowell.'

Wallingford shot a glance at Adrian Garner. 'I heard him ask Lowell if you were in need of a good, solid, management type, Adrian.'

'If Lowell was smart, he said no,' Garner snapped.

Adrian Garner certainly didn't believe in taking his gracious pill in the morning, but to a certain extent I realized that I was overcoming my irritation at his abrupt manner. In the media business you hear so much bifurcation that someone who says things straight can be a refreshing change.

'Be that as it may,' Wallingford said, 'I do think that

Barry West had the opportunity to see Nick often enough and up close enough that whoever he saw either *was* Nick or else looked a great deal like him.'

It had been my first impression at Lynn's apartment on Sunday that these men cordially disliked each other. War, however, makes strange bedfellows, and so does a failed company, I thought. But it was also clear to me that I was not here solely to help Lynn explain to the world that she was a helpless victim of her husband's infidelity and larceny. It was important to all of them to get some sense of the way the cover story in *Wall Street Weekly* would turn out.

'Mr. Wallingford,' I said.

He raised his hand. I knew he was going to ask me to call him by his given name. He did. I did.

'Charles, as you well know, I'm only writing the human interest element of the Gen-stone failure and Nick Spencer's disappearance. I believe you've been speaking extensively with my colleague Don Carter?'

'Yes. In cooperation with our auditors, we have given full access to our books to outside investigators.'

'He stole all that money, yet he wouldn't even go with me to look at a house in Darien that was a great bargain,' Lynn said. 'I wanted so much to make our marriage work, and he couldn't understand that I hated living in another woman's house.'

In fairness I had to agree that she had a point. I wouldn't want to live in another woman's house if I married. Then for the quickest of moments I realized that if Casey and I ended up together, we wouldn't have that problem.

'Your associate Dr. Page has been given free access to our laboratory and to the results of our experiments,' Wallingford continued. 'Unfortunately for us, there were some promising results early on. This is not uncommon in the search for a drug or vaccine to prevent or slow down the growth of cancer cells. Too often, hopes have been dashed and companies gone under because the early research simply did not prove out. That's what happened at Gen-stone. Why would he steal so much money? We'll never know why he started to steal it. When he knew the vaccine didn't work and the stock would start to tumble, there was no way he could cover his theft, and that was probably when he decided to disappear.'

Journalists are taught in Journalism 101 to ask five basic questions: Who? What? Why? Where? When?

I chose the middle one. 'Why?' I asked. 'Why would he do that?'

'Initially perhaps to buy more time to try and prove the vaccine would work,' Wallingford said. 'Then, when he knew it could not work and that he'd been falsifying data, I think he decided he had only one choice: to steal enough money to live on for the rest of his life and then to run away. Federal prison is not the country club that the media depict it to be.'

It crossed my mind to wonder if anyone had ever seriously thought of federal prison as a country club. What Wallingford and Garner were saying was that in essence I had proven myself to be true blue by standing by Lynn. Now we could agree on the best way to summarize her innocence, and then I could help rebuild their credibility through the manner in which I submitted my part of the research for the cover story.

It was time to once again say what I thought I'd been saying right along: 'I have to repeat something that I hope you realize,' I told them.

Our salads were being served, and I waited to finish my statement. The waiter offered ground pepper. Only Adrian Garner and I accepted. Once the waiter was gone, I told them that I would write the story as I saw it, but in the interest of writing it well and of getting everything right, I would need to schedule in-depth interviews with both Charles Wallingford and Mr. Garner, who I suddenly realized had not encouraged me to call him Adrian.

They both agreed. Reluctantly? Probably, but that was too hard to call.

Then with business somewhat out of the way, Lynn held her hands out to me, reaching across the table. I was forced to meet the gesture by touching the tips of my fingers to hers.

'Carley, you've been so good to me,' she said with a deep sigh. 'I'm so glad you agree that while I might have burned hands, they're also clean hands.'

The famous words of Pontius Pilate raced through my mind: 'I wash my hands of the blood of this innocent man.'

But Nick Spencer, I thought, no matter how pure his motives may have been originally, was certainly guilty of theft and deception, wasn't he?

Clearly that's what the bulk of evidence indicated.

Or did it?

# Chapter 30

Before leaving the restaurant, we agreed on times for my interviews with Wallingford and Garner. I pushed my advantage and suggested I meet them at their homes. Wallingford, who lives in Rye, one of the toniest suburbs in Westchester County, readily said that I could call on him on either Saturday or Sunday afternoon at three o'clock.

'Saturday would be better for me,' I responded, thinking of Casey and the cocktail party I was attending with him on Sunday. Then, crossing my fingers, I slipped him a curve. 'I do want to go to your headquarters and speak to some of your employees, just to get them to express their feelings about the loss of their 401k's and the bankruptcy and how all that is going to affect their lives.'

I saw him trying to think quickly of a polite way to refuse me, so I added, 'I took names of stockholders at the meeting last week, and I'll be talking to them as well.' Of course, what I really wanted to talk to the employees about was whether it was common knowledge that Nick

Spencer and Vivian Powers were emotionally involved.

Wallingford clearly didn't like the request at all, but yielded because he was trying to get good press out of me. 'I don't suppose that would be a problem,' he said after a moment, his tone icy.

'Tomorrow afternoon, about three o'clock, then,' I said quickly. 'I promise I won't be long. I just want to get an overall reaction to put in the story.'

Unlike Wallingford, Garner flatly refused to be interviewed in his home. 'A man's home is his castle, Carley,' he said. 'I never conduct business there.'

I would love to have reminded him that even Buckingham Palace was open to tourists, but I held my tongue. By the time we'd finished espresso, I was more than ready to put on my traveling shoes. A journalist is not supposed to let emotion get in the way of a story, but as I sat there, I could feel my anger rising. It seemed to me that Lynn was downright cheerful at the thought that her husband had been involved in a serious romance before he disappeared. It made her look better, even sympathetic, and that was all that mattered to her.

Wallingford and Garner were also on that same page. Show the world that we are victims – that was the thrust of everything they told me. Of the four of us, I thought, I'm the only one who seems remotely interested in the possibility that if Nicholas Spencer could be tracked down, there might be a way to recoup at least *some* of that money. That would be great news for the stockholders. Maybe I'd get back part of my $25,000. Or perhaps Wallingford and Garner were assuming that even if Nick could be found and extradited, he'd probably have buried the money so deep that it would never be found.

After denying me a home visit, Garner did agree that I could call on him in his office in the Chrysler Building. He said he could give me a quick interview at 9:30 on Friday morning.

Realizing how very few journalists got this far with Adrian Garner – he was famous for not giving interviews – I thanked him with reasonable warmth.

Just before we left, Lynn said, 'Carley, I've been starting to sort through Nick's personal things. I came across the plaque they gave him in February in his hometown. He'd shoved it in a drawer. You went up to Caspien to get background material on him, didn't you?'

'Yes, I did.' I wasn't about to admit that I'd been up there less than twenty-four hours ago.

'How do people there feel about him now?'

'The way people feel about him everywhere. He was so persuasive that the Caspien Hospital board put a lot of money in Gen-stone after he was honored. As a result of their losses, they've had to cancel plans for the children's wing addition.'

Wallingford shook his head. Garner looked grim, but I could also see that he was growing impatient. The luncheon was over. He was ready to go.

Lynn offered no response to the fact that the hospital had lost money intended to benefit sick children, and instead asked, 'I mean, what did they say about Nick *before* the scandal broke?'

'There were glowing eulogies in the town newspaper after the plane crash,' I said. 'Apparently Nick was an excellent student, a nice kid, and excelled in sports. There was a great picture of him when he was about sixteen, holding a trophy. He was a champion swimmer.'

'Which may have been the reason he was able to stage the crash, then swim to shore,' Wallingford suggested.

Maybe, I thought. But if he was smart enough to pull that off, it sounds pretty strange to me that he wasn't smart enough not to be spotted in Switzerland.

I went back to the office and checked my messages. A couple of them were pretty disconcerting. The first e-mail I read was 'When my wife wrote to you last year, you never bothered to answer her question, and now she's dead. You're not that smart. Have you figured out who was in Lynn Spencer's house before it was torched?'

Who was this guy? I wondered. Obviously, unless the whole thing was a crank message, he was in pretty bad shape mentally. From the address I could tell that he was the same guy who'd sent me a weird message a couple of days earlier. I had kept that e-mail, but now I wished I'd kept the other one that had seemed weird, the one that said, 'Prepare yourself for Judgment Day.' I'd deleted it because at the time I thought it was from a religious nut. Now I wondered if the same guy had sent all three.

Had someone been in that house with Lynn? I knew from the Gomez couple that it was entirely possible she had late visitors. I wondered if I should show this e-mail to her and say, 'Isn't this ridiculous?' It would be interesting to get her reaction.

The other communication that rattled me was a message on my answering machine from a supervisor in the X-ray office at Caspien Hospital. She said she felt it was important that I clear up something for her.

I returned the call right away.

'Miss DeCarlo, you were here yesterday speaking to my assistant?' she said.

'Yes, I was.'

'I understand that you asked for a copy of the Summers baby X rays, saying that Mrs. Summers was willing to fax you permission to take them.'

'That's right.'

'I gather my assistant told you we did not retain copies. But as I explained to Mrs. Summers's husband when he picked them up on November 28 last year, he was taking our final set, and if he wished, we would make duplicates for him. He said that wouldn't be necessary.'

'I see.' I had to fish for words. I knew Caroline Summers's husband had not picked up those X rays any more than he had picked up the MRI results in Ohio. Whoever had read and taken seriously the letter Caroline Summers wrote to Nicholas Spencer had certainly covered all the bases. Using Nick Spencer's name, he had stolen Dr. Spencer's early records from Dr. Broderick, then he'd stolen the X rays from Caspien Hospital which showed that the baby had multiple sclerosis, and finally he'd stolen the MRI results from the hospital in Ohio. He'd gone to a lot of trouble, and there had to be a good reason.

Don was alone in his office. I went in. 'Got a minute?'

'Sure.'

I told him about The Four Seasons lunch.

'Good going,' he said. 'Garner's a hard guy to pin down.'

Then I told him about the X rays that someone purporting to be Caroline Summers's husband had taken from Caspien Hospital.

'They sure covered all their bases, whoever they are,' Carter said slowly, 'which certainly proves that Gen-stone has – or had – a serious mole in the office. Did you talk about any of this at lunch?'

I looked at him.

'Sorry,' he said. 'Of course you didn't.'

I showed him the e-mail. 'I can't decide whether or not this guy is a crank,' I said.

'I don't know, either,' Don Carter told me, 'but I think you should notify the authorities. The cops would love to track this guy down, because he may very well be an important witness to that fire. We got a tip that the cops in Bedford stopped a kid for driving while under the influence of drugs. His family has a high-powered lawyer who wants to make a deal. Their bargaining chip would be the kid's testimony against Marty Bikorsky. The kid says he was coming home from a different party a week ago, around three o'clock Tuesday morning, and passed the Spencer house. He swears he saw Bikorsky driving his van slowly in front of the house.'

'How would he know it was Marty Bikorsky's van, for heaven's sake?' I protested.

'Because the kid had a fender bender in Mount Kisco and ended up at the service station where Marty works. He saw Marty's car and got a kick out of the license plate. Talked to him about it. It's M.O.B. Bikorsky's full name is Martin Otis Bikorsky.'

'Why didn't he come forward before now?'

'Bikorsky had already been arrested. The kid had sneaked out to the party and is in enough trouble with his parents. He claims that if the wrong guy were arrested, he would have come forward then.'

'Isn't *he* the little model citizen?' I said, but actually I was dismayed at what Don had told me. I remembered asking Marty if he'd been sitting in the car when he went outside to smoke. I caught his wife giving him a warning glance. Was that what that was about? I wondered now as I had then. Had he driven around rather than sit in the car with the engine running? The houses in his neighborhood were very close to each other. An engine running in the middle of the night might have been noticed by a neighbor who had a window open. How natural it would have been if, angry, upset, and having had a couple of beers, Bikorsky had driven past the pristine and beautiful Bedford mansion and thought of losing his own home. And then he might have done something about it.

The e-mails I was getting seemed to verify this version of events, something I found very troubling.

I could see that Don was observing me. 'Are you thinking that my judgment of people isn't panning out?' I asked him.

'No, I was thinking that I'm sorry it isn't panning out for this guy. From what you tell me, Marty Bikorsky has an awful lot on his plate. If he did go nuts and torch that house, he'll do a long stretch, I can guarantee you that. There are too many high rollers in Bedford to let anyone burn down one of their houses and get off lightly. Trust me, if he can cop a plea, he'll be a lot better off in the long run.'

'I hope he doesn't,' I said. 'I'm convinced he's not guilty.'

I went out to my desk. A copy of the *Post* was still there; I turned to page three, which contained the story about Spencer being seen in Switzerland and about the disappearance of Vivian Powers. Earlier I'd read only the first couple of paragraphs. The rest was mostly a rehash of the Gen-stone story, but I did find the information I was hoping might be there – the name of Vivian Powers's family in Boston.

Allan Desmond, her father, had issued a statement: 'I absolutely do not believe that my daughter has joined Nicholas Spencer in Europe. In these past weeks she has spoken frequently on the phone to her mother, her sisters, and me. She was deeply grieved by his death and is planning to move back to Boston. If he is alive, she did not know it. I *do* know that she would not willingly have put her family through this anguish. Whatever has happened to her occurred without her cooperation or consent.'

I believed that, too. Vivian Powers *was* grieving for Nicholas Spencer. It takes a special kind of cruelty to deliberately disappear and leave your family to agonize every moment of every day, wondering what happened to you.

I sat at my desk and looked at the notes I had made about my visit to Vivian's home. One thing jumped out at me. She said that the letter from the mother of the child who had been cured of multiple sclerosis had been answered with a form letter. I remembered that Caroline Summers had told me she never received an answer. So someone in the typist pool had not only passed the letter along to a third party but also had destroyed any record that it ever existed.

I did decide I had an obligation to call the Bedford police and tell them about the e-mails. The detective I reached was cordial, but he didn't sound particularly impressed. He asked me to fax him a copy of both. 'We'll pass the information along to the arson unit in the D.A.'s office,' he said. 'And we'll run our own trace on whoever sent them, but I get the feeling it's a crank letter, Miss DeCarlo. We're absolutely sure we have the right man.'

There was no use telling him that I was still absolutely sure he was wrong. My next call was to Marty Bikorsky. Once again I got the answering machine. 'Marty, I know how bad it looks for you, but I'm still in your corner. I'd really like a chance to sit down with you again.'

I started to leave my cellphone number just in case Marty had mislaid it, but he picked up the receiver before I was finished. He agreed to see me when I left work. I was just walking out when I thought of something and turned on the computer again. I knew I'd read an article in *House Beautiful* in which Lynn was photographed at the house in Bedford. If I remembered correctly, the piece contained a number of exterior shots. What I was particularly interested in was a description of the grounds. I found the article, downloaded it, and congratulated myself that my memory had been accurate. Then I took off.

This time I got stuck in the five o'clock traffic to Westchester and didn't get to Bikorsky's house until twenty of seven. If he and Rhoda had looked stricken when I saw them on Saturday, they looked positively ill today. We sat in the living room. I could hear the sound of the television coming from the little den off the kitchen and assumed Maggie was in there.

I got right to the point. 'Marty, I had the feeling there was something wrong about your either sitting in a cold car or letting an engine run that night, and I don't believe that's what happened. You went for a drive, didn't you?'

It wasn't hard to see that Rhoda had strenuously objected to Marty's telling me to come there at all. Her face flushed, her voice low, she said, 'Carley, you seem like a nice person, but you're a journalist and you want a story. That kid was wrong. He didn't see Marty. Our lawyer will make holes in his story. The kid is trying to get out of trouble himself by taking advantage of the accusation against Marty. He'll say anything to make a deal. I received some calls from people who don't even *know* us who say that kid is always lying. Marty never left our driveway that night.'

I looked at Marty. 'I want to show you these e-mails,' I said. I watched as he read them and then handed them to Rhoda.

'Who is this guy?' he asked me.

'I don't know, but right now the police are putting a trace on these messages. They'll find him. He sounds like a wacko to me, but he may have been hanging around somewhere on the grounds. He may even be the one who set the fire. The point is that if you stick to the story that you didn't drive past the Spencer house ten minutes before it was torched, and you're lying, there may be a few more witnesses who will come forward. Then you really *are* finished.'

Rhoda had begun to cry. He patted her knee and for a few moments said nothing. Finally he shrugged his shoulders. 'I was there,' he said, his voice heavy, 'just the way you figured it, Carley. I had had a couple of beers after work, as I told you, and I had a headache and was driving around. I was still mad, I'll admit that – mad clear through. It wasn't even just the house. It's the fact that the cancer vaccine was no good. You don't know how hard I've prayed that it would be available in time to help our Maggie.'

Rhoda buried her face in her hands. Marty put his arm around her.

'Did you stop at the house at all?' I asked him.

'I stopped only long enough to open the window of the van and spit at the house and all that it stood for. Then I came home.'

I believed him. I would have taken an oath that he was telling the truth. I leaned forward. 'Marty, you were there within a few minutes of the fire starting. Did you see anyone leave the house or perhaps another car driving by? If that kid is telling the truth, and he did see you, did you see him as well?'

'A car came from the other direction and passed me. That may have been the kid. About half a mile away another car heading in the direction of the house went by.'

'Did you notice anything about it?'

He shook his head. 'Not really. I may have thought from the shape of the headlights that it was pretty old, but I couldn't swear on that.'

'Did you see anyone in the driveway coming down from the house?'

'No, but if that guy who sent this message was there, he could be right. I remember there *was* a car parked inside the gate.'

'You saw a car there!'

'Just a glimpse of one.' He shrugged. 'I noticed it when I stopped and rolled my window down, but I was there only a few seconds.'

'Marty, what did that car look like?'

'It was a dark sedan, that's as much as I could tell. It was parked off the driveway, behind the pillar, on the left side of the gate.'

I pulled the article I'd downloaded from the Internet out of my shoulder bag and found a picture of the estate taken from the road. 'Show me.'

He leaned forward and studied the photograph. 'See, this is where the car was parked,' he said, pointing to a spot just beyond the gate.

The caption under the picture stated, 'A charming cobblestone walkway leads to a pond.'

'The car must have been on the cobblestones. The pillar just about hides it from the street,' Marty said.

'If whoever sent the e-mail did see a man in the driveway, that may have been his car,' I told them.

'Why wouldn't he have driven up to the house?' Rhoda asked. 'Why park there and walk up the driveway?'

'Because whoever was there didn't want the car to be seen,' I said. 'Marty, I know you have to talk to your lawyer about this, but I've read the accounts of the fire pretty darn carefully. No one mentioned anything about a car parked at the gate, so whoever was there was gone before the fire engines came.'

'Maybe he was the one who set the fire,' Rhoda said with something like hope creeping into her voice. 'What was he doing there if he was hiding the car?'

'There are plenty of unanswered questions,' I said as I stood up. 'The cops can trace the e-mails. That may prove to be a break for you, Marty. They promised to let me know who it is. I'll get back to you as soon as I can.'

As he got to his feet, Marty asked the question that was also on my mind. 'Did Mrs. Spencer say she had company that night?'

'No, she did not.' Then out of loyalty I added, 'You've seen the size of the place. Somebody could have been on those grounds without her ever knowing it.'

'Not with a car, unless he knew how to punch in the combination for the gate or someone in the house released it for him. That's how those things work. Have the cops checked out people who worked up there, or are they just concentrating on me?'

'I can't answer that. But I can tell you that I'm going to find out. Let's start with the e-mail and see where it takes us.'

The antagonism Rhoda had shown toward me when I got to the house had vanished. She said, 'Carley, do you really think there's a chance that they will find the guy who did set the fire?'

'Yes, I do.'

'Maybe miracles still happen?'

She was talking about more than the fire. 'I believe in them, Rhoda,' I said firmly, and I meant it.

But as I drove home, I was certain that the one miracle she wanted most of all was going to be denied her. I knew I couldn't help her there, but I would do everything I could to help Marty prove his innocence. It would be terrible enough for her to endure the death of her child, but it would be made that much worse if she couldn't have her husband at her side.

I should know, I thought.

# Chapter 31

'Sufficient unto the day is the evil thereof.' That was the way I felt when I got home from being with Marty and Rhoda Bikorsky. It was nearly nine o'clock. I was tired and hungry. I didn't want to cook. I didn't want pizza. I didn't want Chinese food. I looked in my refrigerator and was positively disconsolate. What greeted me was a pathetic jumble of cheese drying at the edges, a couple of eggs, a soft tomato, some brown lettuce, and a quarter loaf of French bread I'd forgotten about.

Julia Child could turn this into a gourmet delight, I reminded myself. Let's see what I can do.

Keeping that charmingly eccentric chef in mind, I set to work and didn't do a bad job of it at all. First I poured a glass of chardonnay. Then I stripped the brown leaves off the lettuce, tossed some garlic, oil, and vinegar together, and made a salad. I sliced the French bread thin, shook Parmesan cheese over it, and stuck it under the broiler. The good part of the cheese and the tomato contributed to an omelet that tasted great.

Not everyone can make an omelet, I thought, congratulating myself.

I ate from a tray while sitting in the club chair that had been in our living room when I was growing up. I had my feet on a hassock; it was comforting to be home and unwind. I opened a magazine I'd been wanting to read, but I found I couldn't concentrate on it because the events of the day kept churning through my mind.

Vivian Powers. I could see her standing at the door of her home as I drove off. I can understand why Manuel Gomez commented that he was happy Nick had known her. Somehow I could not imagine those two people, both of whom had lost loved ones to cancer, living it up in Europe on money that should have been used for cancer research.

Vivian's father had sworn his daughter would not leave her family in anguish, wondering what had happened to her. Nick Spencer's son was clinging to the hope that his father was alive. Would Nick really allow a child who'd lost his mother to live hoping from day to day that he'd hear from his father?

The earliest local TV news came on at ten o'clock, and I tuned in, anxious to see if there were any updates about Spencer or Powers. I was in luck. Barry West, the stockholder who claimed he had seen Nick, was going to be interviewed. I couldn't wait. After the usual barrage of commercials, he was the lead story.

West certainly did not look the part of Sherlock Holmes. He was a medium-sized, pudgy guy, with apple dumpling cheeks and a receding hairline. For the interview, he was seated in the outdoor cafe where he said he had spotted Nicholas Spencer.

The Fox News correspondent in Zurich got right to the point. 'Mr. West, this is where you were seated when you believe you saw Nicholas Spencer?'

'I don't *believe* I saw him. I *saw* him,' West said emphatically.

I don't know why I expected him to have a voice that was either nasal or whiney. I was wrong – his voice was forceful, but modulated.

'My wife and I had to decide whether to cancel this vacation,' he went on. 'It's our twenty-fifth wedding anniversary, and we planned it for a long time, but then we lost a lot of money in Gen-stone. Anyhow, we got here last Friday, and on Tuesday afternoon we were sitting here talking about how glad we were that we hadn't stayed home when I happened to look over there.'

He pointed to a table on the outside rim of the ones connected with the cafe. 'He was right there. I couldn't believe it. I've been at enough Gen-stone stockholder meetings to know Spencer. He'd changed his hair – it used to be dark blond and it's black now – but it wouldn't be any different if he had a ski hat on. I know his face.'

'You tried to speak to him, didn't you, Mr. West?'

'Speak to him, I shouted to him, "Hey, Spencer, I want to talk to you." '

'Then what happened?'

'I'll tell you exactly what happened. He jumped up, threw some money on the table, and ran. That's what happened.'

The newscaster pointed to the table where Spencer allegedly had been sitting. 'We'll leave it to you viewers. As we record this, the weather conditions and time are the same as they were on Tuesday evening when Barry West believes he saw Nicholas Spencer at that table. We have one of our staff, who is approximately Mr. Spencer's height and build, at that table now. How clearly can you see him?'

From that distance the staff member they had picked indeed could have been Nicholas Spencer. Even his features were the same type. But I didn't see how anyone looking at him from that distance and angle could make a positive identification.

The camera went back to Barry West. 'I saw Nicholas Spencer,' he said positively. 'My wife and I put one hundred and fifty thousand dollars into his company. I demand that our government send people to track this guy down and make him tell where he put all that money. I worked hard for it, and I want it back.'

The Fox correspondent continued, 'According to the information we have, several different investigative bodies are following this lead, as well as looking into the disappearance of Vivian Powers, the woman who is reputed to be Nicholas Spencer's lover.'

The telephone rang, and I snapped off the television. Even if the phone hadn't rung, I was about to do that anyhow. I'd had more than enough of hearing people put their improbable spin on events.

I know my greeting sounded quick and impatient: 'Hello.'

'Hey, did somebody walk on your grave today? You sound feisty.'

It was Casey.

I laughed. 'I'm a bit weary,' I said. 'Maybe a bit sad, too.'

'Tell me about it, Carley.'

'Doctor, you sound as though you're asking, "Where does it hurt?" '

'Maybe I am.'

I gave him a thumbnail sketch of the day and ended with 'The bottom line is that I think Marty Bikorsky is being railroaded, and I think something very bad happened to Vivian Powers. The guy who said he saw Nick Spencer in Zurich may be right, but it's a long shot, a *very* long shot.'

'The cops can absolutely trace the e-mails you received?'

'Unless the guy is one of those whiz-kid cyber geniuses, they can, or so they say.'

'Then unless he's a crank, as you say yourself, you may have a breakthrough that will help Bikorsky. On another matter, we may not be going up to Greenwich on Sunday, so what else would you like to do? If the weather is good, a suggestion would be to take a drive and get a shore dinner somewhere.'

'Did your friends call off their party? I thought it was an anniversary or a birthday?'

I could hear the hesitation in Casey's voice. 'No, but when I called Vince to tell him that you'd be able to come with me, I bragged about your new job and the fact that you're writing a cover story on Nicholas Spencer.'

'And . . .'

'And I could tell something was wrong. He said that he was thinking of you as the financial advice columnist when he and I talked earlier about you coming. The problem is that Nick Spencer's first wife's parents, Reid and Susan Barlowe, are his neighbors, and they are coming to the party. Vince says that they're on a roller coaster as it is with all that's going on about Spencer.'

'They have Nick's son, don't they?'

'Yes. In fact, Jack Spencer is best friends with Vince's son.'

'Look, Casey,' I said, 'I'm not going to stand in the way of you being at that dinner. I'll bow out.'

'Not an option,' he said flatly.

'We can go out Saturday or Monday or whenever. But having said that, I would absolutely give my eye teeth to talk to Nick's former in-laws. They refuse to talk to the media, and I don't think they're doing their grandson a favor. On my word of honor, I won't mention Nick Spencer if I'm at that party or ask them one single question, either leading or oblique, but maybe if they get some sense of me, they might give me a call later on.'

Casey didn't answer, and I heard my voice rise when I said, 'Damn it, Casey, the Barlowes can't put their heads in the sand. Something big is going on, and they should be aware of it. I'd put my own life on the line that that jerk Barry West, who says he saw Spencer in Zurich, only saw someone who happened to look a little like him!

'Casey, Vivian Powers, Nick's assistant, is missing. I told you about Dr. Broderick. He's still on the critical list. Nick's house in Bedford was burned down. Nick saw his former in-laws all the time. He entrusted his son to them. Isn't it possible he told them something that might shed some light on all this?'

'What you say makes a lot of sense, Carley,' Casey said quietly. 'I'll talk to Vince. I gather from what he said that the Barlowes are pretty much at the end of their rope with all the conflicting reports about Nick Spencer. His son, Jack, is going to be in deep trouble if something isn't resolved. Maybe Vince can persuade them to talk to you.'

'I'll keep my fingers crossed.'

'Okay. But one way or the other, we're on for Sunday.'

'Terrific, Doctor.'

'One more thing, Carley.'

'Uh-huh.'

'Call me when you find out who sent those e-mails. I think you're right – I'll bet all of them came from the same source, and I don't like the one that talks about judgment day. That guy sounds wacky, and maybe he's getting fixated on you, which worries me. Just be careful.'

Casey sounded so serious that I wanted to cheer him up. 'Judge not lest ye be judged,' I suggested.

'A word to the wise is sufficient,' he countered. 'Good night, Carley.'

# Chapter 32

Now that his rifle was safe in Annie's grave, Ned felt secure. He knew the cops would be back, and he wasn't even surprised when they rang his doorbell again. This time he opened up right away. He knew he looked better than he had on Tuesday. After he had buried the rifle Tuesday afternoon, his clothes and hands were muddy, but he didn't care. When he got home, he opened the new bottle of scotch, settled into his chair, and drank until he fell asleep. All he could think of when he buried the rifle was that if he kept digging, he could get to Annie's coffin and pry it open and touch her.

He had to force himself to smooth down the dirt and leave her grave alone; he just missed her too much.

The next day he woke up at about five o'clock in the morning, and even though the window was streaked and dirty, he could see the sun as it came up. The room got so bright that he noticed his hands and saw how dirty they were. His clothes were caked with dried mud, too.

If the cops had walked in on him then, they'd have said,

'You been digging somewhere, Ned?' Maybe they'd have thought to check Annie's grave and find his rifle.

That was why he'd gotten in the shower yesterday and stood under it for a long time, scrubbing himself with the long-handled brush that Annie had bought for him. Then he even washed his hair, shaved, and cut his fingernails. Annie was always telling him that it was important to look clean and respectable.

'Ned, who's going to hire you if you don't shave or change your clothes or brush your hair so that it doesn't look wild,' she had cautioned. 'Ned, sometimes you look so terrible that people don't want to be near you.'

On Monday, when he'd driven over to the library in Hastings to send the first two e-mails to Carley DeCarlo, he noticed that the librarian looked at him strangely, as if he didn't belong there.

Then Wednesday, yesterday, he'd gone to Croton to send the new e-mails, and he'd worn clean clothes. Nobody paid any attention to him at all.

And so, even though he'd slept in his clothes last night, he knew that he looked better today than he had on Tuesday.

When they came, it was the same two cops, Pierce and Carson. Right away he could see that they noticed he looked better. Then he saw them look at the chair where all his dirty clothes had been lying. After they'd left on Tuesday, he'd thrown them all in the washing machine. He had known the cops would be back and didn't want them to see the clothes all caked with mud.

Ned followed Carson's eyes and saw that he was looking at the muddy boots by his chair. Damn! He had missed putting them away.

'Ned, can we talk to you for a couple of minutes?' Carson asked.

Ned knew he was trying to sound like an old friend who just happened to drop in. He wasn't fooled, though. He knew how cops worked. The time he'd been arrested about five years ago because he got into a fight with that jerk in the bar, the landscaper who worked for the Spencers in Bedford and who said he'd never hire him again, the cops had acted nicey-nicey at first. But then they'd said the fight was his fault.

'Sure, come in,' he told them. They pulled out the same chairs they had in the previous visit. The pillow and blanket were where he had left them on the couch the other day. He'd been sleeping in the chair the past two nights.

'Ned,' Detective Carson said, 'you were right about the fellow who was behind you in Brown's drugstore the other night. His name is Garret.'

So what? Ned wanted to say. Instead he just listened.

'Garret says he thought he saw you parked outside the drugstore when he left. Is he right?'

Should I admit that I saw him? You had to have seen him, Ned told himself. Peg was trying to make her bus. She'd finished with him fast. 'Sure, I was still there,' he said. 'That guy was about a minute behind me coming out of the store. I got in my car, turned the key, changed the radio station to get the ten o'clock news, and then took off.'

'Where did Garret go, Ned?'

'I don't know. Why should I care where he went anyhow? I pulled out of the lot, made a U-turn, and came home. Maybe you want to arrest me because I made a U-turn, huh?'

'When the traffic is light, I've been known to do one myself,' Carson said.

Now we get the buddy-buddy act, Ned thought. They're trying to trap me. He looked at Carson and said nothing.

'Ned, do you have any guns?'

'No.'

'Have you ever fired a gun?'

Be careful, Ned warned himself. 'As a kid, a BB gun.' He bet they already knew that.

'Have you ever been arrested, Ned?'

Admit it, he told himself. 'Once. It was all a misunderstanding.'

'And did you spend time in jail?'

He'd been in the county jail until Annie scraped together the bail. That was where he'd learned how to send e-mails that couldn't be traced. The guy in the next cell said that all you had to do was go to a library, use one of their computers, go on the Internet, and punch in 'Hotmail.' 'It's a free service, Ned,' the guy had explained. 'You can put in a fake name, and they don't know the difference. If anybody gets sore, they can trace that it came from that library, but they can't trace it to you.'

'I was only in overnight,' he said sullenly.

'Ned, I see your boots over there are pretty muddy. Did you happen to be in the county park the other night, after going to the drugstore?'

'I told you, I came straight home.' The county park was where he had dumped Peg.

Carson was studying the boots again.

I didn't get out of the car at the park, Ned told himself. I told Peg to get out and walk home, and then when she started to run, I shot her. They don't have any reason to talk about my boots. I didn't leave footprints in the park.

'Ned, would you mind if we took a look at your van?' Pierce, the tall detective, asked.

They had nothing on him. 'Yeah, I mind,' Ned snapped. 'I mind a lot. I go to the drugstore and buy something. Something happens to a very nice lady who had the hard luck to miss her bus, and you try to tell me I did something to her. Get out of here.'

He saw the way their eyes went dead. He had said too much. How did he know she had missed the bus? That's what they were thinking.

He took a chance. Had he heard it or had he dreamt it? 'They said on the radio that she missed her bus. That's right, isn't it? Someone saw her running for it. And, yes, I do mind you looking at my van, and I mind you coming here and asking me all these questions. Get out of here. You hear me? Get out of here and stay out of here!'

He hadn't meant to shake his fist at them, but that's what he did. The bandage on his hand shook loose, and they could see the blistering and the swelling.

'What was the name of the doctor who treated your hand, Ned?' Carson asked quietly.

# Chapter 33

A good night's sleep means that all parts of my brain come awake at the same time. It doesn't happen all that often, but I was blessed enough that when I woke up on May 1, I felt bright and alert, which as the day evolved turned out to be a lucky thing.

I showered, then dressed in a lightweight gray pin-striped suit that I bought at the end of last season and had been dying to wear. I opened the window to get some fresh air, and also to find out the temperature outside. It was a perfect spring day, warm with a little breeze. I could see flowers pushing through the soil in the pots on my neighbor's windowsill, and above there were blue skies with puffs of fluffy clouds drifting by.

Every May 1 when I was growing up, we had a ceremony at Our Lady of Mount Carmel Church in Ridgewood in which we crowned the Blessed Mother. The words of the hymn we used to sing then drifted through my head as I applied a touch of eye shadow and lip blush.

*O Mary, we crown thee with blossoms today,*
*Queen of the angels, Queen of the May . . .*

I knew why that tune was coming back to me now. When I was ten, I was chosen to crown the statue of the Blessed Mother with a wreath of flowers. Each year the honor alternated between a ten-year-old boy and a ten-year-old girl.

Patrick would have been ten next week.

It's funny how, even long after you've accepted the grief of losing someone you love and truly have gotten on with your life, every once in a while something comes up that plays 'gotcha,' and for a moment or two the scar tissue separates and the wound is raw again.

Enough, I told myself, firmly closing my mind to that kind of thinking.

I walked to work and got to my desk at twenty of nine, filled a cup with coffee, and went into Ken's office where Don Carter was already seated. I wasn't there long enough to have my first sip of coffee before things started to heat up.

Detective Clifford of the Bedford Police called, and what he had to say was a real shocker. Ken, Don, and I listened on the speaker phone as Clifford informed us that they had traced the e-mails, including the one I hadn't kept but had told them about – the one telling me to prepare myself for judgment day.

All three had been sent from Westchester County. The first two had come from a library in Hastings, the other from a library in Croton. The sender had used 'Hotmail,' a free Internet service, but had entered what they believe must have been false information on his ID.

'What does that mean?' Ken asked.

'The sender gave his name as Nicholas Spencer and used the address of the Spencer home in Bedford that burned down last week.'

Nicholas Spencer! We all gasped and looked at each other. Could it be possible?

'Wait a minute,' Ken said. 'They have tons of recent pictures of Nicholas Spencer in the newspaper files. Did you show some of them to the librarians?'

'Yes, we did. Neither one of them recognized Spencer as someone who used one of their computers.'

'Even on Hotmail you have to give a password,' Don said. 'What kind of password did this guy use?'

'He used a woman's name. Annie.'

I ran out to get the original e-mails from my desk and read the last one:

When my wife wrote to you last year, you never bothered to answer her question and now she's dead.
You're not that smart. Have you figured out who was
. in Lynn Spencer's house before it was torched?

'I'll bet anything that guy's wife's name was Annie,' I said.

'There's just one more thing that we think may be interesting,' Detective Clifford said. 'The librarian from Hastings distinctly remembers that a disheveled guy who used the computer had a serious burn on his right hand. She can't be sure he sent these e-mails, but she couldn't help noticing him.'

Before he hung up, Clifford assured us that he was widening the net and alerting libraries in other Westchester towns to be on the lookout for a guy using the computer who was in his fifties, around six feet tall, may be disheveled and has a burn on his right hand.

He had a burn on his hand! I was sure that the man who had been sending me e-mails in which he claimed to have seen someone run down the driveway of the Spencer home was the one with the burn on his right hand. It was an exciting piece of news.

Marty and Rhoda Bikorsky deserved a nugget of hope. I phoned them. God, if we could only realize what's really important in our lives, I thought as I heard their stunned reaction to the fact that the sender of the e-mails was possibly using Nick Spencer's name and had a burned hand. 'They'll get him, won't they, Carley?' Marty asked.

'He may just turn out to be a lunatic,' I cautioned, 'but, yes, I'm sure they'll get him. They're sure he lives around there somewhere.'

'We've had another piece of good news,' Marty said, 'and this has really knocked our socks off. The growth of Maggie's tumor slowed up last month. It's still there, and it's still going to take her, but if it doesn't accelerate again, we'll have one more Christmas with her almost for sure. Rhoda's already starting to plan the gifts.'

'I'm so glad.' I swallowed over the lump in my throat. 'I'll stay in touch.'

I wanted to sit for a few minutes and savor the joy I'd heard in Marty Bikorsky's voice, but instead it was necessary to make a call that I knew would quickly dissipate it. Vivian Powers's father, Allan Desmond, was listed in the Cambridge, Massachusetts, directory. I called him.

Like Marty Bikorsky, the Desmonds let the answering

machine filter their messages. Like Marty, they picked up before I could disconnect. I began by saying, 'Mr. Desmond, I'm Carley DeCarlo from *Wall Street Weekly*. I interviewed Vivian the afternoon of the day she disappeared. I'd very much like to meet you, or at least *talk* to you. If you're willing – '

I heard the receiver being picked up. 'This is Vivian's sister Jane,' a strained but well-bred voice said. 'I know my father would like very much to talk with you. He's staying at the Hilton Hotel in White Plains. You can reach him there now. I just spoke with him.'

'Will he take my call?'

'Give me your number. I'll have him call you.'

Less than three minutes later my phone rang. It was Allan Desmond. If ever a man sounded weary, it was he. 'Miss DeCarlo, I have agreed to hold a press conference in just moments. Could we possibly speak a little later?'

I did a quick calculation. It was nine-thirty. I had some calls to make, and I was due at the Gen-stone office in Pleasantville to talk with the employees there at three-thirty. 'If I drove up, would you be able to have a cup of coffee around eleven?' I asked.

'Yes, I would.'

We agreed that I'd call him from the lobby of the Hilton. Once again I paused to calculate time. I was sure I wouldn't be with Allan Desmond for more than forty minutes to an hour. If I left him by twelve, I could be in Caspien by one o'clock. I felt in my bones that it was time for me to try to persuade Dr. Broderick's wife to talk to me.

I punched in the number of Dr. Broderick's office, figuring that the worst that could happen would be that she'd turn me down.

The receptionist, Mrs. Ward, remembered me and was quite cordial. 'I'm so happy to say that the doctor is improving a little each day,' she said. 'He's always kept in shape and is basically a strong man, and that's helping him now. I know Mrs. Broderick feels he's going to make it.'

'I'm so glad. Do you know if she's at home?'

'No. She's at the hospital, but I do know that she's planning to be here for the afternoon. She's always worked in the office, and now that the doctor's doing better, she's coming in for a few hours each day.'

'Mrs. Ward, I'm going to be in Caspien, and it's very important that I speak to Mrs. Broderick. It's about the doctor's accident. I'd rather not say more than that right now, but I'm planning to stop at your office around two o'clock, and if she can give me fifteen minutes, I think it would be worth her while. I gave her my cell phone number when I spoke to her the other day, but let me give it to you again. Also, I'd appreciate it if you would call me if Mrs. Broderick absolutely refuses to see me.'

I had one more call to make, and that one was to Manuel and Rosa Gomez. I reached them at their daughter's house in Queens. 'We have read about the disappearance of Miss Powers,' Manuel said. 'We are so troubled that something has happened to her.'

'Then you don't believe that she is joining Mr. Spencer in Switzerland?'

'No, I do not, Miss DeCarlo. Of course, who am I to say?'

'Manuel, you know that cobblestone walkway that leads to the pond, just behind the left pillar at the gate?'

'Of course.'

'Is that a spot where anyone was likely to park a car?'

'Mr. Spencer parked his car there regularly.'

'Mr. Spencer!'

'Especially during the summer. Sometimes when Mrs. Spencer had friends at the pool, and he was coming from New York on his way to Connecticut to see Jack, he'd park there where his car wouldn't be noticed. Then he'd slip upstairs to change.'

'Without telling Mrs. Spencer?'

'She might have been aware of his plans, but he said that if he got talking to people, it was hard to get away.'

'What kind of car did Mr. Spencer drive?'

'A black BMW sedan.'

'Did any other people who were friends of the Spencers park on those cobblestones, Manuel?'

There was a pause, and then he said quietly, 'Not during the day, Miss DeCarlo.'

# Chapter 34

Allan Desmond looked as if he hadn't slept in three days, and I'm sure he hadn't. In his late sixties, his pallor was as gray as his steel gray hair. He was a naturally thin man, and that morning he looked pinched and exhausted. Still, he was trimly dressed in a suit and tie, and I had the feeling he was one of those men who probably never was without a tie except on the golf course.

The coffee shop wasn't crowded, and we chose a table in the corner where no one could possibly overhear our conversation. We ordered coffee. I was sure he hadn't eaten a thing all morning and took a chance, saying, 'I'd like a Danish, but only if you'll have one, too.'

'You're very subtle, Miss DeCarlo, but you're right – I haven't eaten anything. A Danish it is.'

'Cheese for me,' I told the waitress.

He nodded to her affirmatively.

Then he looked at me. 'You saw Vivian on Monday afternoon?'

'Yes, I did. I had phoned to try to get her to agree to see me, but she refused. I think she was convinced that I was out to do a hatchet job on Nicholas Spencer, and she wouldn't have any part of it.'

'Why wouldn't she have wanted to take the opportunity to defend him?'

'Because, unfortunately, it doesn't always work out like that. It's sad to say, but there is a segment of the media who, by eliminating part of an interview, can turn a positive endorsement into a scathing putdown. I think Vivian was heartsick about the terrible press Nick Spencer was getting and didn't want in any way to give the appearance of contributing to it.'

Vivian's father nodded. 'She was always fiercely loyal.' Then his face twisted in pain. 'Do you hear what I'm saying, Carley? I'm talking about Vivian as though she's not alive. That absolutely terrifies me.'

I wish I could have been a convincing liar and said something comforting, but I simply could not. 'Mr. Desmond,' I said, 'I read the statement you gave to the media about having been on the phone with Vivian frequently in the three weeks since Nicholas Spencer's plane crashed. Did you know that she and Nicholas Spencer were romantically involved?'

He took a sip of coffee before answering. I didn't have the feeling that he was trying to figure out a way to sidestep the question; I think he was trying to look back and sort out an honest response. 'My wife says I never answer a question directly,' he said, 'and perhaps I don't.' A brief smile flickered across his lips and disappeared as quickly as it had come. 'So let me give you some background. Vivian is the youngest of our four daughters.

She met Joel in college, and they were married nine years ago, when she was twenty-two. Unfortunately, as you must know, Joel died of cancer a little over two years ago. At that time we tried to persuade her to return to Boston, but she took the job with Nicholas Spencer. She was very excited about being part of a company that was going to bring out a cancer vaccine.'

Nick Spencer had been married to Lynn a little over two years before Vivian went to work for him, I thought. I bet that marriage was already going south.

'I'm going to be absolutely honest with you, Carley,' Allan Desmond said. 'If – and it's a very strong if – Vivian did become romantically involved with Nicholas Spencer, it did not happen immediately. She went to work for him six months after Joel died. She came home on weekends at least once a month. Her mother or I or one of her sisters made it a point of speaking to her virtually every evening during this time. If anything, we were all concerned about the fact that she always seemed to be home. We urged her to join a bereavement group, sign up for courses, and work toward a master's degree at night – in short, do something just to get out of the house.'

The Danish had arrived. Needless to say it looked absolutely wonderful, and I could read the warning label that came with it: one thousand calories. Clog your veins. Have you thought about your cholesterol level?

I cut off a piece and picked it up. Heavenly. It's a treat I almost never allow myself. So it's bad for me. It was just too good to worry about that.

'I think you're going to tell me that at some point the picture changed,' I said.

Allan Desmond nodded.

I was glad to see that as he was answering my questions, he was absentmindedly also eating the Danish.

'I would say that at the end of last summer Vivian seemed different. She sounded happier even though she was very concerned that some unforeseen problems had showed up with the cancer vaccine. She didn't go into it, though. I gathered it was privileged information, but she did say that Nicholas Spencer was deeply worried.'

'Did she ever indicate in any way that there was an intimate relationship developing or already going on between them?'

'No, she did not. But her sister Jane, the one who spoke to you earlier, picked up on it. She said something like "Viv's had enough heartbreak. I hope she's smart enough not to fall in love with her married boss." '

'Did you ever directly ask Vivian if she was involved with Nick Spencer?'

'I jokingly asked her if there was an interesting man on her horizon. She told me I was an incurable romantic and said that if anyone ever did show up, she'd let me know.'

I sensed that Allan Desmond was getting ready to ask me questions, so I quickly slipped in one more to him. 'Throwing out the romance factor, did Vivian ever tell you how she felt about Nicholas Spencer?'

Allan Desmond frowned, then looked me straight in the eye. 'In the last seven or eight months when Vivian spoke about Spencer, you would have thought that he walked on water. Which is why, if she had sent us a note saying she was joining him in Switzerland, I would not have approved, but with all my heart I would have understood.'

I watched as tears came to his eyes 'Carley, I would so

happily have that note delivered to me now, but I know it's not going to happen. Wherever Vivian is, and I pray God she is alive, she is not able to communicate with us, or she would have done so by now.'

I knew he was right. As our coffee grew cold, I told him about meeting with Vivian and hearing her plan to live with her parents until she found a place of her own. I told him about her phone call to me saying that she thought she could identify the man who had taken Dr. Spencer's records.

'And shortly after that, she vanished,' he said.

I nodded.

We both left the Danishes half-eaten. I know we shared the visual image of that beautiful young woman whose home had not been her sanctuary.

That thought gave me an idea. 'It's been terribly windy, lately. Did Vivian have any trouble with her front door?'

'Why do you ask that?'

'Because the fact that her front door was open almost seemed like an invitation for a neighbor who was passing by to be curious and ring the bell to see if there was a problem. That, in fact, is what happened. But if that door happened to blow open because the catch was not fastened, Vivian's disappearance might not have been noticed for another day at least.'

I could visualize Vivian at the doorway watching me drive away.

'You could be right. I know that her front door needed to be firmly closed before the lock would click,' Allan Desmond said.

'Let's assume that the door was *blown* open, not *left* open,' I said. 'Was the overturned lamp and table an attempt to make her disappearance look like a burglary and kidnapping?'

'The police think she deliberately left the appearance of foul play. She called you Saturday afternoon, Miss DeCarlo. How did she sound?'

'Agitated,' I admitted. 'Worried.'

I think I sensed their presence before I saw them coming. Detective Shapiro was one of the grim-faced men. The other was a uniformed police officer. They came over to the table. 'Mr. Desmond,' Shapiro said. 'We'd like to talk to you privately.'

'You've found her?' Allan Desmond demanded.

'Let's say we've traced her. Her neighbor, Dorothy Bowes, who lives three doors away from Ms. Powers, is a good friend of your daughter's. She's been on vacation. Your daughter had a key to her house. Bowes got home this morning to find her car missing from the garage. Has she ever had any psychiatric problems?'

'She ran away because she was frightened,' I said. 'I know she did.'

'But where did she go?' Allan Desmond asked. 'What would have frightened her so much that she would run away?'

I thought I might have the answer to that. Vivian had suspected that Nick Spencer's phone had been tapped. I wondered if something made her realize right after she called me that her phone was tapped as well. It would explain a panic-driven escape, but not her failure to contact her family in some way. And then I mentally echoed her father's question: *Where did she go? And was she followed?*

# Chapter 35

The arrival of the officers brought an end to our conversation, so I didn't stay much longer with Allan Desmond. Detective Shapiro and Officer Klein sat with us for a few minutes as we reconfirmed the timetable as we knew it. Vivian had gone to a friend's house and had taken her car. Whatever had frightened her enough to send her fleeing from her own home, at least she had gotten that far safely. I knew that when Vivian's father and I saw Shapiro and Klein approaching our table, we both feared they were bringing bad news. At least now there was hope.

Vivian had called me around four o'clock on Friday to say she thought she knew who had taken the records from Dr. Broderick. According to Allan Desmond, her sister Jane had tried to phone her at ten o'clock that evening and got no answer but assumed – and hoped – she'd had plans. In the early morning the neighbor walking his dog noticed the open front door.

I asked if they thought it was possible that Vivian had

heard or seen someone at the back of the house and ran out the front, and that perhaps she had knocked over the lamp and table in her rush to get out.

Shapiro's response was that anything was possible, including his first reaction – that the disappearance had been staged. Following that scenario, the fact that Vivian left with her neighbor's car did nothing to reduce that possibility.

I could see that Shapiro's comment absolutely infuriated Allan Desmond, but he said nothing. Like the Bikorskys, who were grateful that their child might see another Christmas, he was grateful that his daughter might at least have gone somewhere of her own volition.

I had figured there was a 90 percent chance that I would get a phone call from either Mrs. Broderick or Mrs. Ward, the receptionist, telling me not to come to Caspien, but since I did not, I left Allan Desmond with the investigators, after agreeing that we would keep in close touch.

Annette Broderick was a handsome woman in her mid-fifties with salt and pepper hair. Its natural wave softened her somewhat angular face. When I arrived, she suggested that we go upstairs to their living quarters over the medical office.

It really was a wonderful old house, with spacious rooms, high ceilings, crown molding, and polished oak floors. We sat in the study. The sun streamed in and added to the mellow comfort of the room, already cozy with its wall of bookcases and high-backed English couch.

I realized that I had spent this past week in the company of people who were very much on the edge, fearful of what life was doing to them. The Bikorskys, Vivian

Powers and her father, the employees of Gen-stone whose lives and hopes had been shattered – all these people were under great stress, and I couldn't get them out of my mind.

It occurred to me that the one person who should have leaped to my mind and did not was my stepsister, Lynn.

Annette Broderick offered me coffee, which I refused, and a glass of water, which I accepted. She brought in a glass for herself as well. 'Philip is doing better,' she said. 'It may take a long time, but they expect him to have a complete recovery.'

Before I could tell her how glad I was to hear that, she said, 'I frankly thought at first that your suggesting what happened to Philip wasn't an accident was pretty far-fetched, but now I'm beginning to wonder.'

'Why?' I asked quickly.

'Oh, I'm going too far,' she said hastily. 'It's simply that when he began to come out of the coma, he was trying to tell me something. The best I could make out of what he said was "car turned." The police think because of a skid mark that it's possible the car that ran him down was coming from the other direction and made a U-turn.'

'Then the police agree that your husband may have been deliberately run over?'

'No, they believe it was a drunken driver. They've had a lot of problems around here with underage kids drinking or smoking pot. They think someone may have been going in the wrong direction, turned, and didn't see Phil until it was too late. Why do you keep suggesting that it wasn't an accident, Carley?'

She listened while I told her about the missing letter from Caroline Summers to Nick Spencer, and the theft of her daughter's records not only from Dr. Broderick but also from the Caspien Hospital and the hospital in Ohio.

'Do you mean that someone may have put some credence in what would surely be considered a miraculous cure?' she asked incredulously.

'I don't know,' I said. 'But my suspicion is that somebody certainly thought there was sufficient promise in Dr. Spencer's early records to steal them, and Dr. Broderick could identify that person. With all the publicity swirling around Nicholas Spencer, your husband may have become a liability.'

'You say that copies of the X rays were picked up at Caspien Hospital and a copy of the MRI from one in Ohio. Did the same person pick them up?'

'I checked that out. The clerks simply don't remember, but both are sure there was nothing outstanding or significant about the man who claimed to be Caroline Summers's husband. On the other hand, from what I gather, Dr. Broderick clearly remembers the man who came to him for Dr. Spencer's records.'

'I was home that day and happened to glance out the window when that man, whoever he was, got back in his car.'

'I didn't know you saw him,' I said. 'The doctor didn't mention that. Would you recognize him?'

'Absolutely not. It was November, and he had his coat collar turned up. Thinking back, I will say my impression was that he used one of those brownish red rinses on his hair. You know how they can get that orange look in the sun.'

'Dr. Broderick didn't mention that when I spoke to him.'

'It's not the sort of thing he'd be likely to say, especially if he wasn't sure.'

'Has Dr. Broderick begun to talk about the accident?'

'He's under a lot of sedation, but when he's lucid, he wants to know what happened to him. So far he doesn't seem to have any memory of it other than what he tried to tell me as he was coming out of the coma.'

'From what Dr. Broderick told me, he did some research with Dr. Spencer, which is why Nick Spencer left the early records here. How much did Dr. Broderick actually work with Nick's father?'

'Carley, my husband was probably dismissive of his work with Dr. Spencer, but the fact is that he was keenly interested in the research and thought Dr. Spencer was a genius. That was one of the reasons Nick left those records with him. Philip intended to go on with some of the research but realized that it was far too time-consuming for him and that what was an obsession for Dr. Spencer would have to be a hobby for him. Don't forget that Nick at that time was planning a career in medical supplies, not in research, but then about ten years ago, when he began to study his father's records, he realized that he had been on to something, perhaps even something as important as a cure for cancer. And from what my husband told me about it, the preclinical testing was very promising, as was phase one in which they worked with healthy subjects. It was during later experiments that things suddenly went sour. Which makes you wonder why anyone would steal Dr. Spencer's records.'

She shook her head. 'Carley, I'm just grateful that my husband is still alive.'

'I am, too,' I said fervently. I didn't want to tell this very nice woman that if Dr. Broderick had been the deliberate victim of a hit-and-run driver, I felt responsible for its happening. Even though it might not be connected, the fact that after I spoke to him I went straight to the Gen-stone office in Pleasantville and started asking about a man with reddish hair, and then the next day Dr. Broderick ended up in the hospital, seems too connected to be a coincidence.

It was time for me to go. I thanked Mrs. Broderick for seeing me and once again made sure she had my card with my cell phone number on it. I know when I left her that she was not at all convinced her husband had been targeted, which was probably just as well. He would be in the hospital for several weeks at least, and would surely be safe there. I was determined to have some answers by the time he got out.


If the mood at Gen-stone was somber when I was there last week, the atmosphere on this visit was positively mournful. The receptionist had clearly been crying. She said that Mr. Wallingford had asked me to stop by for a moment before I chatted with any of the employees. She then dialed his secretary to announce me.

When she put down the phone, I said, 'I can see that you're upset. I hope it's nothing that can't be straightened out.'

'I got my notice this morning,' she said. 'They're closing the doors this afternoon.'

'I'm terribly sorry.'

The phone rang and she picked it up. I think it must have been a reporter because she said she was not permitted to comment and referred all calls to the company attorney.

By the time she hung up the phone, Wallingford's secretary was a few feet away. I would have liked to talk to the receptionist longer, but that wasn't possible. I remembered the secretary's name from the other day. 'It's Mrs. Rider, isn't it?' I asked.

She was the kind of woman my grandmother would have referred to as a 'Plain Jane.' Her navy blue suit, tan stockings, and low-heeled shoes were in keeping with her short brown hair and total lack of makeup. Her smile was polite but disinterested. 'Yes, it is, Miss DeCarlo.'

The doors to the offices off the long corridor were all open, and I glanced into them as I followed her. Every single one of them appeared to be empty. The whole building seemed empty, and I felt that if I shouted, I'd hear an echo. I tried to engage her in conversation. 'I'm so sorry to hear that the company is closing down. Do you know what you're going to do?'

'I'm not sure,' she said.

I figured that Wallingford had warned her not to talk to me, which, of course, made her all that much more interesting.

'How long have you been working for Mr. Wallingford?' I tried to sound casual.

'Ten years.'

'Then you were with him when he owned the furniture company?'

'Yes, I was.'

The door to his office was closed. I managed to throw out one more line, fishing for information. 'Then you must know his sons. Maybe they were right that he shouldn't have sold the family business.'

'That didn't give them the right to sue him,' she said

indignantly as she tapped at the door with one hand and opened it with the other.

A lovely piece of information, I thought. His *sons* sued him! What made them do that? I wondered.

Charles Wallingford was clearly not thrilled to see me, but he tried not to show it. He got up as I entered the room, and I saw that he wasn't alone. A man was seated opposite him at the desk. He, too, stood up and turned when Wallingford greeted me, and I had the impression of being looked over very carefully. I judged him to be somewhere in his mid-forties, about five feet ten, with graying hair and hazel eyes. Like Wallingford and Adrian Garner, he had an air of authority about him, and I wasn't surprised when he was introduced as Lowell Drexel, a member of Gen-stone's board of directors.

Lowell Drexel – I had heard that name recently. Then I remembered where. At the luncheon, Wallingford had joked with Adrian Garner that the stockholder who claimed to have seen Nick Spencer in Switzerland had asked Drexel for a job.

Drexel's voice was notably devoid of warmth. 'Miss DeCarlo, I understand you have the unenviable job of writing a cover story for *Wall Street Weekly* about Gen-stone.'

'Of *contributing* to a cover story,' I corrected him. 'Three of us are working on it together.' I looked at Wallingford. 'I heard that you're closing down today. I'm so sorry.'

He nodded. 'This time I won't have to worry about a new place to invest my money,' he said grimly. 'As sorry as I am for all our employees and stockholders, I do wish they could understand that, far from being the enemy, we've been on the battlefield with them.'

'We'll still have our appointment on Saturday, I hope,' I said.

'Yes, of course.' He brushed aside as absurd the suggestion that he might want to cancel it. 'I wanted to explain that with a few exceptions, such as the receptionist and Mrs. Rider, we gave our employees the choice of staying for the day or going home. Many of them chose to leave immediately.'

'I see. Well, that is a disappointment, but perhaps I can get a few comments from those who are still here. I hoped it didn't show in my face that I wondered if the sudden closing had anything to do with my request to come here for interviews today.'

'Perhaps I can answer any questions you have, Miss DeCarlo,' Drexel offered.

'Perhaps you can, Mr. Drexel. I understand that you're with Garner Pharmaceuticals.'

'I head the legal department there. As you may know already, when my company decided to invest one billion dollars in Gen-stone, pending FDA approval, Mr. Garner was asked to join the board. In such cases he delegates one of his close associates to take the seat for him.'

'Mr. Garner seems very concerned about the fact that Garner Pharmaceuticals is sharing in the bad press of Gen-stone.'

'He is *extremely* concerned and may be doing something about it soon, which I'm not at liberty to disclose today.'

'And if he doesn't do anything?'

'The assets of Gen-stone, such as they are, will be sold at a sheriff's sale and the proceeds distributed to the creditors.' He gave a sweeping wave of his hand, which I took to mean the building and furnishings.

'Would it be too much to hope that if there is an announcement, my magazine will get the scoop?' I asked.

'It would be too much to hope, Miss DeCarlo.' His slight smile had the finality of a door closing in my face. Lowell Drexel and Adrian Garner were a pair of icebergs, I decided. At least Wallingford put on a veneer of cordiality.

I nodded to Drexel, thanked Charles Wallingford, and followed Mrs. Rider out of the room. She took time to close the door to the private office behind us. 'There are a few telephone operators and keyboarders and some maintenance people still here,' she said. 'Where would you want to start?'

'I think probably the keyboarders,' I said. She tried to lead me, but I fell in step beside her. 'Is it all right if I talk to you, Mrs. Rider?'

'I would prefer not to be quoted.'

'Not even to comment on Vivian Powers's disappearance?'

'Disappearance or flight, Miss DeCarlo?'

'You believe that Vivian staged her disappearance?'

'I would say that her decision to stay after the plane crash is suspect. I personally observed her carrying files out of the office last week.'

'Why do you think she would take records home, Mrs. Rider?'

'Because she wanted to be absolutely certain that there was nothing in the files that would give a hint about where all our money went.' The receptionist had been tearful, but Mrs. Rider was furious. 'She's probably over there in Switzerland with Spencer right now, laughing at the rest of us. It isn't just my pension that I lose, Miss DeCarlo. I'm another one of the fools who invested most of her life savings in this company's stock. I wish Nick Spencer really had been killed in that plane crash. His rotten, oily tongue would be on fire in hell for all the misery he caused.'

If I wanted a reaction to how an employee felt, I certainly had it now. Then her face became scarlet. 'I hope you don't print that,' she said. 'Nick Spencer's son, Jack, used to come in here with him. He always stopped by my desk to talk to me. He has enough to live down without someday reading what I said about his contemptible father.'

'What did you think of Nicholas Spencer before all this came out?' I asked.

'What we all thought, that he walked on water.'

It was the same comment Allan Desmond had made in describing Vivian's reaction to Nicholas Spencer. It was the same reaction I'd had to him myself.

'Off the record, Mrs. Rider, what did you think of Vivian Powers?'

'I'm not stupid. I could see that there was a relationship developing between her and Nicholas Spencer. I think maybe some of us in the office realized it before he did. And what he saw in that woman he married, I'll never know. Sorry, Miss DeCarlo. I've heard she's your stepsister, but whenever she happened to be here – which wasn't often – she'd treat us all as if we didn't exist. She'd sail right past me into Mr. Wallingford's office as though she had every right to interrupt anything he was doing.'

I *knew* it, I thought. There *was* something going on between them. 'Was Mr. Wallingford annoyed when she interrupted him?' I asked.

'I think he was embarrassed. He's a very dignified man,

and she'd mess up his hair or kiss the top of his head, and then laugh when he would say something like "Don't do that, Lynn." I'm telling you, Miss DeCarlo, on the one hand she ignored people, on the other, she acted as though she could say or do anything she wanted.'

'Did you have much chance to observe Vivian's interaction with Nicholas Spencer?'

Now that she'd opened up, Mrs. Rider was a journalist's dream. She shrugged. 'His office is in the other wing, so I didn't see much of them together. But one time when I was leaving to go home, he was ahead of me and walked Vivian to her car. The way their hands touched and the way they looked at each other, I could tell there was something very, very special going on, and at the time I thought, "Good for them. He deserves better than the ice queen." '

We were in the reception area, and I could see that the receptionist was looking at us, her head bent as if trying to pick up scraps of our conversation.

'I'll let you go, Mrs. Rider,' I said. 'And I promise you that this has been off the record. Give me one more impression. You now believe Vivian stayed in the office to cover traces of the money. Right after the plane crash, did she seem genuinely grieved?'

'We all were heartsick and couldn't believe it had happened. Like a bunch of dopes, we were all standing around here crying and saying how wonderful Nick Spencer was, and we were all kind of looking at her because we suspected that they had become lovers. She didn't say a thing. She just got up and went home. Guess she didn't think she could put on a convincing act for our benefit.'

Abruptly, the woman turned away from me. 'What's the use?' she snapped. 'Talk about a den of thieves.' She pointed to the receptionist. 'Betty can show you around.'

As it turned out, I wasn't interested in talking to the people who would be made available to me. It was immediately clear that none of them held a position where they would know anything about the letter Caroline Summers wrote to Nicholas Spencer last November. I asked the receptionist about the laboratory. 'Could that be shut down overnight like everything else?'

'Oh, no. Dr. Celtavini and Dr. Kendall and their assistants will be here for a while.'

'Are Dr. Celtavini and Dr. Kendall here today?' I asked.

'Dr. Kendall is.' She looked uncertain. Dr. Kendall had obviously not been on her list of people to be interviewed, but Betty did call her.

'Miss DeCarlo, do you have any idea how difficult it is to get a new drug approved?' Dr. Kendall asked. 'In fact, only one in fifty thousand chemical compounds discovered by scientists make it to the public market. The search for a cancer cure has been unrelenting, going on for decades. When Nicholas Spencer started this company, Dr. Celtavini was extremely interested and enthusiastic about the results reported in Dr. Spencer's files, and he gave up his position with one of the most prestigious research laboratories in the country to join Nick Spencer – as did I, I might add.'

We were in her office above the laboratory. When I met Dr. Kendall last week, I had thought of her as not being particularly attractive, but now when she looked directly at me, I realized that there was a compelling, almost smoldering fire that had not then been apparent to me. I had noticed her determined chin, but her dark blunt-cut hair had been tucked behind her ears, and I had not taken in the curious shade of her grayish green eyes. Last week I had the sense that she was a fiercely intelligent woman. Now I realized she was also a very attractive one.

'Were you with a laboratory or a pharmaceutical house, Doctor?' I asked.

'I was with Hartness Research Center.'

I was impressed. It doesn't get higher quality than Hartness. I wondered why she had given up that job to go with a new company. She herself had just said that only one in fifty thousand new drugs makes it to the market.

She answered my unasked question: 'Nicholas Spencer was a most persuasive salesman in recruiting personnel, as well as money.'

'How long have you been here?'

'It's a little over two years.'

It had been a long day. I thanked Dr. Kendall for seeing me and left. On the way out I stopped to thank Betty and wish her well. Then I asked her if she kept in touch with any of the girls who had been in the keyboarding pool. 'Pat lives near me,' she said. 'She left a year ago. Edna and Charlotte, I wasn't close to. But if you wanted to get in touch with Laura, just ask Dr. Kendall. Laura's her niece.'

# Chapter 36

It wasn't a question of *if* the cops would come back. It was *when* they'd come back that bothered Ned. He thought about it all day. His rifle was out of the way, but if they had a search warrant for his van, they'd probably find some of Peg's DNA there. She had bled a little when her head hit the dashboard.

Then they'd keep searching until they found the rifle. Mrs. Morgan would tell them that she knew he went to the grave a lot. Eventually they'd figure it out.

At four o'clock he decided not to wait any longer.

It was deserted in the cemetery. He wondered if Annie was lonesome for him the way he was for her. The ground was still so muddy that it was easy to dig up the rifle and the box of ammunition. Then he sat on the grave for a few minutes. He didn't care that his clothes were getting wet and dirty. Just being there made him feel close to Annie.

There were still some things – some people – he had to take care of, but once he'd done what he had to do, then the next time he came here he wouldn't leave. For just a minute Ned was tempted to do it now. He knew how it was done. Take off his shoes. Put the rifle barrel in his mouth and hook the trigger with his toe.

He started to laugh, remembering how he'd done that once when the rifle wasn't loaded, just to tease Annie. She had screamed and burst into tears, and then had run over to him and pulled his hair. It hadn't hurt. He'd laughed at first, but then he'd felt sorry because she was so upset. Annie loved him. She was the only one who had ever loved him.

Ned got up slowly. His clothes were so dirty again that he knew wherever he went people would stare at him. So he went back to the van, wrapped the rifle in the blanket, and drove back to the apartment.

Mrs. Morgan would be first.

He showered and shaved and brushed his hair. Then he took his dark blue suit from the closet and laid it on the bed. Annie had bought it for him on his birthday, four years ago. He'd worn it only a couple of times. He hated to dress up like that. But now he put it on, along with a shirt and tie. He was doing it for her.

He went to the dresser where everything was just the way Annie had left it. The box with the pearls he had given her for Christmas was in the top drawer. Annie had loved them. She said he shouldn't have spent $100 for them, but she loved them. He picked up the box.

He could hear Mrs. Morgan walking around upstairs. She always complained that he was messy. She had complained to Annie about all the stuff in his part of the garage. She'd complained about the way he emptied the garbage, saying that he didn't tie the sacks but just threw them into the big pails at the side of the house. She used to get Annie so upset, and now that Annie was dead, she wanted to throw him out.

Ned loaded his rifle and walked up the stairs. He knocked on the door.

Mrs. Morgan opened it, but she kept the chain on. He knew she was afraid of him. But when she saw him, she smiled and said, 'Why, Ned, you look so nice. Do you feel better?'

'Yes, I do. And I'm going to feel even better in a minute.'

He kept the rifle at his side so that she couldn't see it with the door open only a few inches.

'I'm starting to sort things out in the apartment. Annie liked you very much, and I want you to have her pearls. Can I come in and give them to you?'

He could see the suspicious look in Mrs. Morgan's eyes, and could tell she was nervous from the way she bit her lip. But then he heard the chain slide.

Ned quickly shoved the door open and pushed her back. She stumbled and fell. As he aimed the rifle, he saw the look he wanted on her face – the look that said she knew she was going to die, the look he'd seen on Annie's face when he ran out to the car after the truck slammed into it.

He was only sorry that Mrs. Morgan closed her eyes before he shot her.

They wouldn't find her until sometime tomorrow, maybe even the day after. That would give him time to get the others.

He found Mrs. Morgan's pocketbook and took her car keys and wallet. There was $126 in it. 'Thank you, Mrs. Morgan,' he said looking down at her. 'Now your son can have the whole house.'

He felt calm and at peace. In his head he could hear a voice telling him what to do: *Ned, take your van and park it somewhere so they won't find it for a while. Then take Mrs. Morgan's car, her nice, clean, black Toyota that nobody will notice.*

An hour later he was driving the Toyota down the block. He had parked the van in the hospital parking lot, where no one would think anything of it. People came and went there twenty-four/seven. Then he'd walked back, looked up at the second floor of the house, and got a good feeling thinking about Mrs. Morgan. At the corner, he stopped for the light. In the rearview mirror he saw a car slow down in front of the house, and then he watched as the detectives got out. On their way to talk to him again, Ned figured. Or to arrest him.

Too late, Ned thought, as the light turned green and he headed the car north. Everything he was doing, he was doing for Annie. In her memory he wanted to visit the ruin of the mansion that had started him dreaming of giving her a home like that. In the end, the dream became a nightmare that had taken her life, so he had taken the mansion's life. As he drove, it felt as if she were sitting with him now. 'See, Annie,' he would say when he stopped in front of the ruined mansion. 'See, I got even with them. Your house is gone. Their house is gone.'

Then he would drive to Greenwood Lake, where he and Annie would say good-bye to the Harniks and Mrs. Schafley.

# Chapter 37

I had the radio on as I was driving home from Pleasantville, but I wasn't hearing a word of what was being said. I could not avoid the feeling that my expected presence in the Gen-stone office today contributed to the decision to abruptly close the company's doors. I also had a feeling that no matter what other business Lowell Drexel had to discuss with Charles Wallingford, he was also there to get a good look at me.

It was sheer good fortune that Betty, the receptionist, had mentioned by chance that one of the women who sorted the mail and sent out the form letters was Dr. Kendall's niece, Laura. If she had been the one assigned to respond to Caroline Summers's letter, would she have thought it interesting enough to tell Dr. Kendall about it? I wondered.

But even if she had, why wouldn't she have answered the letter? According to company policy, all letters were to receive a response.

Vivian had said that after he learned his father's records

had been taken, Nick Spencer stopped putting his appointments on the calendar. If he and Vivian were as close as the people in the office seemed to think, I wonder why he had not told her the reason for his concerns.

Didn't he trust her?

That he might not was a new, interesting possibility.

Or was he protecting her by his silence?

'Vivian Powers has been . . .'

I realized suddenly that I was not only *thinking* her name, I was *hearing* it on the radio. With a snap of my finger I turned up the volume, and then listened with growing dismay to the news report. Vivian had been found, still alive but unconscious, in her neighbor's car. The car was parked off the road in a wooded area only a mile from her home in Briarcliff Manor. It was believed that she had attempted suicide, this assumption based on the fact that there was an empty bottle of pills found on the seat beside her.

My God, I thought. She disappeared sometime between Saturday evening and Sunday morning. Could she have been in the car all this time? I was almost crossing the county line as I headed into the city. I debated for a split second, then made the next possible turn to go back to Westchester.

Forty-five minutes later I was sitting with Vivian's father in the waiting room outside the intensive care unit of Briarcliff Manor Hospital. He was crying, both from relief and fear. 'Carley,' he said, 'she's slipping in and out of consciousness, but she seems not to remember anything. They asked her how old she is, and she said sixteen. She thinks she's sixteen years old. What has she *done* to herself?'

Or what has someone else done to her? I thought as I closed my hand over his. I tried to come up with some words to comfort him. 'She's alive,' I said. 'It's a miracle that after five days in the car she's still alive.'

Detective Shapiro was at the door of the waiting room. 'We've been talking with the doctors, Mr. Desmond. There was no way your daughter was in that car for five days. We know that as recently as two days ago she was dialing Nick Spencer's cell phone number. Do you think you can get her to come clean with us?'

# Chapter 38

I stayed with Allan Desmond for four hours, until his daughter Jane, who flew down from Boston, arrived at the hospital. She was a year or two older than Vivian, and looked so much like her that I felt a wrench of surprise when she came into the waiting room.

They both insisted I be with them when Jane spoke – or tried to speak – to Vivian. 'You heard what the police said,' Allan Desmond said. 'You're a journalist, Carley. Make your own decision.'

I stood with him at the foot of the bed as Jane bent over Vivian and kissed her forehead. 'Hey, Viv, what do you think you're doing? We've been worried about you.'

An IV was dripping fluid into Vivian's arm. Her heartbeat and blood pressure were being recorded on a monitor over her bed. She was chalk white, and her dark hair provided a stark contrast to her complexion and the hospital bedding. When she opened them, even though they were cloudy, I noticed again her soft brown eyes.

'Jane?' The timbre of her voice was different.

'I'm here, Viv.'

Vivian looked around then focused on her father. A puzzled expression came over her face. 'Why is Daddy crying?'

She sounds so young, I thought.

'Don't cry, Daddy,' Vivian said as her eyes began to close.

'Viv, do you know what happened to you?' Jane Desmond was running her finger along her sister's face, trying to keep her awake.

'Happened to me?' Vivian was clearly trying to focus. Again, a look of confusion came over her face. 'Nothing happened to me. I just got home from school.'

When I left a few minutes later, Jane Desmond and her father walked with me to the elevator. 'Do the police have the nerve to think she's faking this?' Jane asked indignantly.

'If they do, they're wrong. She's not faking it,' I said grimly.

It was nine o'clock when I finally opened the door of my apartment. Casey had left messages on my answering machine at four, six, and eight o'clock. They were all the same. 'Call me no matter what time you get in, Carley. It's very important.'

He was home. 'I just got in,' I said by way of apology. 'Why didn't you call me on my cell phone?'

'I did. A couple of times.'

I had obeyed the sign in the hospital to turn it off and then had forgotten to turn it on again and check for messages.

'I gave Vince your message about talking to Nick's in-laws. I must have made a convincing case – either that or hearing about Vivian Powers has shaken them up. They want to talk to you, anytime, at your convenience. I assume you've heard about Vivian Powers, Carley.'

I told him about being at the hospital. 'Casey, I could have learned so much more from her,' I said. I didn't realize that I was close to tears until I heard them in my voice. 'I think she wanted to talk to me, but she was afraid to trust me. Then she decided she *did* trust me. She left that message. How long was she hiding in her neighbor's house? Or did somebody see her go there?'

I was talking so fast that I was tripping over my own words. 'Why didn't she use her neighbor's phone to ask for help? Did she ever make it to the car, or did somebody drive her away in it? Casey, I think she was scared. Wherever she was, she kept trying to call Nick Spencer on his cell phone. Did she believe those reports that he was seen in Switzerland? The other day when I spoke with her, I swear she believed he was dead. She couldn't have been in that car for five days. Why didn't I help her? At the time, I knew something was terribly wrong.'

Casey interrupted me. 'Hold it, hold it,' he said. 'You're rambling. I'll be there in twenty minutes.'

It actually took him twenty-three minutes. When I opened the door, he put his arms around me, and for the moment at least, even the terrible burden of having somehow failed Vivian Powers was lifted from my shoulders.

I think that was the moment when I stopped trying to fight being in love with Casey and trusted that maybe he was falling in love with me, too. After all, the greatest proof of love is to be there for someone when she needs you most, isn't it?

# Chapter 39

'This is their pool, Annie,' Ned said. 'It's covered now, but when I worked here last summer for that landscaper, it was open. There were tables out on those terraces. The gardens were really pretty. That's why I wanted you to have the same thing.'

Annie smiled at him. She was starting to understand that he hadn't meant to hurt her by selling her house.

Ned looked around. It was getting dark. He hadn't intended to come onto the property, but he remembered the code to open the service gate, having watched the landscaper use it last summer. That was how he had gotten in when he torched the house. The gate was way over on the left side of the property, past the English garden. Rich people didn't want to look at the help. They didn't want their ratty cars or trucks cluttering up their driveways.

'That's why they have a buffer zone, Annie,' Ned explained. 'They plant trees just to make sure they don't have to see us come in or out. Serves them right that we can turn the tables on them. We can come in and out, and they don't even know it.'

When he was here, he had worked on the lawn, mulched the plants, and put flowers in around the pool. As a result, he knew every inch of this place.

He explained it all to Annie when he drove in. 'You see, we had to use *this* gate when I worked here. See, the sign says service entrance. For most deliveries or for people coming to do a job, the housekeeper would have to buzz to let them in but the landscaper – that lousy guy I got in trouble for punching out – had the code. Every day we parked outside this garage. They don't use this one for anything except storing lawn furniture and that kind of stuff. Guess they won't be using it *this* year. Nobody wants to sit around a place like this, with the house gone and everything still a mess.

'There's a little bathroom with a toilet and sink at the back of the garage. That's for people like me. You don't think they're going to let us go into their house, even their pool house, do you? No way, Annie!

'The guy and his wife who cleaned this place were nice people. If we'd run into them, I'd have said something like "I was just stopping by to say how sorry I was about the fire." I look nice today, so it would have been okay. But I had a feeling we wouldn't run into them, and it turns out I was right. In fact, it looks as if they're gone. There's no car. The house they used to live in is dark. The shades are down. There's no big house to take care of now. They had to use the service gate, too, you know. All those trees are there so you don't have to look at that gate or the garage.

'Annie, I was working out here a couple of years ago when I heard that guy Spencer on the phone telling people that he knew this vaccine worked, that it would change the world. Then last year when I was here for just those couple of weeks, I kept hearing the other guys saying they had bought the stock and that it had doubled in value and was still going up.'

Ned looked at Annie. Sometimes he could see her very clearly; other times, like now, it was like seeing her shadow. 'Anyhow, that's the way it happened,' he said.

He went to take her hand, but even though he knew it was there, he couldn't feel it. He was disappointed, but he didn't want to show it. She was probably still a little mad at him. 'It's time to go, Annie,' he said finally.

Ned walked past the pool, past the English garden, and through the wooded area to the service road where he'd parked the car in front of the garage, which was where they stored the lawn furniture. 'Want to take a look before we go, Annie?'

The garage door wasn't locked. That was somebody's mistake, he thought. But it didn't matter. He could easily have punched out a window. Ned went inside. The lawn furniture was stored there, but there was also a space where the housekeepers used to keep their car. The cushions for the furniture were piled on the shelves in the back. 'See, Annie. You'd even like the garage for the working guys. Nice and neat.'

He smiled at her. She knew he was teasing.

'Okay, honey. Now let's go to Greenwood Lake and take care of those people who were so mean to you.'

Greenwood Lake was in New Jersey, and it took Ned an hour and ten minutes to get there. He heard nothing on the news about Mrs. Morgan, so the police didn't know about her yet. But a couple of times he heard them say that Nicholas Spencer's girlfriend had been found. A wife *and* a girlfriend, Ned thought. Just what you'd expect of him. 'The girlfriend's real sick, honey,' he told Annie. 'Real sick. She's getting hers, too.'

He didn't want to get to Greenwood Lake too soon. The Harniks and Mrs. Schafley went to bed after the ten o'clock news, and he didn't want to get there before then. He stopped at a diner and ate a hamburger.

It was ten o'clock sharp when he drove down the block and parked in front of where their house used to be. Mrs. Schafley's light was on, but the Harniks' house was dark. 'We'll drive around for a while, honey,' he told Annie.

But at midnight the Harniks still weren't home, and Ned decided he couldn't take a chance on waiting anymore. If he put the rifle inside Mrs. Shafley's window, he could finish her off but then he couldn't come back.

'We'll have to wait, honey,' he told Annie. 'Where should we go now?'

'Back to the mansion,' he heard her say. 'Put the car in the garage and fix a nice bed for yourself on one of those long couches. You'll be safe there.'

# Chapter 40

I was the first to arrive at the *Wall Street Weekly* offices on Friday morning. Ken, Don, and I had arranged to meet at eight o'clock to go over everything before my 9:30 appointment with Adrian Garner. They were only a few minutes behind me, and, clutching our coffees, we filed into Ken's office and got right down to business. I think we all felt from the get-go that the pace of events had changed, and not just because Gen-stone had closed its doors. We all instinctively knew that the developments were happening thick and fast, and that we needed to get a handle on them.

I started by telling them about my rush to the hospital when I heard that Vivian Powers was there, and I described how I found her. Then it turned out that Ken and Don were also looking at the investigation with fresh eyes, but with conclusions quite different from mine.

'There's a scenario I see developing that's starting to make sense,' Ken said, 'and it's not a pretty one. Dr. Celtavini phoned me yesterday afternoon and asked me if we could meet last night at his home.' He looked at us, paused, then continued. 'Dr. Celtavini is well connected in the scientific community in Italy. He got a tip a few days ago that several labs there have been funded by an unknown source, and seem to be pursuing different phases of the Gen-stone research for a cancer vaccine.'

I stared at him. 'What unknown source would fund that?'

'Nicholas Spencer.'

'Nicholas Spencer!'

'It's not the name he used over there, of course. If it's true, it probably means that Spencer was using Gen-stone money to fund research at separate labs. Then he fakes his disappearance. Gen-stone goes bankrupt. Nick gets himself a new identity, probably a new face, and becomes sole owner of the vaccine. Maybe the vaccine is promising after all, and he deliberately falsified the results to destroy the company.'

'Then he may have been seen in Switzerland?' I wondered aloud. I can't believe that, I thought, I simply *cannot* believe it.

'I'm beginning to think that it's not only possible but probable – ' Ken began.

'But, Ken,' I protested, interrupting him, 'I'm sure Vivian Powers believes Nick Spencer is dead. And I believe they really were seriously involved with each other.'

'Carley, you told me she was missing for five days, but the doctors say she wasn't in the car that long and couldn't have been. So what *did* happen? There are a couple of answers to all that. Either she's a great actress or, far-fetched as it may seem, she has a dissociative personality. That would account for blackouts and a sixteen-year-old persona.'

I was starting to feel like a voice crying in the wilderness. 'The scenario I'm coming up with is quite different,' I said. 'Let's start from another point of view, shall we? Somebody stole Dr. Spencer's records from Dr. Broderick. Somebody stole the X rays and MRI of Caroline Summers's child. And if Vivian is to be believed, the letter that Caroline Summers wrote to Nick disappeared, and the answer that Caroline was supposed to receive was never sent. Vivian told me she left it to be handled by one of the clerks. She was quite definite about that.'

I was just getting warmed up. 'Vivian also said that after Dr. Spencer's records disappeared, Nick Spencer got very secretive about his appointments and would disappear from the office for days at a time.'

'Carley, I think you're proving my point,' Ken said mildly. 'It's come out that he made two or three trips to Europe between mid-February and April 4 when his plane crashed.'

'But maybe Nick Spencer was getting suspicious that something was going on in his own company,' I said. 'Hear me out. Dr. Kendall's twenty-year-old niece, Laura Cox, was a secretarial assistant at Gen-stone. Betty, the receptionist, told me that yesterday. I asked her if it was general knowledge that they were related, and she told me it wasn't. She said that one day she just happened to remark to Laura Cox that she had the same first name as Dr. Kendall, and her answer was "I'm named after her. She's my aunt." But then later she got terribly upset and begged Betty not to say a word to anyone. Apparently, Dr. Kendall did not want their relationship known.'

'What would have been the harm?' Don asked crisply.

'Betty told me that it was a company rule that family

members of employees were not to apply for jobs. Dr. Kendall certainly knew that.'

'Medical research companies don't believe in letting the left hand know what the right hand is doing,' Don said by way of agreement. 'By even allowing her niece to take a secretarial assistant position, which is really a starter job, Dr. Kendall was breaking the rules. I would have thought she was more of a professional than that.'

'She told me she was with Hartness Research Center prior to coming to Gen-stone,' I said. 'What kind of reputation did she have there?'

'I'll run a check on her.' Ken made a note on his pad.

'And while you're doing it, keep in mind that everything you're saying about Nicholas Spencer possibly deliberately trying to bankrupt his own company and have the vaccine to himself could also apply to someone else.'

'Who?'

'Charles Wallingford, for openers. What do you really know about him?'

Ken shrugged. 'A blueblood. Not a very effective one, but nevertheless a blueblood, and very proud of it. His ancestor started the furniture company as a philanthropic gesture to give employment to immigrants, but he was a heck of a businessman. The family fortunes declined in other areas, as they sometimes do, but the furniture business was very strong. Wallingford's father expanded it; then when he died, Charles took it over and ran it into the ground.'

'Yesterday, when I was in the Gen-stone office, his secretary was indignant about the fact that his sons sued him over the sale of the company.'

Don Carter likes to look unflappable, but his eyes widened at that piece of information. 'Interesting, Carley. Let's see what I can find out about that.'

Ken was doodling again. I hoped that was a sign that had opened him to the possibility of another scenario for what had happened at Gen-stone.

'Have you been able to find out the name of the patient who checked out of the hospice at St. Ann's?' I asked him.

'My source at St. Ann's is still trying to get it.' He grimaced. 'The guy's name has probably already appeared in the obit column.'

I looked at my watch. 'I've got to get on my way. God forbid I keep the mighty Adrian Garner waiting. Maybe he'll break down and tell me the rescue plan that Lowell Drexel was hinting at yesterday.'

'Let me guess what it is,' Don suggested. 'With great fanfare, Garner's public relations department is going to announce that Garner Pharmaceuticals will take over Gen-stone, and as a gesture of good will to the employees and stockholders, they'll pay eight or ten cents on the dollar of the amounts they have lost. They'll announce that Garner Pharmaceuticals will start all over on its never-ending fight to erase the scourge of cancer from the universe. And so on and so on . . .'

I stood up. 'I'll let you know how the scenario checks out. See you guys.' I hesitated but bit back the words I was not yet ready to vocalize – that Nick Spencer, alive or dead, may have been the victim of a conspiracy within his company, and that two other people had already been caught up in it with him, Dr. Philip Broderick and Vivian Powers.

*

The executive offices of Garner Pharmaceuticals are in the Chrysler Building, that wonderful old New York landmark at Lexington and 42nd Street. I was ten minutes early for my appointment, but even so was barely in the reception area when I was ushered into the sanctum sanctorum, Adrian Garner's private office. For some reason I was not surprised to see Lowell Drexel already ensconced there. I was surprised, however, at the sight of the third person in the room: Charles Wallingford.

'Good morning, Carley,' he said, actually sounding genial. 'I'm the surprise guest. We had a meeting scheduled for later, so Adrian was kind enough to invite me to be with you now.'

I suddenly had an image of Lynn kissing the top of Wallingford's head and mussing his hair as his secretary had described it yesterday. I think I'd always subconsciously been aware that Charles Wallingford was a lightweight, but that mental image reinforced it. If Lynn was involved with him, no doubt it was because she wanted another notch on her belt.

Needless to say, Adrian Garner's office was magnificent. It commanded a view from the East River to the Hudson River, and encompassed most of downtown New York. I have a passion for beautiful furniture, and I would swear that the library desk that dominated the room was an authentic Thomas Chippendale piece. It was a Regency design, but the heads of Egyptian figures on the side and center posts looked exactly like the desk I'd seen on a museum trip to England.

I took a chance and asked Adrian Garner if I was right. At least he had the grace not to look surprised that I knew something about antique furniture, but then he did say, 'Thomas Chippendale the Younger, Miss DeCarlo.'

Lowell Drexel was the one who smiled. 'You're very observant, Miss DeCarlo.'

'I hope so. That *is* my job.'

As with most executive offices these days, there was a sit-ting room arrangement with a couch and several club chairs at the far end of the room. However, I was not invited there. Garner sat behind his Thomas Chippendale the Younger desk. Drexel and Wallingford had been seated in leather armchairs in a semicircle facing him when I was ushered into the office. Now Drexel indicated that I should sit in the chair between them.

Adrian Garner got to the point immediately, something I'm sure he did in his sleep. 'Miss DeCarlo, I did not want to cancel our appointment but you can understand that our decision to close Gem-stone yesterday has accelerated the need to make a number of other decisions which we had been debating.'

Clearly this was not going to be the in-depth interview I'd hoped to have. 'May I ask what kind of other decisions you will be making, Mr. Garner?'

He looked directly at me, and I suddenly had a sense of the formidable power that emanated from Adrian Garner. Charles Wallingford was one hundred times better looking, but Garner was the real dynamic force in this room. I'd felt it at lunch last week, and I felt it again now, only much more intensely.

Garner looked at Lowell Drexel. 'Let me answer that question, Miss DeCarlo,' Drexel said. 'Mr. Garner feels a deep sense of commitment to the thousands of investors who put money in Gen-stone because of Garner

Pharmaceuticals' announced decision to invest a billion dollars in the company. Mr. Garner is under no legal obligation to address their plight, but he has made an offer that we expect will be happily accepted. Garner Pharmaceuticals will give all employees and stockholders ten cents on every dollar they lost through the fraud and theft perpetrated in the company by Nicholas Spencer.'

It was the speech Don Carter had told me to expect, with the slight variation that Garner delegated it to Lowell Drexel for delivery.

Then it was Wallingford's turn: 'The announcement will be made on Monday, Carley. So you will understand if I ask to postpone your visit to my home. At a later date I will enjoy meeting with you, of course.'

At a later date there won't be any story, I thought. You three want to get this story off the table and into the shredder as fast as possible.

I was not about to go gently into that good night. 'Mr. Garner, I'm sure that your company's generosity will be greatly appreciated. Speaking for myself, I gather it will mean that at some point I can expect a check for twenty-five hundred dollars in full compensation for the twenty-five thousand dollars I lost.'

'That's right, Miss DeCarlo,' Drexel said.

I ignored him and stared at Adrian Garner. He stared back at me and nodded affirmatively. Then he did open his mouth: 'If that's all, Miss DeCarlo – '

I interrupted him. 'Mr. Garner, I would like to know for the record if you personally believe that Nicholas Spencer was seen in Switzerland.'

'I never comment "for the record" without factual

knowledge. In this case, as you must know, I have no direct factual knowledge.'

'Did you ever have occasion to meet Nicholas Spencer's assistant, Vivian Powers?'

'No, I did not. My meetings with Nicholas Spencer all took place in this office, not in Pleasantville.'

I turned to Drexel. 'But you sat on the board, Mr. Drexel,' I persisted. 'Vivian Powers was Nicholas Spencer's personal assistant. Surely you must have met her at least once or twice. You'd remember her. She's a very beautiful woman.'

'Miss DeCarlo, every executive I know has at least one confidential assistant, and many of them are attractive. I don't make it a habit of becoming familiar with them.'

'Aren't you even curious as to what happened to her?'

'I understand she attempted suicide. I have heard the rumors that she was romantically involved with Spencer, so perhaps the end of that relationship, whichever way it ended, brought on serious depression. It happens.' He stood up. 'Miss DeCarlo, you'll have to excuse us. We have a meeting in the conference room in less than five minutes.'

I think he would have dragged me out of the chair if I had tried to say another word. Garner did not bother to lift his bottom off the seat when he said briskly, 'Good-bye, Miss DeCarlo.' Wallingford took my hand and said something about my getting together with Lynn soon because she needed cheering up; then Lowell Drexel escorted me from the sanctum sanctorum.

The largest wall of the reception area contained a map of the world that gave testimony to the global impact of Garner Pharmaceuticals. Key countries and locations were symbolized by familiar landmarks: the Twin

Towers, the Eiffel Tower, the Forum, the Taj Mahal, Buckingham Palace. It was exquisite photography and got across the message to anyone who looked at it that Garner Pharmaceuticals was a worldwide powerhouse company.

I stopped to glance at it. 'It's still painful to look at a picture of the Twin Towers. I guess it always will be,' I told Lowell Drexel.

'I agree.'

His hand was under my elbow. 'Get lost' was the message.

There was a picture on the wall by the door of what I took to be the hotshots at Garner Pharmaceuticals. If I had any thought of getting more than a passing glance at it, I wasn't given the opportunity. Nor did I get a chance to pick up some of the giveaway literature stacked on the table there. Drexel propelled me into the corridor and even stood with me to make sure I got on the elevator.

He pressed the button and looked impatient that there wasn't a door opening magically at his touch. Then an elevator arrived. 'Good-bye, Miss DeCarlo.'

'Goodbye, Mr. Drexel.'

It was an express elevator, and I plunged down to the lobby, waited five minutes, then took the same elevator back again.

This time I was in and out of the executive offices of Garner Pharmaceuticals in a matter of seconds. 'I'm so sorry,' I murmured to the receptionist. 'Mr. Garner asked me to be sure to pick up some of your literature on my way out.' I winked at her, girl to girl. 'Don't tell the great man I forgot.'

She was young. 'Promise,' she said solemnly as I scooped up the giveaways.

I wanted to study the picture of the assembled Garner honchos, but I heard Charles Wallingford's voice in the corridor and quickly moved away. This time, however, I didn't go directly to the elevator but instead scurried around the corner and waited.

A minute later I peeked around cautiously to see Wallingford impatiently pressing the button for an elevator. So much for the big meeting in the conference room, Charles, I thought. If there is one going on, you're not invited to it.

It had been, to say the least, an interesting morning.

It was to be an even more interesting evening. In the taxi on the way back to the office, I checked the messages on my cell phone. There was one from Casey. Last night when he came to my apartment, he had felt it was too late to phone Nick Spencer's former in-laws, the Barlowes, in Greenwich. He had already spoken to them this morning, though. They would be home by five o'clock today and he asked if it would be convenient for me to come at that time. 'I'm off this afternoon,' Casey finished. 'If you want, I'll drive you up there. I can have a drink with Vince next door while you're with the Barlowes. Then we'll find a place to have dinner.'

I liked that idea a lot. Some things don't need to be put into words, but I had the feeling the minute I opened the door for Casey last night that everything had changed between us. We both knew where we were heading, and we were both glad to be going there.

I called Casey briefly, confirmed that he'd pick me up at four o'clock, and went back to the office to start to put together a preliminary draft of a profile of Nicholas

Spencer. I had a great idea for a caption: *Victim or Crook?*

I looked at one of the most recent pictures taken of Nick before the plane crash and liked what I saw. It was a close-up and showed a serious and thoughtful expression in his eyes, and a firm, unsmiling mouth. It was the picture of a man who looked deeply concerned but trustworthy.

That was the word: *trustworthy.* I could not see the man who had so impressed me that night at dinner, or who was now looking steadily back into my eyes as I stared at his photograph, lying, cheating, and faking his own death in a plane crash.

That thought opened another avenue of thought that I had accepted without question. The plane crash. I knew that Nick Spencer gave his position to the air controller in Puerto Rico only minutes before communications ceased. Because of the heavy storm, the people who believed he was dead assumed that the plane had been struck by lightning or had been caught in a wind shear. The people who believed he was alive thought he had somehow managed to get out of the plane before the crash, which he had somehow engineered.

Was there another explanation? How well had the plane been maintained? Had Spencer shown any signs of illness before he left? People under stress, even men in their early forties, can have a sudden heart attack.

I picked up the phone. It was time to have a quiet visit with my stepsister, Lynn. I called her and told her I'd like to come by for a talk. 'Just the two of us, Lynn.'

She was on her way out and sounded impatient. 'Carley, I'm spending the weekend in the guest house in Bedford. Would you like to come up on Sunday afternoon? It's quiet there, and we'll have plenty of time to talk.'

# Chapter 41

On the way back to Bedford, Ned stopped and filled up on gas; then he picked up sodas and pretzels, and bread and peanut butter, in a hole-in-the wall convenience store next to the service station. That was the kind of food he liked to eat when he watched television and while Annie puttered around the apartment or the Greenwood Lake house. She wasn't much of a television watcher, except for a couple of shows like *Wheel of Fortune*. She was usually good at figuring out the answers before the contestants did.

'You should write to them. You should go on the program,' he used to tell her. 'You'd win all the prizes.'

'I'd be a big dummy standing there. If I knew all those people were looking at me, I wouldn't be able to say a word.'

'Sure you would.'

'Sure I *wouldn't*.'

Sometimes lately he would just think about her, and it was as if she was speaking to him – for instance, when he was about to put the soda and stuff on the counter, he could hear Annie telling him to get milk and cereal for the morning. 'You need to eat right, Ned,' she said.

He liked it when she scolded him.

She'd been with him when he stopped for gas and food, but the rest of the way back to Bedford, he couldn't see or feel her in the car. He couldn't even see her shadow anymore, but maybe that was because it was dark.

Arriving at the Spencer property, he was careful to make sure that there was no one else on the road before he pulled up to the service gate and pressed in the code. When he had torched the house, he had gloves on so he wouldn't leave fingerprints on the panel. Now it didn't matter. By the time he left here for good, everybody would know who he was and just what he had done.

He parked his car in the service garage, the way he'd planned it. The room had an overhead light, but even though he knew it couldn't be seen from the road, he didn't take a risk turning it on. He'd found a flashlight in the glove compartment of Mrs. Morgan's car he could use, but when he turned off the car's headlights, he found he didn't need it. There was enough moonlight coming in the window to see the piles of furniture. He went to the stack of lounge chairs, lifted the top one off, and put it between the car and the wall with the shelves.

There was a name for this kind of furniture, but it wasn't chair and it wasn't couch. 'What do you call those things, Annie?' he asked.

'Divan.'

In his head he could hear her saying it.

The long cushions were on the top shelf, and it was a struggle to flip one of them down. It was heavy and thick, but when it was in place on the divan, he tested it. It felt as good as his chair in the apartment. He wasn't ready to go to bed yet, however, so he opened the bottle of scotch.

When he finally got sleepy, it was chilly, so he opened the trunk, unwrapped the blanket from the rifle, picked up the rifle, and laid it down again. It made him feel good to have the rifle next to him, and he shared the blanket with it.

He knew he was safe there, so he could let himself fall asleep. 'You need to sleep, Ned,' Annie was whispering.

When he woke up, he could tell from the shadows that it was late afternoon; he'd slept all day. He got up and walked to the right side of the garage and opened the door to the closetlike space that held a sink and toilet.

There was a mirror over the sink. Ned looked at himself and saw his red-rimmed eyes and the stubble on his face. He'd shaved not even a day ago, and already his beard was growing in. He had loosened his tie and the top button of his shirt before he lay down last night, but he probably should have taken them off. They looked kind of wrinkled and messy now.

But what difference did it make? he asked himself.

He splashed cold water on his face and looked at the mirror again. The image was blurry. Instead of his face he was seeing Peg's eyes and Mrs. Morgan's eyes, wide and staring and scared; like when they had realized what was going to happen to them.

Then images of Mrs. Schafley and the Harniks started to slither around inside the mirror as well. Their eyes were scared, too. They knew something was going to happen to them. They could tell he was coming after them.

It was too early to drive to Greenwood Lake. In fact, he

decided he shouldn't leave the garage until ten o'clock – that would mean he'd get there about quarter past eleven. Last night it wasn't smart when he kept driving around the same mile or two, waiting for the Harnicks to get home. The cops might have noticed.

The soda wasn't cold anymore, but he didn't care. The pretzels were filling enough. He didn't even need the bread and peanut butter, or the cereal. He turned on the car radio and found the news. On both the nine o'clock and the nine-thirty editions, there was nothing about a nosy landlady in Yonkers being found shot dead. The cops had probably rung her bell, saw her car was missing, and thought she was out visiting, Ned decided.

Tomorrow they might get more nosy, though. Also, tomorrow her son might start wondering why he hadn't heard from her. But that would be tomorrow.

At a quarter of ten Ned raised the garage door. It was cool outside, but it was the nice kind of cool that comes after a day that had a lot of sunshine. He decided to stretch his legs for a few minutes.

He walked along the path through the woods until he emerged into the English garden. The pool was beyond it.

Suddenly he stopped. What was that? he wondered.

The shades were pulled down in the guest house, but light was coming from underneath them. There was somebody in the house.

It couldn't be the people who worked here, he thought. They would have tried to put their car in the garage. Keeping in the shadows, he passed the pool, went around the row of evergreens, and inched his way toward the guest house. He could see that one of the shades on a side window was raised a little bit. Keeping as silent as he had when he used to wait in the woods for the squirrels, he edged up to that window and bent down.

Inside he could see Lynn Spencer sitting on the couch, a drink in her hand. The same guy he had seen running down the driveway that night was sitting opposite her. He couldn't hear what they were saying; but from the expressions on their faces, Ned could see that they were worried about something.

If they had looked happy, he would have gone right back for his rifle and finished them off right there, tonight. But he liked the fact that they looked worried. He wished he could hear what they were saying to each other.

Lynn looked as if she was planning to stay there awhile. She was wearing slacks and a sweater, the kind of country clothes that rich people wore. 'Casually dressed' – that was the expression. Annie used to read about 'casual' clothes and laugh: 'My clothes are *real* casual, Ned. I have casual uniforms to carry trays. I have casual jeans and T-shirts for when I clean. And when I dig in the garden, I have nothing *but* casual clothes.'

That thought made him sad again. After the house in Greenwood Lake was gone, Annie threw her gardening gloves and tools into the garbage. She wouldn't listen when he kept promising that he'd get her a new house. She had just kept on crying.

Ned turned from the window. It was late. Lynn Spencer wasn't going home. She would be here tomorrow. He was sure of it. It was time to go to Greenwood Lake and take care of tonight's business.

The garage door didn't make a sound when he opened it, and the gate at the service entrance opened noiselessly.

The people in the guest house had no idea he had been there.

When he returned three hours later, he put the car away, locked the garage, and lay down on the divan, his rifle next to him. The rifle carried the smell of burned powder, a nice smell almost like smoke from a fireplace when there is a fire blazing. He put his arm around the rifle, pulled the blanket up, and tucked it around him and the rifle, cuddling until he felt safe and warm.

# Chapter 42

Reid and Susan Barlowe lived in a Federal-style white brick house, situated on a lovely piece of property that borders Long Island Sound. Casey drove up the circular driveway and dropped me off in front of the house at exactly five o'clock. He was going next door to visit his friend, Vince Alcott, while I was talking to the Barlowes. I was to walk over there when I was finished.

Reid Barlowe opened the door for me and greeted me courteously, then said that his wife was in the sunroom. 'It's a pleasant view looking over the water,' he explained as I followed him down the center hallway.

As we walked in, Susan Barlowe was setting a tray on the coffee table with a pitcher of ice tea and three tall glasses. We introduced ourselves, and I asked them to call me Carley. I was surprised that they were so young – surely not more than their late fifties. His hair was salt and pepper, hers still a dark blond sprinkled with gray. They were a handsome tallish couple, both on the thin side, with attractive features dominated by their eyes. His were brown, hers, a bluish gray, but both held a kind of lingering sadness. I wondered if the remnants of grief I saw there were for their daughter who died eight years ago, or for their former son-in-law, Nicholas Spencer.

The sunroom was well named. The afternoon sun was filtering in, brightening even more the yellow flower pattern on the upholstery of the wicker couch and chairs. White oak walls and floors, and a low planter that ran along the floor-to-ceiling windows, completed the sense of having brought the outdoors inside.

They insisted I sit on the couch that offered a panoramic view of Long Island Sound. The two nearest armchairs formed a conversational group, and they settled in them. I was happy to accept a glass of ice tea, and for a moment we sat quietly, taking each other's measure.

I thanked them for letting me come and apologized in advance for asking any questions that might seem either prying or insensitive.

For a moment I thought I was going to have a problem. They exchanged glances, after which Reid Barlowe got up and closed the door to the foyer.

'Just in case Jack comes in and we don't hear him, I'd prefer that he not pick up scraps of our conversation,' he said when he sat down again.

'It's not that Jack would deliberately eavesdrop,' Susan Barlowe said hastily, 'it's that he's so bewildered, poor kid. He adored Nick. He was grieving for him and handling it pretty well, and then all those stories broke. Now he wants to believe he's alive, but that's a double-edged sword because that brings up the question of why Nick hasn't contacted him.'

I decided to start from square one. 'You know that Lynn Spencer and I are stepsisters,' I said.

They both nodded. I could swear that a look of disdain came over their faces at the sound of her name, but then maybe I thought I saw it because I was anticipating it.

'In truth, I have met Lynn only a few times. I am neither her advocate nor her detractor,' I said. 'I'm here as a journalist to learn everything I can of your perception of Nick Spencer.' I eased my way into discussing how I first met Nick, and I described my own impression.

We talked for well over an hour. It was obvious that they loved Nicholas Spencer. The six years he'd been married to their daughter Janet had been ideal. The diagnosis that she had cancer had come at the very time he planned to fold his medical supply company into a research pharmaceutical firm.

'When Nick knew that Janet was sick and her chances weren't good, he became almost obsessed,' Susan Barlowe said, her voice almost a whisper.

She reached in her pocket for her sunglasses, saying something about the sun getting quite strong. I think she didn't want me to see the tears that she was struggling to hold back. 'Nick's father had been trying to develop a cancer vaccine,' she continued. 'I'm sure you know that. Nick had taken his father's later notes and had begun to study them. By then his own great interest in microbiology had made him very knowledgeable. He felt that his father had been on the verge of a cure and decided to raise the money to fund Gen-stone.'

'You invested in Gen-stone?'

'Yes, we did.' It was Reid Barlowe who answered. 'And I would do it again. Whatever went wrong, it was not because Nick set out to cheat us or anyone else.'

'After your daughter died, did you stay close to Nick?'

'Absolutely. If there was any strain, it began to appear after he and Lynn were married.' Reid Barlowe's lips tensed into a narrow line. 'I swear to you that Lynn's physical resemblance to Janet was the compelling factor in his attraction to her. The first time he brought her up here was like a body blow for my wife and me. And it wasn't good for Jack, either.'

'Jack was six then?'

'Yes, and he had a very clear memory of his mother. After Lynn and Nick were married, and Jack would come up here to visit, he became more and more reluctant to go home. Finally Nick suggested that we enroll him in school here.'

'Why didn't Nick just split with Lynn?' I asked.

'I think eventually it would have come to that,' Susan Barlowe said, 'but Nick was so involved with developing the vaccine that concerns about his marriage – or lack of one – were put on hold. For a while he became terribly worried about Jack, but once Jack started living with us and was obviously happier, Nick concentrated only on Gen-stone.'

'Did you ever meet Vivian Powers?'

'No, we did not,' Reid Barlowe said. 'Of course, we've read about her, but Nick never mentioned her to us.'

'Did Nick ever indicate that he felt there was a problem at Gen-stone that went beyond the fact that many promising drugs fail in the final stages of testing?'

'For the last year there is no doubt that Nick was seriously troubled.' Reid Barlowe looked at his wife, and she nodded. 'He confided to me that he had been borrowing against his shares of Gen-stone because he felt further research was needed.'

'Borrowing against *his* shares, not against company funds?' I asked quickly.

'Yes. We are financially secure, Miss DeCarlo, and the month before his plane crashed, Nick asked if he could arrange a personal loan for further necessary research.'

'Did you give it to him?'

'Yes, I did. I will not tell you how much, but that is why I believe that if Nick took all that money from the company, it was because he was spending it on research and *not* because he planned to put it into his own pocket.'

'Do you believe he is dead?'

'Yes, I do. Nick was not a dissembler, and he never would have abandoned his son.' Reid Barlowe held up a warning hand. 'I think Jack just came in. He was being dropped off after soccer practice.'

I heard feet running down the hall, then stopping at the closed door. The boy looked in through the French windowpanes, then raised his hand to knock. Reid Barlowe waved him in and jumped up to hug him.

He was a skinny kid with spikey hair and enormous gray-blue eyes. When we were introduced, his wide grin for his grandparents became a shy, sweet smile for me. 'I'm very pleased to meet you, Miss DeCarlo,' he said.

I felt a lump in my throat. I could remember Nick Spencer saying, 'Jack's a great kid.' He was right. You could tell he was a great kid. And he was the age my Patrick would be now if he had lived.

'Gran, Bobby and Peter asked me to stay overnight with them. Is that okay? They're having pizza. Their mom says she really wants me to.'

The Barlowes looked at each other. 'If you guys promise not to stay up too late fooling around,' Susan Barlowe said. 'Don't forget, you have early practice tomorrow.'

'I really, *really* promise,' he said earnestly. 'Thanks, Gran. I told them I'd call right away if you said yes.' He turned to me. 'It was very nice to meet you, Miss DeCarlo.'

He walked quietly as far as the door, but once he was in the hall, I could hear him begin to run. I looked at his grandparents. Both of them were smiling now. Reid Barlowe shrugged. 'As you can see, it's the second time around for us, Carley. The joke is that Bobby and Peter are twins, but their parents are only a couple of years younger than we are.'

There was an observation I felt I had to make. 'Despite everything that has happened to him, Jack appears to be a well-adjusted kid, which certainly is a tribute to both of you.'

'He has really down days, of course,' Reid Barlowe said quietly. 'But how could he not? He was very close to Nick. It is the uncertainty of everything that could destroy him. He's a smart kid. Nick's picture and the stories about him have been all over the newspapers and television. One day Jack's trying to cope with his father's death, the next he hears he's been seen in Switzerland. Then he starts to fantasize that Nick might have parachuted out of the plane before it crashed.'

We talked for a few minutes more, and then I got up to leave. 'You've been very kind,' I said, 'and I promise that when I see you on Sunday, I'll simply be another dinner guest, not a journalist.'

'I'm glad we had this time to talk quietly,' Susan Barlowe said. 'We felt it absolutely necessary that our position be known publicly. Nicholas Spencer was an honest man and a dedicated scientist.' She hesitated. 'Yes, I'll call him a scientist, even though he didn't have a Ph.D. in microbiology. Whatever went wrong in Gen-stone was *not* his fault.'

They both walked with me to the front door. As Reid Barlowe opened it, his wife said, 'Carley, I just realized, I haven't even asked about Lynn. Is she fully recovered yet?'

'Just about.'

'I should have contacted her. Truthfully, I resented her from the beginning, but I shall always be grateful to her. Did she tell you that Nick was planning to take Jack with him on the trip to Puerto Rico, and she was the one who persuaded him to change his plans? Jack was so terribly disappointed at the time, but if he had been with Nick that day, he would have been on the plane when it crashed.'

# Chapter 43

I liked Casey's friends, Vince and Julie Alcott, immediately. Vince and Casey had been in class together at Johns Hopkins Medical School. 'How Julie and I had the nerve to get married when I was still in school, I'll never know,' Vince said with a laugh. 'I can't believe we're coming up on the tenth anniversary this Sunday.'

I joined them in a glass of wine. They tactfully stayed away from asking me about my visit next door. All I said about it was how nice the Barlowes were and how much I enjoyed meeting Jack.

I think Casey realized, however, that I was terribly troubled because after a few minutes he stood up. 'Speed the parting guest,' he said. 'I know Carley has work to do on her column, and we're looking forward to coming back on Sunday.'

We drove back to Manhattan in almost total silence. But at a quarter past seven, as we got close to midtown, he said, 'You do have to eat, Carley. What do you feel like having?'

Although I hadn't thought about it, I realized suddenly that I was starving. 'A hamburger. Is that okay?'

P. J. Clarke's, the famous old New York restaurant on Third Avenue, had recently reopened after a total overhaul. We stopped there. After we ordered, Casey said, 'You're really upset, Carley. Want to talk about it?'

'Not yet,' I said. 'It's still kind of spinning around in my mind.'

'Did meeting Jack get to you?'

Casey's voice was gentle. He knows how seeing a boy the age Patrick would have been stabs me in the heart.

'Yes and no. He's a really nice kid.' When our hamburgers arrived, I said, 'Maybe it's better if we *do* talk it out. You see, the problem is that I'm adding two and two, and where that's leading me is pretty bad and a little frightening.'

# Chapter 44

On Saturday morning Ned turned on the car radio. The seven o'clock news was just coming on. As he listened, he began to smile. In Greenwood Lake, New Jersey, three longtime residents had been shot dead while they slept. The police said that their deaths were believed to be connected to the shooting death of Mrs. Elva Morgan of Yonkers, New York. Her tenant, Ned Cooper, had formerly owned a home in Greenwood Lake and was known to have recently threatened the victims there. The report went on to say that Cooper was also a suspect in the death of Peg Rice, the drugstore clerk who had been shot four nights ago. Ballistic tests were being conducted. Cooper was thought to be driving either an eight-year-old brown Ford van or a recent-model black Toyota. He should be considered armed and dangerous.

That's what I am, Ned thought: armed and dangerous. Should he go over to the guest house now and finish off Lynn Spencer and her boyfriend, if he was still around? he wondered. No, maybe not. He was safe here. Maybe he'd wait. He still had to figure out a way to get to Spencer's stepsister, Carley DeCarlo.

Then Annie and he could both rest, and it would be all over, except for the final thing, when he took off his shoes and socks and lay down on Annie's grave and held his rifle close.

There was a song Annie liked to hum, 'Save the last dance for me . . .'

Ned got the bread and peanut butter out of the car, and as he made a sandwich he began to hum that song. Then he smiled as Annie joined in:

'Save . . . the last . . . dance . . . for me.'

# Chapter 45

On Saturday morning I slept until eight o'clock, and when I woke up, I felt better in the sense that it had been a busy and emotional week and I had needed the rest. My head felt clear, too, but that wasn't helping me feel any better about all that I had learned. I was coming to a conclusion that, with all my heart, I wanted to be wrong.

As I was making coffee, I turned on the television to catch the news and heard the headline about the shooting spree that had left five people dead in the last few days.

Then I heard the word 'Gen-stone,' and listened with growing horror to the details of the tragedy. I heard how Ned Cooper, a resident of Yonkers, had sold his home in Greenwood Lake without his wife's knowledge and then invested the money in Gen-stone. I learned that she had died in an accident the day they learned the stock was worthless.

A picture of Cooper flashed on the screen. I *know* him, I thought; I *know* him! I've seen him somewhere recently.

Was it at the stockholders' meeting? I wondered. It was possible, but I wasn't sure.

The announcer said that Cooper's late wife had worked at St. Ann's Hospital in Mount Kisco and that he had been treated for psychiatric problems in the clinic there on and off for years.

St. Ann's Hospital. *That's* where I saw him! But *when?* I was at St. Ann's three times: the day after the fire, a few days later, and when I spoke to the director of the hospice wing.

The roped-off crime scene in Greenwood Lake flashed onto the screen. 'Cooper's house was located between the homes of the Harniks and Mrs. Schafley,' the announcer was saying. 'According to neighbors he was here two days ago and accused the victims of conniving to get rid of him, knowing that his wife would not have allowed him to sell the house if they had notified her of his plans.'

The crime scene in Yonkers was next. 'Elva Morgan's son tearfully told police that his mother had said she was afraid of Ned Cooper, and she had told him he would have to vacate the apartment by June 1.'

Throughout the broadcast Cooper's picture was inset in a corner of the screen. I kept studying it. *When* did I see him at St. Ann's? I wondered.

The TV anchor continued, 'Three nights ago Cooper was the next-to-last customer in Brown's drugstore before it closed. According to William Garret, a college student who was behind him at the register, Cooper had purchased a number of salves and ointments for his burned right hand, and became agitated when the clerk, Peg Rice, inquired about it. Garret is positive that Cooper was sitting outside in his car when Garret left the store at precisely ten o'clock.'

*His burned right hand! Cooper had a burned right hand!*

I saw Lynn in the hospital the first time the day after the fire. I was interviewed by a reporter from Channel 4, I thought. That's where I saw Cooper. He was standing outside watching me. I'm sure of it.

*His burned right hand!*

Something told me I had seen him another time as well, but figuring that out wasn't important now. I knew Judy Miller, one of the producers at Channel 4, and phoned her. 'Judy, I believe I remember seeing Ned Cooper outside St. Ann's Hospital the day after the Spencer mansion was torched,' I told her. 'Would you still have outtakes of the segment of my interview on April 22? Cooper might just happen to be in it.'

I then called the Westchester County District Attorney's Office and asked to be connected to Detective Crest in the arson squad. When I told him why I called, he said, 'We did check St. Ann's emergency room, and Cooper didn't get treated there, but he was well known in the hospital. Maybe he didn't go through the emergency room. We'll let you know what we find out, Carley.'

I kept switching from channel to channel, picking up varying information about Cooper and his wife, Annie. She was reported to have been heartbroken when he sold their house in Greenwood Lake. I wondered how much the news that Gen-stone was worthless had contributed to her accident. Was it just coincidence that the announcement of the stocks being worthless came out the day of her death?

At nine-thirty, Judy called me back. 'You were right, Carley. We have Ned Cooper on camera outside the hospital the day we interviewed you.'

At ten o'clock, Detective Crest called back. 'Dr. Ryan at St. Ann's saw Cooper in the lobby on Tuesday morning, the twenty-second, and noticed a serious burn on his hand. Cooper claimed he burned it on the stove. Dr. Ryan gave him a prescription.'

I was feeling heartsick for Cooper's victims, but at the same time I felt sorry for Cooper himself. In their own tragic way he and his wife had been victims of the Genstone failure, too.

But there was someone else who, at least in one way, might not be victimized any further. 'Marty Bikorsky absolutely did not set the fire at the Spencer mansion,' I told Detective Crest.

'Off the record, we're reopening the investigation,' he told me. 'There'll be an announcement later on this morning.'

'Say it *on* the record,' I snapped. 'Why not say it straight out – Martin Bikorsky did not set that fire.'

Next I called Marty. He had been watching the report on television and talking to his lawyer. I could hear the hope and excitement in his voice. 'Carley, this nut has a burn on his hand. If nothing else, I'll get reasonable doubt at my trial. My lawyer says so. Oh, God, Carley, do you know what this means?'

'Yes, I do.'

'You've been so great, but I have to tell you that I'm glad I didn't take your advice to admit to the cops that I was in Bedford the night of the fire. My lawyer still thinks I'd have handed them a conviction if I'd placed myself there.'

'I'm glad you didn't, too, Marty,' I said. What I didn't tell him was that my reason for not disclosing his presence in front of the mansion that night was different from *his* reason. I wanted to have my talk with Lynn before the subject of the car parked inside the gate became known.

We agreed to keep in close touch, and then I asked the question that I was afraid to ask: 'How is Maggie doing?'

'She's eating better, and that gives her some energy. Who knows, we might even have her with us a little longer than the doctors said. We just keep praying for a miracle. You be sure to pray for her, too.'

'You bet I will, Marty.'

'Because maybe if she can hang on long enough, there will be a cure someday.'

'I believe that, Marty.'

When I hung up the phone, I walked to the window and looked out. I don't have a great view from my apartment. I just look out at the row of converted town houses across the street, but I wasn't seeing them anyhow. My mind was filled with the image of four-year-old Maggie and the terrible thought that for their own greedy motives some people might have deliberately slowed down the development of the cancer vaccine.

# Chapter 46

Every hour or so on Saturday, Ned listened to the news on the car radio. He was glad that Annie had made him buy the groceries the other night. It wouldn't have been safe to go to a store now. He was sure his picture was being shown on television and over the Internet.

*Armed and dangerous.* That's what they said.

Sometimes after dinner Annie would stretch out on the couch and fall asleep, and he'd go over and hug her. She'd wake up and look startled for a minute. Then she'd laugh and say, 'Ned, you're dangerous.'

But that was different from now.

Without refrigeration the milk had gone sour, but he didn't mind eating the cereal dry. Ever since he shot Peg, his appetite had been coming back. It was as if a big stone inside him had started to dissolve. If he hadn't had the cereal and the bread and the peanut butter, he would have gone over to the guest house and killed Lynn Spencer and taken food from her kitchen. He could even have driven her car out of here, and no one would have been the wiser.

But then if her boyfriend came back and found her, they'd know her car was missing. The cops would be on the lookout for it everywhere. It was flashy and cost a lot of money. It would be easy to spot.

'Wait, Ned,' Annie was saying to him. 'Rest for a while. There's no hurry.'

'I know,' he whispered.

At three o'clock, after he'd been dozing on and off for a couple of hours, he decided to go outside. There was little room to walk around in the garage, and his legs and neck felt cramped. The garage had a door on the side next to the car. He opened it very slowly and listened for the sound of anyone outside. But it was all right. There was no one around this part of the property. He would have bet that Lynn Spencer never walked over here anyhow. But just in case he ran into any trouble, he carried his rifle with him.

He went around the back of the pool house as far as the trees that screened the pool from the guest cottage. Now that all the leaves were out, no one in the guest cottage could see him even if they were looking that way.

He could see the cottage, though, by looking through the branches. The shades in the guest house were up, and a couple of the windows were open. Spencer's silver convertible was in the driveway. The top was down. Ned sat on the ground with his legs crossed. It felt a little damp, but he didn't mind.

Because time didn't mean anything to him, he wasn't sure how long he had been there when the door to the house opened and Lynn Spencer came out. As Ned watched, she pulled the door closed and walked to the car.

She was wearing black slacks and a black and white blouse. She looked dressed up. Maybe she was meeting someone for a drink and dinner. She got into the car and started the engine. The car was so quiet that it hardly made a sound as it started, then went around the side of what was left of the mansion.

Ned waited three or four minutes until he was sure she was gone, then he moved quickly across the open space and to the side of the house. He walked from window to window. All the shades were up, and as far as he could see, the house was empty. He tried to open the windows on the side, but they were locked. If he was going inside, he had to take a chance and go in through a front window where anyone who happened to come up the driveway would see him.

He took time to rub the bottom of his shoes back and forth on the driveway so he wouldn't leave any dirt on the windowsill or inside the house. Then, in one quick move, he shoved up the left front window and, propping his rifle against the house, hoisted himself up. When he got one leg over the sill, he reached for his rifle and, once inside, lowered the window back to just the spot it had been when he opened it.

He checked to make sure there was no dirt on the windowsill or that his shoes didn't make any marks on the floor or carpets. He did a quick search of the house. The two bedrooms upstairs were empty. He was definitely alone, but he knew he couldn't count on Lynn Spencer staying out long even though she was dressed up when she left. She could even have forgotten something and come back in a minute.

He was in the kitchen when the sharp peal of the phone

made him clutch the rifle and press his finger on the trigger. The phone rang three times before the answering machine on the counter picked it up. Ned opened and closed cabinet drawers as he heard the recorded message. Then he heard a woman's voice saying, 'Lynn, this is Carley. I'll be doing a draft of the story tonight and wanted to ask you a quick question. I'll try you again later. If I don't reach you, I'll see you tomorrow at three in Bedford. If you've changed your plans and are coming back to New York early, give me a call. My cell phone number is 917-555-8420.'

Carley DeCarlo was coming here tomorrow, Ned thought. That was why Annie had told him to wait and to rest today. Tomorrow it would be all over. 'Thank you, Annie,' Ned said. He decided he should get back to the garage, but first there was something he had to find.

Most people kept an extra set of keys around the house, he thought.

Finally he found them, in almost the last drawer he opened. They were in an envelope. He knew they'd be there somewhere. Each of the housekeepers probably had a key to this house. There were two sets of keys in two different envelopes. One envelope was marked 'Guest House,' the other, 'Pool House.' He didn't care about the pool house, so he left that, taking just one set of the house keys.

He opened the back door and made sure that one of the keys fit into the lock. There were only a couple of things more that he wanted before he went back to the garage. There were six cans of Coca-Cola and club soda, and six bottles of water in the refrigerator, lined up two by two. He wanted to take those, but he knew the Spencer woman would notice if any were missing. But he found that one of the overhead cabinets had boxes of crackers, bags of potato chips and pretzels, and cans of nuts – he didn't think she'd miss one of those.

The liquor cabinet was full as well. There were four bottles of unopened scotch alone. Ned took one of them from the back. You couldn't even tell it was missing unless you pulled the drawer out all the way. They were all the same brand, too.

By then he felt as if he'd been inside the house a long time, even though it really had been only a few minutes. Still, he took the time to do one more thing. Just in case there was anyone in the kitchen when he came back, he'd leave a side window unlocked in the room with the television.

As he hurried down the hall, Ned's eyes darted from the floor to the staircase to be sure there wasn't a single mark from his shoes anywhere. As Annie used to say, 'You can be neat when you want to be, Ned.'

When the window in the study was unlocked, he took long strides to the kitchen, then with the bottle of scotch and box of crackers under his arm, he opened the back door. Before he closed it behind him, he looked back. The blinking red light of the answering machine caught his eye. 'I'll see you tomorrow, Carley,' he said quietly.

# Chapter 47

I kept the volume on the television on low all morning, turning it up only when I heard new information about Ned Cooper or his victims. There was a particularly poignant segment about his wife, Annie. Several of her coworkers at the hospital spoke about how they remembered her energy, her sweetness with the patients, her willingness to work overtime when she was needed.

With increasing pity I watched as her story evolved. She had carried trays all day, five or six days a week, and then went home to a rented apartment in a shabby neighborhood where she lived with an emotionally disturbed husband. The one great joy in her life seems to have been her home in Greenwood Lake. One nurse talked about that. 'Annie couldn't wait to get to start her garden in the spring,' she said. 'She'd bring in pictures of it, and every year it was different and beautiful. We used to tease her that she was wasting her time here. We told her she should be working in a greenhouse.'

She had never told anyone at the hospital that Ned sold the house. But a neighbor who was interviewed said that Ned had bragged about owning Gen-stone stock and had said that he was going to be able to buy Annie a mansion like the one the Gen-stone boss had in Bedford.

That comment sent me scurrying to the phone to call Judy again and ask her to send me a copy of that interview, as well as one of my own. It provided one more direct link between Ned Cooper and the Bedford fire.

I kept thinking of Annie as I e-mailed my column to the magazine. I was certain that the police were checking the libraries, showing Ned Cooper's picture, to see if he was the one who had sent me the e-mails. If so, he had placed himself at the scene of the fire. I decided to call Detective Clifford at the Bedford police station. He was the one I had spoken to last week about the e-mails.

'I was just about to call you, Miss DeCarlo,' he said. 'The librarians have confirmed that Ned Cooper was the man who used their computers, and we're taking very seriously the message he sent you about preparing yourself for judgment day. In one of the other two he said something about your not answering his wife's question in your column, so we think he might be getting fixated on you.'

Needless to say, it wasn't a pleasant thought.

'Maybe you should request police protection until we get this guy,' Detective Clifford suggested, 'although I can tell you that a black Toyota with a man who might have been Cooper was seen an hour ago by a truck driver at a rest stop in Massachusetts. He's sure the car had a New York plate even though he couldn't get the numbers, so it may turn out to be a good lead.'

'I don't need protection,' I said quickly. 'Ned Cooper

doesn't know where I live, and anyhow, I'm going to be out most of the day today and tomorrow.'

'Just to be on the safe side, we phoned Mrs. Spencer in New York, and she called back. She's staying up here in the guest house until we catch him. We told her that it's unlikely that Cooper would come back here, but nonetheless we're keeping an eye on the roads near her property.'

He promised to call me if he heard any further definite news about Cooper.

I had brought my thick file on Nick Spencer home from the office for the weekend, and as soon as I was off the phone, I got it out. What I was interested in this time were the reports about the plane crash, ranging from the first headlines to the brief follow-up references in the articles about the stock and the vaccine.

I highlighted as I read. The accounts were straightforward. On Friday, April 4, at 2 p.m., Nicholas Spencer, a seasoned pilot, had taken off in his private plane from Westchester County Airport, destined for San Juan, Puerto Rico. He planned to attend a weekend business seminar there, returning late Sunday afternoon. The weather forecast was for moderate rainfall in the San Juan area. His wife had dropped him off at the airport

Fifteen minutes before he was to land in San Juan, Spencer's plane disappeared from the radar screen. There had been no indication that he was having a problem, but the rainfall had developed into a heavy storm, with considerable lightning in the area. The speculation was that the plane had been hit by lightning. The next day, bits of wreckage from his plane began to wash ashore.

The name of the mechanic who had serviced the plane

just before takeoff was Dominick Salvio. After the accident he said that Nicholas Spencer was a skillful pilot who had flown under severe weather conditions before but that a direct lightning strike could have sent the plane into a spin.

After the scandal broke, questions about the flight began to surface in the newspaper accounts. Why hadn't Spencer used the Gen-stone company plane, which he normally did on company-related trips? Why had the number of calls made and received on his cell phone decreased so drastically in the weeks before the crash? Then, when his body was not recovered, the questions changed. Had the crash been staged? Had he actually been on the plane when it went down? He always drove his own car to the airport. On the day he left for Puerto Rico, he had asked his wife to drop him off at the airport. Why?

I called the Westchester airport. Dominick Salvio was at work, and I was put through to him and learned that he would be finished work at two o'clock. He reluctantly agreed to meet me for fifteen minutes in the terminal.

'Fifteen minutes only, Miss DeCarlo,' he said. 'My kid has a little league game today, and I want to see it.'

I looked at the clock. It was eleven forty-five, and I was still in my robe. One of the great luxuries to me on Saturday mornings, even if I'm working at my desk, is not having to rush to shower and dress. But now it was time to get moving. I had no idea how much traffic I might encounter and wanted to leave myself a full hour and a half to get to the Westchester airport.

Fifteen minutes later, thanks to the noise of the blow-dryer, I almost didn't hear the phone, but then I ran to get it. It was Ken Page. 'I found our cancer patient, Carley,' he said.

'Who is he?'

'Dennis Holden, a thirty-eight-year-old engineer who lives in Armonk.'

'How is he doing?'

'He wouldn't say over the phone. He was very reluctant to even talk to me, but I persuaded him, and he finally invited me to come to his house.'

'What about me?' I asked. 'Ken, you promised –'

'Hold it. It took a bit of doing, but you're in. He's willing to see you, too. We have our choice: today or tomorrow at three o'clock. That's not much notice, so does either work for you? I can make whichever works best for you. I have to call him right back.'

Tomorrow I was scheduled to see Lynn at three o'clock, and I didn't want to change that. 'Today is perfect,' I told Ken.

'I'm sure you've been watching the news about that Cooper guy. Five people dead because the Gen-stone stock tanked.'

'Six,' I corrected. 'His wife was a victim, too.'

'Yes, you're right, she was. Okay, I'll call Holden, tell him we're on for later, get directions, and get right back to you.'

Ken called back a few minutes later. I took down Dennis Holden's address and phone number, finished drying my hair, put on a quick touch of makeup, chose a steel blue pantsuit – another of my end-of-the-season sales purchases from last summer – and took off.

Given all that I had learned about Ned Cooper, I looked around very carefully as I opened the outer door. These old brownstones have high, fairly narrow stoops, which means that if anyone wanted to take aim, I'd make a pretty easy target. But the traffic was moving fast. There were a fair number of people walking on the sidewalk outside my building, and I couldn't see anyone sitting in the parked cars near the house. It looked safe enough.

Even so, I ran down the stairs and walked quickly to my garage, three blocks away. As I walked, I wove in and out of the people who were just sauntering along, and all the time I had a feeling of guilt about it. If Ned Cooper *did* have me in his sights, I was exposing these others to danger.

Westchester County Airport is situated at the border of Greenwich, the town I'd visited less than twenty-four hours ago, and where I would be returning tomorrow with Casey, for dinner with his friends. I knew the airport had started out as a sleepy airfield created primarily for the convenience of the wealthy residents in the surrounding area. Now, however, it was a major terminal and the preferred choice of thousands of travelers, including those not necessarily counted among the well-heeled.

Dominick Salvio met me in the terminal lobby at 2:04. He was a large-framed man with confident brown eyes and an easy smile. He had about him the comfortable air of a guy who knew exactly who he was and where he was going. I gave him my card and explained that I went by the name of Carley, and he said, 'Marcia DeCarlo and Dominick Salvio turn into Carley and Sal. You figure.'

Since I knew the timer was clicking away, I didn't waste a minute getting to the point. I was absolutely frank with him. I told him that I was doing the story and that I had met Nick Spencer. Then I briefly explained my relationship to Lynn. I said that I did not and would not believe that Nick Spencer had survived the crash and was now hiding away in Switzerland, thumbing his nose at the world.

At that moment Carley and Sal bonded. 'Nick Spencer was a prince,' Sal said emphatically. 'They don't come any better than that guy. I'd like to get my hands on all those liars who are making him out to be a crook. I'd wrap their tongues around their feet.'

'We're agreed,' I said, 'but what I need to know from you, Sal, is how Nick seemed when he got on the plane that day. You know he was only forty-two years old, but everything I uncover about him, especially the things that happened in those last months, seems to suggest that he was under a tremendous amount of stress. Even men as young as he get heart attacks, the kind that kill you before you have a chance to react in any way.'

'I hear you,' he said, 'and it's possible that's what happened. What gets me mad is that they act as if Nick Spencer was an amateur-night-in-Bridgeport kind of pilot. He was good, damn good, and he was smart. He'd flown in plenty of storms and knew how to handle them – unless he did get slammed with lightning, and that's tough for anyone to handle.'

'Did you see or speak to him before he took off that day?'

'I always service his plane myself. I saw him.'

'I know Lynn dropped him off. Did you see her?'

'I saw her. They were sitting at a table in that coffee shop nearest to where the private planes are kept. Then she walked him to the plane.'

'Did they seem affectionate with each other?' I hesitated, then said bluntly, 'Sal, it's important to know Nick Spencer's state of mind. If he was distressed or distracted because of something that had happened between them, it could have had a bearing on his physical condition or his concentration.'

Sal looked past me. I sensed he was weighing his words, not so much to be cautious as to be honest. He looked at his watch. My allotted time with him was going by too quickly.

Finally he said, 'Carley, those two people were never happy together, I can tell you that.'

'Was there anything special about their behavior that day?' I persisted.

'Why don't you talk to Marge? She's the waitress in the coffee shop who waited on them.'

'Is she here today?'

'She works long weekends, Friday through Monday. She's there now.'

Taking my arm, Sal walked with me through the terminal to that coffee shop. 'That's Marge,' he said, pointing to a matronly looking woman in her sixties. He caught her eye, and she came over to us, smiling.

The smile vanished when Sal told her why we were there.

'Mr. Spencer was the nicest man,' she said, 'and his first wife was a lovely person. But that other one was one cold fish. She must have really upset him that day. I will say for her that she was apologizing, but I could tell that he was mad clean through. I couldn't hear all of what they were saying, but it was something about how she had changed her mind about going to Puerto Rico with him, and he said if he'd known sooner, he would have taken Jack. Jack is Mr. Spencer's son.'

'Did they eat or drink anything?' I asked.

'They both had ice tea. Listen, it's a good thing that neither she nor Jack was on that plane. It's just a damn shame that Mr. Spencer wasn't that lucky.'

I thanked Marge and walked back through the terminal with Sal. 'She gave him a big kiss in front of everybody when she left him,' he said. 'I had figured that at least the poor guy might have been feeling good about his marriage, but then Marge tells me what she just told you. So maybe he was upset, and maybe that did affect his judgment. That can happen to the best of pilots. I guess we'll never know.'

# Chapter 48

I got to Armonk early and sat in the car outside Dennis Holden's house, waiting for Ken Page to arrive. Then, almost like an automaton, I called Lynn at the Bedford number. I wanted to ask her point-blank why she had talked Nick Spencer out of taking his son with him to Puerto Rico, then backed off from going herself. Had someone hinted to her that it wasn't smart to get on that plane?

She was either out or chose not to pick up the phone. Thinking about it, I decided it was just as well. It would be better to see for myself how she reacted when I did ask her that question. She had traded on my mother's marriage to her father to make me her unpaid public relations spokesperson. She was the sad widow, the abandoned stepmother, the bewildered wife of a man who turned out to be a crook. The truth was that she didn't give a damn about Nick Spencer, and she didn't give a damn about his son, Jack, and she had probably been carrying on with Charles Wallingford all along.

Ken pulled up and parked behind me, and we walked together to the house. It was a handsome Tudor-style stucco and brick home, enhanced by the setting. Expensive shrubbery, flowering trees, and a velvety green lawn testified that Dennis Holden was either a successful engineer or had family money.

Ken rang the bell, and the door was opened by a thin boyish-faced man with very short brown hair and warm hazel eyes. 'I'm Dennis Holden,' he said. 'Come in.'

The house was as attractive on the inside as it had appeared from the street. He took us into the living room where two creamy white couches faced each other on either side of the fireplace. The antique rug was a wonderful amalgam of colors, shades of red and blue, gold and crimson. As I sat down next to Ken on one of the couches, the thought ran through my head that a few months ago Dennis Holden had left this house for what he expected to be the last time to check into a hospice. What did it feel like for him to come home? I could only imagine the emotions that were churning inside him.

Ken was handing his card to Holden. I fished in my bag for mine, found it, and handed it to him as well. He examined them carefully. 'Dr. Page,' he said to Ken, 'do you have a practice?'

'No. I write about medical research full-time.'

Holden turned to me. 'Marcia DeCarlo. Don't you also write a financial advice column?'

'Yes, I do.'

'My wife reads it and enjoys it very much.'

'I'm glad.'

He looked at Ken. 'Doctor, on the phone you said that you and Miss DeCarlo are writing a cover story on Nicholas

Spencer. In your opinion is he still alive, or is the man in Switzerland who claims to have seen him mistaken?'

Ken looked at me, then back at Holden. 'Carley has been interviewing Spencer's family. Why don't I let her answer that?'

I told Holden about visiting the Barlowes and about meeting Jack, and I finished by saying, 'From everything I've heard about Nick Spencer, he would never abandon his son. He was a good man and absolutely dedicated to finding a cure for cancer.'

'Yes, he was.' Holden leaned forward and linked his fingers together. 'Nick was not a man who would fake his own disappearance. Having said that, I feel his death releases me from a promise I made to him. I had hoped his body would be found before I broke the promise, but it has been nearly a month since the plane crash, and it may never surface.'

'What was that promise, Mr. Holden?' Ken asked quietly.

'That I would not reveal to anyone that he had injected me with his cancer vaccine while I was in the hospice.'

Ken and I were both hoping that Dennis Holden had received the vaccine and would admit it to us. To actually hear it from his lips felt like going down the last deep drop on a roller coaster. We both stared at him. This man was thin, but he did not appear at all frail. His skin was pink and healthy. I realized now why his hair was so short – it was growing back in.

Holden got up, walked across the room, and picked up a framed picture that had been lying facedown on the mantel. He brought it over and handed it to Ken, who held it between us. 'This is the picture my wife took at what was supposed to be my last dinner at home.'

Gaunt. Emaciated. Bald. In the picture Dennis Holden was sitting at the table, a weak smile on his face. The open-necked shirt he was wearing hung on his body. His cheeks were sunken, his hands looked skeletal. 'I was down to eighty pounds,' he said. I'm one hundred and forty now. I had colon cancer that was operated on successfully, but the cancer had spread. It was all through my body. My doctors call it a miracle that I'm still alive. It is a miracle, but it came from God through his messenger Nick Spencer.'

Ken could not take his eyes off the picture. 'Do your doctors know you received the vaccine?'

'No. They had no reason to suspect it, of course. They're just astonished that I'm not dead. My first reaction to the vaccine was not to die. Then I started feeling a little hungry and began to eat again. Nick visited me here every few days and kept a chart on my progress. I have a copy, and he had a copy. But he swore me to secrecy. He said that I was never to call him at his office or leave a message for him there. Dr. Clintworth at the hospice suspected that Nick had given me the vaccine, but I denied it. I don't think she believed me.'

'Have your doctors been doing X rays or MRIs, Mr. Holden?' Ken asked.

'Yes. They call it a one-in-a-trillion spontaneous remission. A couple of them are writing medical briefs on me. When you called today, my first inclination was to refuse to see you. But I read every issue of *Wall Street Weekly*. I'm so sick of seeing Nick's name dragged through the mud that I thought it was time to speak out. The vaccine may not work for *everybody*, but it gave me back my life.'

'Will you let me see the notes Nick made on your progress?'

'I already made a copy in case I decided to give them to you. They show that the vaccine attacked the cancer cells by coating them and then smothering them. Healthy cells immediately started to grow in those areas. I went into the hospice on February 10. Nick was a volunteer there. I'd done all the research available on the treatment and potential treatment of cancer. I knew who Nick was and I'd read about his research. I begged him to try the vaccine on me. He injected me on February 12, and I came home on the twentieth. Two and a half months later, I'm cancer free.'

As we were about to leave an hour later, the front door opened. A very pretty woman and two girls in their early teens came in. All three had beautiful red hair. They obviously were Holden's wife and daughters, and they all went straight to his side.

'Hi,' he said, smiling. 'You guys are early. Did you run out of money?'

'No, we didn't run out of money,' his wife said, linking her arm with his. 'We just wanted to make sure that you were still here.'

We talked as Ken walked with me to my car. 'It *could* be a one-in-a-trillion spontaneous remission,' he said.

'You know it's not.'

'Carley, drugs and vaccines act differently on different people.'

'He's cured, that's all I know.'

'Then why did the lab tests go wrong?'

'You're not asking me, Ken, you're asking yourself. And you've come up with the same answer: Somebody wanted the vaccine to appear to have failed.'

'Yes, I have considered that possibility, and what I think is that Nicholas Spencer suspected the tests on the vaccine were being deliberately manipulated. That would explain the blind tests he was funding in Europe. You heard Holden say that he was sworn to secrecy, and under no circumstances was he to phone Nick or leave a message for him at the office. He didn't trust anyone.'

'He trusted Vivian Powers,' I said. 'He had fallen in love with her. I believe he didn't tell her about Holden or his suspicions because he felt that it might be dangerous for her to have that knowledge, and it turns out he was right. Ken, I want you to come with me and look at Vivian Powers for yourself. That girl isn't faking, and I have an idea as to what may have happened to her.'

Vivian's father, Allan Desmond, was in the waiting room next to the intensive care section of the hospital. 'Jane and I are taking turns being here,' he said. 'We don't want Vivian to be alone when she's awake. She's confused and frightened, but she is going to make it.'

'Has her memory improved?' I asked.

'No. She still thinks she's sixteen. The doctors tell us that she may never recover the last twelve years. She will have to accept that fact when she's well enough to understand. But the important thing is she's alive, and we'll be able to take her home soon. That's all we care about.'

I explained that Ken was working with me on the Spencer story and that he was a doctor. 'It's important that he have a chance to see Vivian,' I said. 'We're trying to piece together what happened to her.'

'On that basis, yes, you can see her, Dr. Page.'

It was only a few minutes later that a nurse came into the waiting room. 'She's waking up, Mr. Desmond,' she said.

Vivian's father was at her side when her eyes opened. 'Daddy,' she said softly.

'I'm here, dear.' He took her hands in his.

'Something happened to me, didn't it? I had an accident.'

'Yes, dear, you did, but you're going to be fine.'

'Is Mark all right?'

'He's fine.'

'He was driving too fast. I told him that.'

Her eyes were closing again. Allan Desmond looked at Ken and me and whispered, 'Vivian was in an automobile accident when she was sixteen. She woke up in the emergency room.'

Ken and I left the hospital and walked to the parking lot. 'Do you have anybody you could consult about mind-altering drugs?' I asked.

'I know where you're going with that question, and, yes, I do. Carley, there's a battle among the pharmaceutical companies to find drugs to cure Alzheimer's and restore memory. The other side of that research is that in the process, the laboratories are learning a lot more about *destroying* memory. It's not a very well kept secret that for sixty years mind-altering drugs have been used to get information from captured spies. Today those kinds of drugs are infinitely more sophisticated. Think of the so-called date rape pills. They're tasteless and odorless.'

Then I voiced the suspicion that had been forming in my mind for some time. 'Ken, let me try this out on you. I believe that Vivian ran to her neighbor's house in a panic and was afraid to call for help even on that phone. She took the car and was followed. I believe she may have been given mind-altering drugs to try to learn whether it was possible that Nick Spencer somehow survived the crash. In the office I learned that a number of people suspected she and Nick were emotionally involved. Whoever kidnapped her might have hoped that if Nick was alive, he would respond to her phone call. When that didn't happen, they gave her a drug that would erase her short-term memory and left her in the car.'

I arrived home an hour later and turned on the television first thing. Ned Cooper was still missing. If he had gone to the Boston area, as was speculated, he might have managed to find a place to hide. It sounded as though every lawman in the state of Massachusetts was out looking for him.

My mother phoned. She sounded worried. 'Carley, I've hardly spoken to you in the last two weeks, and that isn't like you at all. Poor Robert almost never hears from Lynn, but you and I are always close. Is anything wrong?'

There's a lot wrong, Mom, I thought, but not between us. Of course I couldn't tell her what was really troubling me. Instead I calmed her down with the excuse that the cover story was practically a 24/7 commitment, but almost choked at her suggestion that it would be so nice if some weekend Lynn and I came down together and the four of us spent some quality time together.

When I hung up, I made myself a peanut butter sandwich and a pot of tea, put it on a tray, and settled down at my desk for a couple of hours of work. The Spencer files were piled on it, and the newspaper clippings I had been studying for references to the air crash were scattered around as well. I gathered them up, put them back in the proper file and then picked up the house organs and other literature that I'd grabbed at Garner Pharmaceuticals.

I decided they were worth skimming through to see if there were any references to Gen-stone. When I got to the one that was in the middle of the pack, my blood went cold. It was what I had seen in the reception office that had registered in my subconscious.

For long minutes, maybe even as long as a half hour, I sat there sipping at the second cup of tea and barely noticing that it was already chilled.

The key to everything that had happened was in my hand. It was like opening a safe and finding inside everything I'd been searching for.

Or it was like having a deck of cards and arranging them all in sequence by suit. Maybe that's a better example because in cards the joker is wild and in some games it can belong anywhere. In the deck we were playing with, Lynn was the wild card, and where she belonged was going to affect both her life and mine.

# Chapter 49

When he got back to the garage from the guest house, Ned sat in the car drinking scotch and occasionally listening to the car radio. He enjoyed hearing the news reports about himself, but on the other hand, he didn't want to drain the car's battery. After a while he felt himself dozing, and gradually he drifted off to sleep. The sound of a car coming up the service road and driving past the garage woke him abruptly and made him reach for his rifle. If it was the cops and they tried to come after him, he'd at least blow some of them away before he died.

One window of the garage faced the road, but he couldn't see out of it. There were too many chairs stacked in the way. That was good, though, because it means they couldn't look in from the road and see the car, either.

He waited nearly half an hour, but no one drove out again. Then he thought of something – he bet he could guess who had shown up: the boyfriend, the guy she'd had with her the night he set the fire.

Ned decided to take a look and see if he was right. With his rifle tucked under his arm, he noiselessly opened the side door and made his now familiar way to the guest house. The dark sedan was parked where the housekeepers used to leave their car. The shades in the house had all been pulled down except for the one in the study that he had looked through the other night. That one was raised an inch or so from the sill again. It must be stuck, he decided. The window was still open, so when he squatted down, he was able to peek in and see through to the living room where Lynn Spencer and that guy had been sitting last night.

They were there again, only this time they had someone else with them. He could hear another voice, a man's voice, but couldn't see the face. If Spencer's boyfriend and the other guy were here tomorrow when the DeCarlo woman came to visit, they'd be out of luck, too. Fine with him. None of them deserved to live.

As he strained to listen to their conversation, he could hear Annie telling him to go back to the garage and get some sleep. 'And don't drink anymore, Ned,' she said.

'But . . .'

Ned clamped his lips shut. He had started to talk out loud to Annie, the way he'd gotten in the habit of doing. The man who was talking, the boyfriend, didn't hear, but Lynn Spencer raised her hand and told him to be quiet.

He could tell that she was saying she thought she had heard something outside. Ned slipped away and was back behind the tall evergreens before the front door opened. He couldn't see the face of the guy who walked out and looked at the side of the house, but he was taller than the boyfriend. He only glanced around quickly, then went back inside. Before he closed the door, Ned could hear him say, 'You're crazy, Lynn.'

She's not crazy, Ned thought, but this time he kept his mouth shut until he was safely back inside the garage. Then, as he opened the bottle of scotch, he began to laugh. What he had started to tell Annie was that it was okay to drink the scotch as long as he didn't take the medicine as well. 'You keep forgetting, Annie,' he said. 'You always keep forgetting.'

# Chapter 50

On Sunday morning I got up early. I simply couldn't sleep. It wasn't just that I was dreading having to face Lynn; I also had an odd sense that something terrible was going to happen. I had a quick cup of coffee, dressed in comfortable slacks and a light sweater, and walked uptown to the cathedral. The eight o'clock Mass was about to start, and I slipped into a pew.

I prayed for those people who had lost their lives because Ned Cooper had invested in Gen-stone. I prayed for all the people who were going to die because Nick Spencer's cancer vaccine had been sabotaged. I prayed for Jack Spencer, whose father had loved him so much, and I prayed to my little guy, Patrick. He's an angel now.

It wasn't even nine o'clock when the congregation streamed out. Still feeling restless, I walked up to Central Park. It was a perfect April morning, promising a day filled with sunshine and freshly blossomed trees. People were already walking and roller-blading and bicycling through the park. Others were stretched out on blankets on the grass, preparing for picnics or for sunbathing.

I thought of the people like the ones in Greenwood Lake who had been alive last week and now were dead. Did they have any premonition that their time was running out? My Dad did. He went back and kissed my mother before he set out for his usual morning walk. He'd never done that before.

Why was I thinking like that? I wondered.

I wanted to wish the day away, making the time disappear until the evening, when I'd be with Casey. We were good together. We both knew it. Then why did I have this overwhelming sadness when I thought of him, as though we were going in different directions, as though our paths were dividing again?

I started back home and on the way stopped for coffee and a bagel. That perked me up a bit, and when I saw that Casey had already called twice, that perked me up even more. He'd gone to a Yankee game last night with one of his friends who has a box there, so we hadn't talked.

I called him back. 'I was getting worried,' he said. 'Carley, this Cooper guy is still out there somewhere, and he's dangerous. Don't forget that he has contacted you three times.'

'Well, don't worry. I'm keeping a lookout,' I said. 'He certainly won't be in Bedford, and I doubt if he's in Greenwich.'

'I agree. I don't think he'd be in Bedford. He's more likely looking for Lynn Spencer in New York. The Greenwich police are watching the Barlowes' house. If he blames Nick Spencer for the failure of the vaccine, he might be crazy enough to go after Nick's son.'

The cancer vaccine is not a failure, I wanted so much to tell Casey, but I couldn't, not over the phone, not now.

'Carley, I've been thinking. I could drive you to Bedford this afternoon and wait for you.'

'No,' I said quickly. 'I don't know how long I'll be with Lynn, and you should get to the party on time. I'll join you there. Casey, I won't go into it now, but I learned some things yesterday that mean there'll be criminal charges coming out of all this, and I only pray that Lynn is not involved. If she does know anything or suspect anything, now is the time for her to come forward. I've got to convince her of that.'

'Just be careful.' Then he repeated the words that I had heard from his lips for the first time the other night: 'I love you, Carley.'

'I love you, too,' I whispered.

I showered and washed my hair and paid more attention than usual to my makeup. I'd plucked a pale green silk slack suit out of the closet. It was one of those outfits that I always felt good in, and people told me I looked good in, too. I decided to carry the necklace and earrings I usually wear with that suit in my purse. They seemed too festive for the conversation I was going to have with my stepsister. Instead, I put on plain gold earrings.

At one forty-five I got in my car and started the drive to Bedford. At ten of three I rang the bell and Lynn released the gate. As I had done last week when I interviewed the housekeepers, I drove around the remains of the mansion and parked in front of the guest house.

I got out of the car, walked to the door, and rang the bell. Lynn opened it for me. 'Come in, Carley,' she said. 'I've been waiting for you.'

# Chapter 51

At two o'clock Ned was positioned behind the trees near the guest house. At quarter after two a man he'd never seen before came walking up the driveway that ran to the service gate. He didn't look like a cop – his clothes were too expensive. He had on a dark blue jacket and tan pants, and wore an open-necked shirt. He had a look and attitude about him, reflected in the way he walked, that said he felt as if he owned the world.

If you're around here in an hour, you won't be owning it anymore, Ned thought. He wondered if this guy was the same one who was here last night – not the boyfriend, the other one. Could be, he decided. They were about the same size.

Today Ned could again see Annie standing near him. She was stretching out her hand to him. She knew that soon he was coming to her. 'It won't be long, Annie,' he whispered. 'Just give me a couple of hours, okay?'

His head hurt, in part because he'd finished the bottle of scotch, but some of the discomfort was due to the fact that he hadn't yet figured out how he was going to get to the cemetery. He couldn't take the Toyota – the cops everywhere were looking for it. And Lynn Spencer's car was too flashy – people would notice it.

He watched as the guy walked up to the house and knocked at the door. Lynn Spencer opened it for him. Ned decided the guy was probably a neighbor who had walked over to see her. Whichever way, he either knew the code to open the service gate or she had opened it from the house.

Twenty minutes later, at ten of three, a car drove in through the front driveway and parked in front of the guest house.

Ned watched as a young woman got out of the car. He recognized her right away – it was Carley DeCarlo. She had arrived right on time, maybe even a little early. Everything was going to happen just the way he had planned.

Only that new guy was still inside. Too bad for him.

DeCarlo was dressed up as if she was going to a party, Ned thought. She was wearing a pretty suit, the kind he would have liked to buy Annie.

DeCarlo could afford clothes like that. But, of course, she was one of them – the cheats taking everybody's money, breaking Annie's heart and then telling the world, 'I didn't have a thing to do with it. I'm a victim, too.'

*Sure* you are! That's why you drive up in a sporty-looking, dark green Acura, wearing a fancy outfit that cost a ton of money.

Annie had always said that if they ever could afford a new car, she'd want it to be dark green. 'Think about it, Ned. Black can be kind of dreary, and a lot of the dark blue cars look as though they're black, so what's the difference? But dark green – looks really classy and still has some punch to it. So when you win the lottery, Ned, you just march yourself out and buy me a dark green car.'

'Annie, honey, I never bought you one, but I'll be driving to meet you today in a dark green car,' Ned said. 'Okay?'

'Oh, Ned.' He heard her laugh. She was close by. He felt her kiss. He felt her rub the back of his neck the way she used to do when he was all uptight about something, like having a run-in with somebody at work.

He had left the rifle leaning against a tree. Now he retrieved it and began to calculate the best way to proceed. He wanted to get inside the house. That way there'd be less chance that the shots would be heard from the road.

Getting down on all fours, he crept along the shrubbery line until he was at the side of the house, under the window of the TV room. Today the door leading to the living room was almost closed, so he couldn't see inside. But he could see the guy who had just come up the driveway. He was in the TV room, standing behind the door.

'I don't think Carley DeCarlo knows he's here,' Annie said. 'I wonder why.'

'Why don't we find out,' Ned suggested. 'I have a key for the kitchen door. Let's go inside.'

# Chapter 52

Lynn really is a beautiful woman. She usually wore her hair swept back in a French knot, but today she had allowed tendrils to fall around her face, splashes of golden blond that softened the iciness of her cobalt blue eyes. She was wearing perfectly tailored white silk slacks and a white silk blouse. My concern about looking too festive for our serious discussion certainly was not shared by her. Her jewelry included a narrow gold necklace sprinkled with diamonds, diamond and gold earrings, and the solitaire diamond ring I had noticed at the shareholders' meeting.

I complimented her on her appearance, and she said something about having cocktails at a neighbor's house later. I followed her into the living room. I'd been in this room only last week, but I had no intention of telling her that. I was sure she would resent my visit to Manuel and Rosa Gomez.

She sat on the couch, reclining just enough to suggest that this was going to be a relaxed social exchange, body

English that told me I was in for a hard time. I certainly didn't want anything to drink, even water, but her failure to make even a token offer of hospitality was, I thought, my message to say my piece and get out.

Your call, I thought, and took a deep breath. 'Lynn, this isn't going to be easy, and, frankly, the only reason I'm here and trying to help you is that my mother is married to your father.'

Her eyes fastened on me, and she nodded. We're in agreement, I thought, and I continued. 'I know we don't like each other very much, and that's fine, but you used our family connection – if you can call it that – to make me your mouthpiece. You were the sad widow who had no idea what her husband was up to, you were the stepmother who yearned for her stepson. You were out of a job, friendless, just about broke. It was all a lie, wasn't it?'

'Was it, Carley?' she asked politely.

'I think it was. You didn't give a damn about Nick Spencer. The one honest thing you said was that he married you because you resembled his first wife. I believe that's true. But, Lynn, I'm here to warn you. There's going to be a criminal investigation into why the vaccine suddenly developed problems. I happen to know that the vaccine works – I saw living proof of that myself yesterday. I saw a man who, three months ago, was at death's door, and now he is one hundred percent cancer free.'

'You're lying,' she snapped.

'No, I'm not. But I'm not here to talk about that man now. I'm here to tell you that we know Vivian Powers was kidnapped and probably given mind-altering drugs.'

'That's ridiculous!'

'No, it isn't, and neither is the fact that Nick's father's files were stolen from Dr. Broderick, who was holding them for Nick. I'm pretty positive I know who it was who took them. I found his picture yesterday in a Garner Pharmaceuticals house organ. It was Lowell Drexel.'

'Lowell?' Her voice was nervous now.

'Dr. Broderick said it was a man with reddish brown hair who picked up the files. I guess the dye job was so good that he didn't see it for what it was. The picture was taken last year before Drexel stopped coloring it. I intend to call the investigators and tell them about it. Dr. Broderick was almost killed by a hit-and-run driver, and that may not have been an accident. At least I don't believe it was. He's recovering, and he'll be shown that picture. If, or maybe when, he identifies Drexel, the next thing the investigators are going to do is start looking into the plane crash. You were heard quarrelling with Nick in the coffee shop at the airport just before he took off. The waitress heard him ask you why you changed your mind at the last minute and didn't join him on the flight. You'd better have some answers ready when the police come to see you.'

Lynn was visibly nervous now. 'I was hoping to patch up our marriage – that's why I said I would go with him in the first place. I told Nick that and asked him to take Jack with him on a trip some other time. He agreed, but very unhappily. Then he was brusque with me all day Friday, so by the time we were leaving for the airport, I decided to leave my suitcase home. I waited until we were in the car to tell him, which is why he exploded. It simply hadn't occurred to me that he might run up and get Jack at the last minute.'

'That's a pretty thin story,' I told her. 'I'm trying to help you, but you're making it difficult. You know what they'll start to speculate about next? I'll tell you. They'll start to wonder whether or not you slipped something into Nick's drink in that coffee shop. I'm starting to wonder about that myself.'

'That's ridiculous!'

'Then start thinking about how serious your situation is. The investigators have been concentrating on Nick, and it's been your good fortune so far that they haven't found his body. Once word gets out about the vaccine and they change that focus, you're going to start to look pretty bad. So if you know anything about what was going on in the lab, or if you were tipped off not to get on that flight with Nick, then you'd better come forward now and cut a deal with the prosecutor.'

'Carley, I loved my husband very much. I wanted to patch up our marriage. You're making all this up.'

'No, I'm not. That lunatic Ned Cooper, who just shot all those people, is the one who set the fire here. I'm sure of it. He saw someone leaving the house that night. He sent me e-mails about it, which I've turned over to the police. I think you're involved with Wallingford, and when that revelation comes out, your alibi won't hold water.'

'You think I'm involved with Charles?' She began to laugh, a nervous, high-pitched, mirthless sound. 'Carley, I thought you were smarter than that. Charles is nothing but a weak-kneed crook who steals from his own company. He did it before, which is why his sons won't talk to him, and he started doing it at Gen-stone when he realized that Nick was taking loans against his own stock. He decided to help himself by looting the medical-supply division.'

I stared at her. 'Wallingford was *allowed* to steal! You *knew* he was stealing and did nothing about it?'

'It wasn't her problem, Carley,' a deep male voice said.

The voice came from behind me. I gasped and jumped up. Lowell Drexel was standing in the doorway. He was holding a pistol.

'Sit down, Carley.' His voice was quiet, unemotional.

My knees were suddenly weak as I sank back into the chair and looked at Lynn for an explanation.

'I was hoping it wouldn't go this far, Carley,' she said. 'I'm really sorry, but . . .' Suddenly she was looking past me, toward the back of the room, and the contemptuous expression she'd worn an instant ago had transformed into a look of sheer horror.

I jerked my head around. Ned Cooper was standing in the dining area, his hair matted, his face covered with stubble, his clothes stained and wrinkled, his eyes wide, his pupils dilated. He was holding a rifle, and as I watched, he shifted it a hairbreadth and pulled the trigger.

The sharp cracking sound, the smell of acrid smoke, Lynn's terrified scream, and the thud of Drexel's body as it hit the hardwood floor assaulted my senses. *Three!* That was all I could think. *Three* in Greenwood Lake; *three* in this room. I'm going to die!

'Please,' Lynn was moaning, 'please.'

'No. Why should you live?' he asked. 'I've been listening. You're dirt.'

He was aiming the rifle again. I buried my face in my hands.

'Plea –'

I heard the explosive sound again and smelled the smoke and knew that Lynn was dead. Now it was my turn. Now he's going to kill me, I told myself, and waited for the impact of the bullet.

'Get up.' He was shaking my shoulder. 'Come on. We're taking your car. You're a lucky girl. You get to live another half hour or so.'

I stumbled to my feet. I couldn't look at the couch. I didn't want to see Lynn's body.

'Don't forget your pocketbook,' he said with eerie calm.

It was on the floor next to the chair where I'd been sitting. I bent down and scooped it up. Then Cooper grabbed my arm and propelled me back through the dining area and into the kitchen. 'Open the door, Carley,' he commanded.

He pulled it shut behind us and shoved me to the driver's side of the car.

'Get in. *You* drive.'

He seemed to know I hadn't locked the car. Had he been watching for me? I wondered. Oh, God, why did I come here? Why didn't I take his threat seriously?

He walked around the front of the car, never taking his eyes off me and keeping his rifle at the ready. He got in the passenger seat. 'Open your pocketbook and get out the keys.'

I fumbled with the catch. My fingers were numb. My whole body was trembling so much that when I did get the catch open and pulled out the keys, it was hard to fit the key into the ignition.

'Drive down this road. The number for the gate is 2808. Punch it in when we get there. When the gate opens, turn right. If there are any cops around, don't try anything.'

'I won't,' I whispered. I could barely form the words.

He leaned down so that his head wasn't visible to

anyone on the street. But when the gate opened and I drove out, there were no other cars on the road.

'Turn left up at the corner.'

When we passed the charred remains of the mansion, I saw a police car drive slowly by. I kept looking straight ahead. I knew Ned Cooper meant what he said: If they came near us, he'd kill them and me.

Cooper remained slumped in the seat, the rifle between his legs, speaking only to give directions. 'Turn right here. Turn left here.' Then he said in a markedly different tone of voice, 'It's over, Annie. I'm on the way. Guess you're glad, honey.'

*Annie.* His dead wife, I thought. He was talking to her as if she was in the car. Maybe if I tried to talk to him about her, if he saw I felt sorry for both of them, then I might have a chance. Maybe then he wouldn't kill me. I wanted to live. I wanted to have a life with Casey. I wanted another child.

'Turn left here, then drive straight for a while.'

He was avoiding main roads, anyplace there was likely to be police looking for him.

'All right, Ned,' I responded. My voice was trembling so much that I bit my lip to try to get control of it. 'I heard people talking about Annie on the television yesterday. Everybody said they loved her.'

'You didn't answer her letter.'

'Ned, sometimes, if I get the same question from a lot of people, I do answer the letter, but I don't use one particular name because that wouldn't be fair to all the others. I bet I answered Annie's question even though I didn't use her name.'

'I don't know.'

'Ned, I bought stock in Gen-stone, too, and I lost money, just like you. That's why I'm writing a story for the magazine, to let everybody know about people like us who got cheated. I know how much you wanted to give Annie a nice big home. The money I used to buy the stock was money I had been saving for an apartment. I live in a rented place that's really small, just like the one you lived in.'

Was he listening? I wondered. I couldn't tell.

My cell phone rang. It was in my purse which was still lying in my lap.

'Someone supposed to call you?'

'That's probably my boyfriend. I'm supposed to meet him.'

'Pick it up. Tell him you'll be late.'

It *was* Casey. 'Everything okay, Carley?'

'Yes. I'll tell you about it.'

'How long before you get here?'

'Oh, about twenty minutes.'

'Twenty minutes?'

'I just started.' How could I let him know I needed help? 'Tell everybody that I'm on my way,' I said. 'It's good to know I'll be seeing Patrick soon.'

Cooper took the phone out of my hand. He pushed the end button and dropped it on the seat. 'You'll be seeing Annie soon, not Patrick.'

'Ned, where are we going?'

'To the cemetery. To be with Annie.'

'Where is the cemetery, Ned?'

'Yonkers.'

Yonkers was less than a ten-minute drive from where we were.

Did Casey understand that I needed him? I wondered. Would he call the police and tell them to be on the lookout for my car? But even if they saw it and followed us, it would only mean that some of them would be killed, too.

I was now sure that Ned Cooper was planning to kill himself in the cemetery, after he killed me. The only way I could hope to survive was if he decided to let me live. To do that I had to get his sympathy. 'Ned, I think that it's a shame all the terrible things they said about you on the television yesterday. It wasn't fair.'

'Annie, hear that? She doesn't think it's fair, either. They don't know what it was like for you to lose your house, all because I believed their lies. They don't know how it felt for me to see you die when that garbage truck hit your car. They don't know that those people you were so nice to all the time didn't want you to know that I was going to sell the house to them. They didn't like me, so they wanted us both to go away.'

'I'd like to write about all that, Ned,' I said. I tried to keep from sounding as if I was pleading. It wasn't easy.

We drove through Yonkers. There was a lot of traffic, and Cooper slumped lower in the seat.

'I'd like to write about Annie's beautiful gardens, how she planted a new one every year,' I continued.

'Keep driving straight. We're almost there.'

'And I'll let everyone know that the patients loved her at the hospital. I'll write about how much she loved *you*.'

The traffic had thinned out. On the right, down the block, I saw a cemetery. 'I'll call it "Annie's Story," Ned.'

'Turn into that dirt road. It goes through the cemetery. I'll tell you when to stop.' There was no discernible emotion in his voice.

'Annie,' I said, 'I know you can hear me. Why don't you tell Ned that it's better if you two are alone together, and that I should go home and write about you and tell everyone how much you and Ned loved each other. You don't want me to be in the way when you finally get your arms around Ned, do you?'

He didn't seem to be listening. 'Stop here and get out of the car,' he commanded.

Ned made me walk ahead of him to a grave that was still freshly dug and covered with mud. The ground had begun to settle, and there was a depression in the middle.

'I think Annie's grave should have a beautiful tombstone with flowers carved around her name,' I said. 'I'll do that for her, Ned.'

'Sit down. Over there,' he said, pointing to a space about six feet from the foot of the grave.

He sat down on the grave, the rifle pointing at me. With his left hand he pulled off his right shoe and sock.

'Turn around,' he said.

'Ned, I promise you, Annie wants to be alone with you.'

'I said turn around.'

He was going to kill me. I tried to pray, but I could only whisper the word that Lynn had died trying to say, 'Please – '

'What do you think, Annie?' Ned said. 'What should I do? You tell me.'

'Please.' I was too numb with terror to even move my lips. In the distance I heard the scream of sirens racing down the road. Too late, I thought. Too late.

'All right, Annie. We'll do it your way.'

I heard the crack of the rifle and everything went black.

\*

I kind of remember a cop saying, 'She's in shock,' and seeing Ned's body lying on Annie's grave. Then I guess I passed out again.

When I woke up, I was in a hospital. I had not been shot. I knew I was alive, that Annie had told Ned not to kill me.

I guess I was heavily sedated, because I fell asleep again. When I woke up, I heard someone say, 'She's in here, Doctor.' Two seconds later I was wrapped in Casey's arms, and that was when I knew I was safe at last.

# Epilogue

When confronted with the admissions Lynn had made to me before she died, Charles Wallingford rushed to cooperate with the investigators. He admitted that he had stolen all the money that was missing, except for what Nick had borrowed against his own stock. The theft was to be his payoff for cooperating in the scheme to send Gen-stone into bankruptcy. Charles's most stunning statement was that Adrian Garner, the billionaire head of Garner Pharmaceuticals, had masterminded the entire plan and directed every step of what had happened.

It was Garner who had recommended Dr. Kendall as Dr. Celtavini's assistant and sent her there deliberately to sabotage the experiments.

Garner was also Lynn's lover and the man Ned Cooper saw in the driveway the night he set the fire. After the mansion burned, Lynn dismissed the housekeepers in order to continue seeing Garner without being observed.

When Garner learned that the cancer vaccine did indeed work, he was not satisfied just to distribute it – he wanted to *own* it as well. When the vaccine seemed to be a failure and Gen-stone went bankrupt, he planned to pick up the patent on the vaccine for a comparative pittance. Then Garner Pharmaceuticals would own a vaccine that did in fact show great promise, and would in all likelihood prove to be very lucrative.

The mistake had been to have Lowell Drexel pick up Dr. Spencer's records personally. Vivian Powers's phone had been tapped. When she left a message for me saying that she knew who had taken the records, she was kidnapped and drugged to keep her from connecting the now grayhaired Drexel to the man Dr. Broderick had described as coming to his office.

Garner gave Lynn the tablet she put in the iced tea Nick drank in the airport coffee shop. It was a new drug, one that did not take effect for a few hours, and when it did, would knock the victim out without warning. Nick Spencer never had a chance.

Since then, Garner has been indicted for murder. Another major pharmaceutical company stepped in and worked out a deal to absorb Gen-stone in a stock exchange. The investors who initially thought they were defrauded now have stock that is worth most of what they invested, but it will be worth a great deal more someday if the vaccine continues to succeed without serious complications.

As I suspected, Dr. Kendall's niece was the one who passed the letter from Caroline Summers about her daughter having been cured of multiple sclerosis. When it reached Adrian Garner's desk, he told Drexel to get Dr. Spencer's records from Dr. Broderick. Now the new pharmaceutical company is bringing in top microbiologists from all over the world to study those records and to try to discover what combination of drugs may have produced that astonishing cure.

It is still hard for me to believe that Lynn not only helped to kill her husband, but also would have allowed Lowell Drexel to kill me that terrible day in the guest house. Lynn's father has had to endure not only her death, but also the heartbreak and humiliation of the media stories. My mother has done her best to help him, but it has not been easy. As she sympathizes with him, she has to struggle with her own awareness of what Lynn would have done to me to keep me from telling the true story.

Casey knew what I was trying to tell him when I was in the car with Ned and contacted the police. They had been watching the cemetery. They always thought Ned might go back there. When he explained that Patrick was my dead son, and knowing how often Ned went to Annie's grave, they raced there at once.

Today is June 15. There was a memorial service for Nick Spencer this afternoon, and Casey and I attended. The Gen-stone employees and stockholders, the ones who had denounced Spencer the loudest, were quietly respectful and attentive when tributes were paid to his dedication and genius.

Dennis Holden was electrifying when he spoke. The picture of him, gaunt and near death, that he had shown to Ken Page and me was flashed on a billboard-sized screen. 'I am here because Nick Spencer took a risk and injected me with his vaccine,' he declared.

Nick's son, Jack, was scheduled to pay the final tribute. 'My father was a great dad,' he began. Tears filled everyone's eyes as he said, 'He promised me that if he could make it happen, no little kid would ever again lose his mother to cancer.'

He's clearly the worthy son of a splendid father. I watched Jack take his seat between his grandparents. I knew that with all that had happened, he was blessed to have been granted people like them to care for him.

Then there was a stir as Vince Alcott said, 'Nicholas Spencer is believed to have given the cancer vaccine to one other person. She is with us now.'

Marty and Rhoda Bikorsky walked onto the stage, their daughter, Maggie, between them. Rhoda was the one who stepped forward to the microphone. 'I met Nicholas Spencer at St. Ann's Hospice,' she said, fighting back tears. 'I was visiting a friend there. I had heard about the vaccine. My little girl was dying. I begged him to give it to her. I brought her to him the day before he died in the plane crash. Even my husband didn't know about it. When I heard the drug was worthless, I was so afraid that we'd lose her even sooner. That was two months ago. Since then, the tumor in Maggie's brain has shrunk a little more every day. We don't yet know what the final outcome will be, but Nick Spencer has given us so much hope.'

Marty held up Maggie to let the audience see her. The child who had been so fragile and pale when I saw her six weeks ago now had color in her cheeks and was putting on weight. 'We were promised we'd have her till Christmas,' Marty said. 'Now we're beginning to believe we'll get to see her grow up.'

As people filed out of the service, I overheard someone repeat what Maggie's mother had said. 'Nick Spencer has given us so much hope.'

Not bad for an epitaph, I thought.

**POCKET
BOOKS**

### Also by

## MARY HIGGINS CLARK
# Daddy's Little Girl

Ellie Cavanaugh was only seven years old when her
teenage sister, Andrea, was murdered. It was Ellie
who led her parents to the secret hideout in which
Andrea's body was found. And it was Ellie's
testimony that led to the conviction of the man she
firmly believed to be the killer.

Now, twenty-two years later, the convicted killer is
set free from prison. He returns to Ellie's hometown
intent on white-washing his reputation. Ellie, now an
investigative reporter, also returns home determined
to thwart his attempts and conclusively prove his
guilt. As she delves deeper into her research, she
uncovers horrifying facts that shed new light on her
sister's murder. With each discovery, she comes
closer to a confrontation with a desperate killer.

**PRICE £6.99**
**ISBN 0 7434 4937 1**

**POCKET
BOOKS**

# Before I Say Goodbye

**Mary Higgins Clark**

Nell McDermot is devastated when her husband's
cabin cruiser blows up. Not only is she shattered by
Adam's sudden death, but she is wracked with guilt,
because the last time Nell saw Adam alive, she told
him to leave and never come back.

Nell's feelings are further complicated by her Great-
aunt Gert's insistence that she try to make peace with
Adam through a medium. And despite her
scepticism, the awful burden of guilt finally drives
Nell to consult Bonnie wilson, a well-known psychic.

As Nell searches for the truth about Adam's death,
she relies more and more heavily on Bonnie, who
claims to be receiving instructions from Adam. But
what Nell does not know is that she is being closely
watched, and the nearer she comes to learning what
happened to her husband, the nearer she is to
becoming the next victim of a ruthless killer . . .

**PRICE £6.99**
**ISBN 0 671 01039 5**

**POCKET
BOOKS**

# On the Street Where
You Live

## Mary Higgins Clark

In 1892, in the seaside town of Spring Lake, New Jersey,
a young woman disappears and the house in which she
grew up is immediately sold.

Now, more than a century later, emily Graham buys
back her ancestral home. Recovering from the bitter
break up of her marriage, with a new position as
criminal defence attorney in a major law firm, Emily
begins renovating the Victorian house. In the backyard,
the skeleton of a young woman is found, and identified
as that of Martha Lawrence, the girl who disappeared
from Spring Lake over four years ago. Within her
skeletal hand is the finger bone of another woman,
adorned with a ring – a family heirloom, Emily's family
heirloom.

Seeking desperately to find the link between her
forebear's past and this recent murder, Emily herself
becomes a threat to the killer. Devious and seductive,
he has chosen her as his next victim . . .

**PRICE £6.99**
**ISBN 0 7434 1499 3**

**POCKET
BOOKS**

These books and other **Mary Higgins Clark** titles are available from your bookshop or can be ordered direct from the publisher.

| | | |
|---|---|---|
| ☐ 0 7434 6773 6 | **Second time Around** | £6.99 |
| ☐ 0 7434 4937 1 | **Daddy's Little Girl** | £6.99 |
| ☐ 0 7434 1499 3 | **On the Street Where You Live** | £6.99 |
| ☐ 0 671 01039 5 | **Before I Say Goodbye** | £6.99 |
| ☐ 0 7434 8427 4 | **The Cradle Will Fall** | £6.99 |
| ☐ 0 7434 8430 4 | **Moonlight Becomes You** | £6.99 |
| ☐ 0 7434 8428 2 | **Stillwatch** | £6.99 |
| ☐ 0 7434 8429 0 | **Let Me Call You Sweetheart** | £6.99 |
| ☐ 0 7434 8431 2 | **We'll Meet Again** | £6.99 |
| ☐ 0 7434 8432 0 | **You Belong To Me** | £6.99 |
| ☐ 0 7434 8433 9 | **Pretend You Don't See Her** | £6.99 |
| ☐ 0 7434 4099 4 | **He Sees You When You're Sleeping** | £4.99 |
| ☐ 0 7434 1501 9 | **Deck the Halls** | £4.99 |
| ☐ 0 671 02284 9 | **All Through The Night** | £4.99 |

Please send cheque or postal order for the value of the book, free postage and packing within the UK; OVERSEAS including Republic of Ireland £1 per book. **OR: Please debit this amount from my:**

**VISA/ACCESS/MASTERCARD** ..............................................................

**CARD NO**..........................................................................................

**EXPIRY DATE**....................................................................................

**AMOUNT £** .......................................................................................

**NAME**................................................................................................

**ADDRESS**...........................................................................................

.............................................................................................................

**SIGNATURE**.......................................................................................

Send orders to: SIMON & SCHUSTER CASH SALES
PO Box 29, Douglas, Isle of Man, IM99 1BQ
Tel: 01624 675137, Fax 01624 670923
www.bookpost.co.uk
Please allow 14 days for delivery.
Prices and availability subject to change without notice.